MY
HUSBAND'S
GIRLFRIEND

MY HUSBAND'S GIRLFRIEND

SHERYL BROWNE

bookouture

Published by Bookouture in 2021

An imprint of Storyfire Ltd.
Carmelite House
50 Victoria Embankment
London EC4Y 0DZ

www.bookouture.com

ISBN: 978-1-83888-872-5
eBook ISBN: 978-1-83888-871-8

For every single reader out there.
A massive thank you for your support!

xx

PROLOGUE

'Wake up!' A woman's voice, fraught with anxiety, floats on the edge of her consciousness. Ignoring the excruciating pressure in her chest, she continues to search. Desperately. Blindly. She can't find him. She *has* to.

'You need to wake up!' She feels a hand on her forearm, shaking her, trying to drag her back.

No! she screams silently. *I can't! He's here. I can feel him. I need to find him.*

'You have to get *up*!' the woman hisses. 'You have to …'

A strange whooshing, gurgling sound drowns out the agitated voice. The pressure increases, causing her blood to pump frantically. Her head begins to throb. Her heart thrashes – *thud, thud, thud* – a dull drumbeat in her chest.

'Can you hear me? I *know* you can hear me. Wake up, will you?'

No, please … I can't *leave him. I* won't *leave him.* She blinks wildly around, but the grit and the dirt someone is shovelling into the water burns her eyes. She can't see. Nothing but deep, dark, impenetrable red. Panic engulfs her. And then he's there, an arm's stretch in front of her. He's moving away, floating, swirling; dancing like a fragile anemone. She tries to follow, but her lungs, bursting within her, scream at her to draw air. She can't *reach* him. She tries to hold on to the essence of him, but he's drifting further away, fading into the distance like a soft white djinn.

And then he's gone. And the voice is right next to her, insistent, a demented buzzing bee in her head. 'For God's sake, wake up! The *police* are here.'

She chokes out a strangled sob, snapping her eyes open as the quilt is stripped from her body.

'You need to get dressed.' The woman she thought she knew, but doesn't know at all, scans her eyes urgently, her own tear-filled and anguished, yet holding a warning. 'They want to talk to you.'

She watches her leave, tries to hold onto the fragments of her dream, which hover tauntingly on the periphery of her memory. Scrambling from her bed, she searches for her dressing gown, but it's not there. Not anywhere. Glancing quickly around, her heart thrashing, she grabs a sweatshirt from the bedroom chair, tugs it on and reaches to pull her hair from the back of it. It's damp, hanging in rat's tails, as it does if she showers and goes to bed without drying it. But she didn't do that. Did she? Her mind is fuzzy, a headache forming, pinpricks of sharp white light scorching her eyes. She can't remember. *Why* can't she remember?

With trembling hands, she reaches for her jeans and pulls them on, then pushes her feet into her slippers. Muted voices drift up from the lounge as she slowly descends the stairs: a male voice, a woman's voice; wretched with grief. Her legs leaden, her chest pounding, she places the flat of her hand to the partially open door and pushes it open.

A female police officer stands. 'Hello.' She offers her a smile as she takes a faltering step inside. 'We're told you took a sleeping tablet last night.' Her eyes are kind, curious, assessing. 'Are you okay to talk to us?'

She nods, tries to smile back, but her facial muscles are as frozen as she feels inside. Goosebumps rise over her skin as reality sinks in.

She wasn't dreaming.

CHAPTER ONE

Sarah

Sarah could feel Joe's eyes on her as, stunned, she reread the text she'd just received from her ex. 'Problem?' he asked.

'No,' she said evasively. 'Not really.' Trying to digest the words, she glanced over to where her little boy was throwing his soft football across the pub garden and galloping gleefully after it. 'Careful, Ollie,' she called. 'Don't go too far from the table, sweetheart.'

'I'll get him.' Placing his pint down, Joe was on his feet as Ollie charged on. At three years old, coming up to four, he was definitely a handful. 'Come on, mate.' Scooping him up, Joe headed for the ball and kicked it back towards Sarah. 'Let's go and have another drink and then we'll practise some goal kicks. What do you say?'

Despite the worrying text, Sarah laughed as Ollie answered with a giggling 'Yes.' This was her and Joe's first date since they'd gone out together years ago at school, and she didn't want to spoil it, which going on about her failed relationship certainly would. They were just having a casual drink together, each of them preferring not to read anything too serious into it. They'd broken up at just eighteen, and both had relationships go wrong in between. Now they were treading carefully; Sarah more than Joe possibly, since she had Ollie to consider. They'd both changed since they'd first dated, inevitably, but it was reassuring that Joe seemed fundamentally the same, considerate and caring. He'd spent a good hour with Ollie, playing with Duplo, before they'd left this evening, while – not sure how one did dating any more – Sarah had taken her time making herself presentable enough to be seen out in public. He'd wanted Ollie to feel at ease with him, he'd said, reminding her why she'd once loved him, and causing her a pang of regret at having lost him.

Seating Ollie on the bench table and collecting up his beaker, Joe passed it to him and picked up his own drink. 'Cheers,' he said, clinking with him and taking a glug.

'Cheers,' Ollie said manfully, and did likewise.

Sarah smiled and took a sip of her wine. Joe really was good with him. She couldn't believe he didn't have children of his own. His wife hadn't wanted them apparently, which had become a problem between them. Joe had been glad of it in the end, he'd said. It had made things less complicated when he'd discovered his wife had been stuck on her ex. When he'd talked about it, he had smiled in the *c'est la vie* way he did whenever he wanted people to believe something didn't bother him. He'd clearly been devastated at finding his wife was cheating on him, though. Sarah had seen the pain in his eyes.

'I think you've won him over.' She glanced again at Ollie, who was now emulating Joe's every move, planting his beaker back on the table and twirling it around as Joe did with his glass.

'I'm obviously irresistible,' Joe said with a wink. 'So, is everything okay?' He nodded towards her phone.

'Yes,' Sarah said quickly, though she didn't feel very okay. She felt bewildered. *Do you mind if I bring Ollie to meet Laura?* her ex had asked.

Since she'd never even met the woman, Sarah had had no idea how to respond. She'd had to steel herself to text him back. *It's serious then?*

Steve had taken a minute, then, *Yes*, he'd replied. *We're thinking of living together. Laura has her own place, so it makes sense for me to move in there.*

Sarah felt as if she'd been hit by a thunderbolt. He'd only been going out with this Laura for a few months. He hadn't even found himself a place to live yet; he was still crashing at his mother's, for goodness' sake. Had it really taken him such a short time to move on? She felt cheated on – ridiculously, since she and Steve weren't together any more. She also felt inadequate, as if the failure of their relationship had been all down to her, which was *definitely* ridiculous. They simply hadn't been compatible. Steve was so laid-back sometimes he was horizontal, which had been part of the problem between them. It had taken her a while to realise that his lack of involvement might have something to do with the fact that he hadn't been ready to make the crucial decision to commit, despite the fact that they had a child together.

And then came his father's stroke. Steve, who was close to him, had been distraught. Sarah should have been there more for him, but she'd been struggling herself to look after Ollie whilst also working full time. She'd been so tired, and looking back, she supposed she'd needed support too, especially after an early miscarriage, which, since Steve was dealing with so much emotionally, she hadn't mentioned. She'd told herself she could cope. Both of them exhausted and emotional, they'd ended up arguing. Eventually, they hadn't even argued. They'd simply stopped communicating.

Sarah shook herself. She hated dwelling on the past. She had Ollie, a future to look forward to. It had come out of the blue, though; Steve suddenly making the momentous decision to move in with someone else had rocked the foundations of the life she was trying to rebuild for her and her child.

'Another drink?' Joe asked, indicating her glass – which she'd just emptied rather too quickly, she realised. 'I thought you might want to cheer us on rather than get involved in the footie practice, since you're wearing heels.'

Sarah looked down at her feet. The shoes were wedges, but too high to run around a pub garden in. Should she have another drink? She didn't want to end up tipsy in charge of her son. A small one couldn't hurt, though. She'd hardly been out since splitting with Steve – thus the great 'what to wear' dilemma. And she was with Joe, a police officer, who really was one of the kindest people she knew. She could relax a little, surely? Let her hair down and enjoy herself? 'Why not?' She smiled, grateful that he was taking Ollie under his wing while she was feeling so distracted. 'I'll have another white wine, please. A large one.'

'Sure?' Joe asked. 'I wouldn't want you to think I was plying you with alcohol.' He was joking, but Sarah noted the concern in his eyes; a myriad of rich forest greens that conveyed his every emotion.

'Positive,' she said, her own eyes gliding over him. She doubted the thought would enter Joe's head, but she couldn't deny that the prospect of making love with him was tempting, curling into his firm body afterwards and lying safe in his embrace as she had done years ago. Why had they stopped going out together? Different lives and aspirations, she supposed. Joe had gone off to his police training course in Worcester, while she'd applied to complete her Level 3 in canine care, working one day at the dog rescue trust in Evesham. Somehow their various commitments took over and life ran away with them. They'd moved on. Sarah had loved Steve, thought he'd loved her. She would never regret her relationship with him. Without him, she wouldn't have Ollie, who was her world, but she did wonder now how she'd ever let Joe go. 'I'll try not to go over on my wedges or do anything else to embarrass you,' she added with a teasing smile.

'I doubt there's anything you could do that would embarrass me, Sarah.' Giving her a mischievous wink, Joe moved to help Ollie, who was in the process of scrambling off the bench after his ball. For all her worries – the frightening prospect of single parenthood, Steve now moving on so swiftly he obviously hadn't paused to draw breath – she was content in that moment, watching this capable man filling the gap in Ollie's life. Thinking she might be wise to give herself some breathing space, she hadn't been contemplating going out with anyone again so soon, but maybe Joe was just the man she needed, someone she could depend on, with no baggage or secrets in his closet.

CHAPTER TWO

Joe

'Joe?' someone called behind him as he stood at the bar. Turning around to see who it was, he almost wished he hadn't.

'Fancy meeting you here,' his ex-wife said, her expression somewhere between pleased and shocked.

She wasn't half as shocked as he was. The last time he'd seen her was when he'd stuffed a few clothes in a holdall and walked out three months ago, wishing to God he'd had the strength to do it sooner. Courtney had wanted to talk things through. Joe hadn't. Having witnessed her with her ex the night before, he'd doubted very much he would be able to be civil. It was a work meeting, she'd said, which was bullshit. He'd known way before then that she was cheating on him. He hadn't realised how spectacularly, though. She and her ex both worked in the glitzy world of advertising, so she'd always had an excuse for seeing him. The man drove a fancy car, a BMW Z4 sport model, the kind of car Joe could only ever dream of. The car he'd eventually realised they were having sex in – he hadn't needed to be a detective to work that out. Following her a few times when she'd gone out dressed to kill had given him all the evidence he needed. The bloke enjoyed illicit sex, it seemed; since he was with someone else and Courtney was married, shagging her qualified, obviously. When he'd eventually caught them in the act, Joe felt as if he'd been kicked in the gut. Parked in a secluded spot, they were fucking over the bonnet. Not much room in the back, he'd supposed, feeling sick to his soul. He'd got then why she'd never wanted to start a family. She wasn't in love with him. She never had been. He'd been the bit of rough she'd fancied, that was all, possibly an attempt to make her ex jealous. Somehow they'd ended up getting married. It had been a volatile relationship. It was bound to be, he realised looking back, when it had been so one-sided.

'You're looking good,' she said now, her eyes – meticulously made up as always – roving leisurely over him.

'You too,' he responded with a short smile. She usually did, he reminded himself, dressing in the tightest of clothes to show off her figure. She was showing it off now, wearing slim-cut jeans and a skin-hugging top. Courtney always knew how to turn heads.

'So how are you?' she asked, stepping towards him.

'Fine,' he said. *Better for not constantly doubting myself*, he didn't add. 'You?'

'Okay. You know …' She shrugged, her gaze flitting down and back. 'Are you with someone?' She glanced curiously around.

Joe considered. 'A friend,' he said eventually, not wanting to bring Sarah, who was everything Courtney wasn't – natural and caring – into the conversation.

'Ah.' She nodded knowingly, a flicker of regret in her eyes.

'What brings you to this neck of the woods?' he asked, assuming she and the hotshot were slumming it, since they usually met in more salubrious places than a local pub with a beer garden. He hoped he didn't run into the bastard. He still felt sorely tempted to deck him.

'Girls' night,' she said, waving over her shoulder.

'Oh, right.' Joe was surprised. Courtney didn't generally do girls' nights. Not her type of thing, she'd said. Far too rowdy.

'We should meet up sometime,' she suggested. 'Have a chat.'

A chat? Right. Joe smiled cynically. 'I'm not sure we have anything to chat about, Courtney. Do we?'

She glanced down again. He supposed she had the good grace to look contrite, even if she wasn't. Admitting she was wrong wasn't generally Courtney's thing either.

'There's the apartment,' she reminded him. 'We should probably put it on the market at some point, assuming you don't want to—'

'I think we can pretty much sort that out on the phone,' Joe cut in. 'I'd better go.' He nodded towards the rear exit. 'I have someone waiting.'

'Your friend,' she said with an enigmatic smile.

'That's right.' Giving her another short smile back, he turned away.

'I'll ring you,' she called after him.

'Do that,' he said. He didn't look back. He had no intention of making small talk with the woman who'd ripped his heart from inside him. He wanted to move on.

He was leading Ollie away from the bench ready to play football when he noticed Courtney coming out of the pub, also via the rear entrance. She stopped, looking actually sad as she glanced from Sarah to Ollie, whose hand Joe had firmly in his, and then back to him. Was that what the flash of regret he'd seen was all about, he wondered; the fact that she'd realised she might have wanted kids after all, a family? Wasn't likely to have them with the hotshot, was she? Might cramp his style.

'Who was that?' Sarah asked, noticing him watching her as she headed off.

'No one,' Joe said, turning his attention back to Ollie. 'Just someone I thought I knew. Turns out I didn't.'

CHAPTER THREE

Sarah

She actually had managed to embarrass him. Joe had looked taken aback when, once Ollie was tucked safely in bed with his snuggle bunny, she'd slipped between him and the coffee maker and pressed her mouth over his. He'd soon reciprocated, his tongue finding hers, his hands tracing the contours of her body. When they'd paused for breath, though, the look in his eyes had been troubled. 'Are you sure about this?' he'd asked worriedly.

'Yes. Why? Aren't you?' Thinking he might not fancy her any more, that he was just trying to be a friend to her when she needed one, Sarah had felt her self-esteem plummet.

'Of course I am,' he'd said softly, undeniable heat now in his eyes. 'It's just … Don't you think it might be a little too soon, for you, I mean?'

'No, absolutely not,' she'd assured him, her mouth drawn greedily back to his, her hands finding his buttons, the firm flesh under his shirt. She'd practically undressed him.

And now here she was in her kitchen in the cold light of the morning after, wondering what on earth she'd been thinking. Turning on the kitchen tap, she filled a glass with water and glugged it down. She liked Joe, a lot. So why the bloody hell had she compromised him?

The sex had been amazing, for her anyway, no-holds-barred passionate. She hadn't seen exploding white lights in a long time. Tracing her spine softly with his thumb as he'd held her afterwards, he'd said he'd often thought of her, wondering what might have been if they'd stayed together. He clearly did still care for her, possibly wanted more than the occasional date. But Sarah wasn't sure she could give more. Not yet. She had a child and it complicated things. Ollie would be confused, imagining she'd moved a new man into his life to replace his father.

Steve hadn't had any such qualms, though, had he? A fresh sense of dismay washed through her as she recalled the text he'd sent her telling her he was busy making plans for a future without her. Who was she, she wondered, this woman he'd fallen so quickly in love with? Sarah had no doubt she would be everything she herself wasn't: slim, confident, beautiful, with perfectly behaved hair. Her hand went to her own hair, a mad crop of mousy curls that refused to be tamed no matter what she did.

Stop. She pulled herself up, determined not to go down that road. Her self-esteem was obviously flagging again.

Whoever this woman was, and however suddenly involved with her Steve was, surely he didn't think she would just hand Ollie over to her care knowing nothing about her? A pang of guilt tugged at her conscience as she realised she should have mentioned that she'd become involved with Joe. The difference was, though, that she knew Joe; she'd practically grown up with him. She would trust him implicitly with her son. This woman had only recently come into Steve's life. How much of her history did he actually know? And why the urgent need to introduce her to Ollie? She wouldn't let him use their son, involve him in his life only when it suited him to make him look good. She huffed self-righteously, and then immediately felt bad. Steve would never do anything to hurt Ollie. If anyone was using someone, it was her.

Her eyes flicked to the ceiling. She could hear Joe moving around, obviously up and getting dressed. Sending Steve a quick message – *We need to have a chat. Will call you* – she glugged another glassful of water, attempting to dilute the wine she'd consumed last night, and then dashed up the stairs.

Meeting Joe coming out of her bedroom, his shoes in his hand and clearly making an effort not to wake Ollie, she couldn't help but smile.

Seeing her, his mouth curved into a warm smile back. 'Shh,' he said, pressing a finger to his lips and nodding towards the room where her little boy slept.

She beckoned him away from Ollie's door. 'Thanks, Joe,' she said.

'No problem. I thought you wouldn't want Ollie to know about us yet.'

Sarah dropped her gaze. 'No,' she mumbled, looking uncomfortably back at him. 'Not yet.'

Joe's smile faded. 'I, er, take it you're not desperate for a repeat performance then?' he asked awkwardly.

Oh God, she'd hurt his feelings. 'It's not that, Joe. It's just …'

'Don't beat yourself up, Sarah, I get it,' he said as she fumbled for the right words. 'Sex on the rebound is never a great idea. I, er, should probably go. Duty calls.' Nodding past her to the stairs, he smiled again, a heartbreakingly sad smile this time.

'It wasn't on the rebound,' she said quickly. 'Joe, please don't feel …' Crushed, that was how he looked. 'It's not that I don't want this … us.'

Joe glanced down to the hand she'd placed on his arm. 'Are you sure about that, Sarah? You hit the wine pretty hard after receiving that text.'

She had. She'd promised herself she would only have one more, and it had turned into two, and then another once they'd got back. Joe obviously thought it was something to do with Steve. Hand on heart, Sarah couldn't say that it wasn't. She tried to rescue the situation. 'I just need a little time to make sure Ollie's okay with things. He's had so many changes in his life recently. Can you be patient with me, do you think?'

Joe closed his eyes, looking relieved. 'Of course I can. I do understand. I know you have Ollie to consider and I don't want to push it. I wouldn't dream of it. Look, I'll call you, shall I? In a couple of days, maybe?' His expression was hopeful.

Sarah thought about it. Her emotions were all over the place, but could it really hurt to see Joe discreetly? 'Or I could call you?' she suggested. 'Tonight, possibly? There's no harm in talking on the phone, is there?'

'No harm at all,' he assured her, a playful twinkle in his eye. 'As long as you can't read what might be going on in my mind.'

Sarah laughed and leaned in to kiss the lips of the man she'd fallen in love with all those years ago. The man she suspected she could so easily love again. She had to be sure, though. Ollie had to be her priority.

'I'd better get on.' She eased away as she heard her son's feet pad across his bedroom. No doubt he was heading for his toy box.

'Talk later,' Joe said throatily, and squeezed past her to the stairs.

Watching him go, Sarah traced her lips with her fingertips, a warm sensation spreading through her body. She had to put Ollie first, but she owed it to Joe not to mess him around. She would ring him, and she would see him. She would just take it more slowly, as he'd hinted she should before she threw herself at him, which only went to show how caring he was.

Her mind made up, she turned to Ollie's room, her eyes snagging on the wall clock as she did. God, the time. She was going to be *so* late for work. Needing the extra money now she was on her own, she'd applied for a job as a behavioural therapist at the dog rescue centre, which paid more but also meant working alternate Saturdays. Her friend Becky, who taught at the local primary school, looked after Ollie on those days, and she was wonderful with him, but still Sarah felt guilty spending so much time away from him.

Composing herself, she pushed his bedroom door open. 'Morning, munchkin.' She smiled, finding him sitting cross-legged on his bed, surrounded by a sea of Duplo. 'And what are we making this morning, hmm?'

'A train,' Ollie replied, his brow furrowed in concentration.

'So I see. It's a very smart train.' Sarah made a space and sat down beside him. She was doubtless going to be late, but having got herself in a state one morning while trying to adjust to single parenthood, only to end up shaking her little boy's world further, she'd vowed never to do that again. 'Who's that?' she asked, pointing to the tiny figure in the bright yellow driver's cab.

'Daddy. He's coming to see me,' Ollie answered without missing a beat, and Sarah's heart squeezed for him. He missed him. Of course he would.

'He is coming, darling.' Wrapping an arm around his shoulders, she drew him close. 'He's going to take you to see his new friend. Would you like that?'

'Is he a workmate?' Ollie asked innocently, having met one or two of Steve's employees when he'd collected them in his van on the way to take Ollie to nursery.

'Not a workmate, no. A lady friend,' Sarah answered carefully. 'I think she's a good friend, though.'

The furrow in Ollie's brow deepened as he processed her words. 'Is she a nice friend?' He looked up at her, his wide blue eyes scanning hers unnervingly. It was as if he knew that in order to like her, he would need his mummy's approval.

'I'm sure she's lovely. I bet we'll all get along really well,' she reassured him, her heart aching as the reality of the situation sank in. Steve had to move on. There would inevitably be another woman in his life, but she hated the thought of someone else taking over her responsibilities as a mother, which this Laura inevitably would now they were going to be living together. Steve had seen Ollie regularly, but his time with him had been limited to day visits since his mother didn't have much room. They'd agreed he could stay with him on the weekends Sarah wasn't working once he got a suitable place of his own. That thought caused a flutter of nervous butterflies to take off in her tummy.

'Will she play Lego with me?' Ollie asked, after due consideration.

'Probably. You can ask her when you meet her.' Sarah forced some enthusiasm into her voice, though her nerves were tying themselves into knots as she wondered how soon that would be. 'Now, how about we go and brush your teeth so you can give her and Daddy a big bright smile when you see them?' She gave his shoulders another quick squeeze. 'Becky will be here soon. You like Becky, don't you?'

'Uh-huh.' Nodding, Ollie slid dutifully off the bed. 'She makes scrambly.'

He meant scrambled eggs, his favourite, which Sarah had precious little time to make in the mornings. Burying a sigh, she accompanied him to the bathroom.

After encouraging him to use his Batman toothbrush in all the right places, she was following him down the stairs when Becky arrived. 'Hiya, gorgeous little man,' she said, stepping in and immediately crouching to pull Ollie into a hug. 'And how are we today? Smiley or sad?'

'Smiley,' Ollie said with an assured nod. 'I'm going to meet Daddy's new lady friend.'

'Oh yes?' Straightening up, Becky took hold of his hand, raising an eyebrow at Sarah as she did.

Sarah rolled her eyes. 'Talk later,' she mouthed. Becky knitted her brow. Obviously she'd gathered that Steve was in a new relationship.

'Mummy said she's a nice friend,' Ollie went on as Becky led him to the kitchen.

'Did she?' Becky cast Sarah a surprised glance over her shoulder. 'Well, that's good, isn't it? We wouldn't want him to have a nasty friend, would we?'

'No.' Ollie shook his head in agreement. 'That would make Daddy sad.'

Suppressing another despairing sigh, Sarah left Ollie in Becky's capable care and grabbed her mobile from the hall table. She'd made a decision. She'd been planning to call Steve later, but as she was running late anyway …

'It's just a quick call,' she said when he picked up. 'About your text.'

'Right.' Steve sounded wary, as if girding himself for an argument. Sarah wouldn't go there. Ollie would only be caught up in the middle of it, and she didn't want that.

'I'm okay with your girlfriend meeting Ollie,' she said, making sure to keep any emotion from her voice, 'on one condition.'

'Which is?' Steve asked cautiously.

'I meet her first. On her own.'

CHAPTER FOUR

Laura

Realising that Steve was on the phone, Laura tried not to too obviously eavesdrop as she came into the bedroom to get changed out of her PJs ready to go to work at the hospice. She'd wanted to tell him she'd rearranged her wardrobe to make a bit more room for his clothes, but he seemed deep in conversation. Squeezing past where he sat on the end of the bed, she collected her uniform from its hanger, grabbed a scrunchie from the dressing table and hitched up her hair, giving him a smile through the mirror as she did.

Steve reciprocated and then furrowed his brow as he turned his attention back to his phone. 'No, no problem,' he said to whoever he was talking to. 'I'm sure she'll be fine about it. It's just, wouldn't it be better if you brought Ollie along to meet the two of us together?'

Halfway into her uniform, Laura paused, her stomach somersaulting. He was talking to his ex. They were obviously discussing her meeting Ollie with a view to him coming here. Steve was desperate to maintain regular contact with his son, for him to start visiting now he was moving in, hopefully staying alternate weekends. Laura was desperate to meet him. With Steve's help, she'd been busy turning the box room into a little boy's dream room. But now, realising a meet-up might be imminent, she felt a chill of trepidation run through her. What if he didn't take to her? She couldn't bear that.

'Yes, I get you'd want to check her out …' His expression awkward, Steve's gaze flicked again to Laura.

She turned away on the pretext of slipping her feet into her shoes. She was aware of her hands shaking as she fastened her buttons. She'd mentally prepared herself for this, or thought she had, trying to eliminate anything that would turn her into an incoherent fool, namely stress. She'd forced herself to remain calm, practising talking out loud when she was on her own. She'd even tried recording herself. Running through what she wanted to say beforehand, she was fluent. As soon as she started recording, though, her lips would jam and she would stammer and stutter, finding it almost impossible to spit the words out.

She so wanted their first meeting to go well, to put little Ollie at his ease and welcome him into her life. She was determined to look after him as if he were her own. She didn't intend to say that to his mother, of course. It would be bound to bring the woman's maternal instincts out and make her protective. That was only natural. Laura would quite understand if Sarah didn't immediately trust her, but she hoped she might like her. She and Steve had been separated such a short time, though. It was more likely she would hate her. Laura was, in effect, her replacement after all.

The lack of confidence her mother had instilled in her threatening to stress her out and cause the very thing she was trying to avoid, she willed herself to try to think more positively. Even if she didn't get on with her mother, she got along with the women at work, and the residents all liked her. One sweet old lady, Annie, who always had a warm twinkle in her eye whenever Laura popped into her room to see her, even said she wished she'd had her for a daughter. Laura wished she'd had Annie for a mother. She might not have spent her childhood in purgatory then.

'I do understand, Sarah,' she heard Steve say as she tried to quash the panic rising inside her. 'I would want to do the same. It just seems a bit over-cautious, that's all. She's not a serial killer or a child molester. She's—'

He stopped, sighing heavily. 'Yes, sorry. I know it's not a joking matter. I'll have a word and call you back, okay?'

Another pause, while the knot in Laura's tummy twisted itself tighter. 'Right, yes. It's a bit short notice, but as I say, I'll have a word and get back. Bye, Sarah. Give Ollie my love.'

Shaking his head in despair, he got to his feet and walked towards her. 'Sorry about that. It was Sarah,' he said unnecessarily. 'She wants to meet.'

'Oh. Okay.' Swallowing back her apprehension, Laura nodded and smiled and tried to convince herself that his ex would probably be as anxious as she was. It wouldn't be an easy meeting for her either. The post-separation wounds, Laura knew, would still be raw.

'The thing is …' Hesitating, Steve looked her over worriedly. 'She wants to meet you on your own. Just the two of you.'

Oh God, no. Laura's heart lurched. That was the worst possible scenario. She couldn't do that. Be alone with the woman. Have a whole conversation with her without Steve to step in and rescue her when she got tongue-tied.

'It's just to get to know you,' he added, plainly sensing her alarm. 'You know, for you both to get to know each other before Ollie comes for a visit. I thought it might not be a bad idea. That way everybody will be at their ease, won't they?'

Laura felt the blood drain from her face. No, they wouldn't. It was a bad idea. A terrible idea. She would feel like a complete idiot, which people always assumed she was when she stammered and stumbled over her words. Or said nothing at all, which made her look even worse. 'B-b-but …' she started, completely forgetting her strategy of avoiding trigger words when she was nervous.

'Hey.' Steve stepped towards her, placing his hands gently on her arms. 'It's okay. She doesn't bite,' he attempted to reassure her. 'She's not going to judge you, Laura. Sarah's not like that.'

Of course she would. People did. It was a fact. And this woman would have more reason to want to think badly of her than anyone. Surely Steve wasn't naïve enough to believe that she wouldn't? 'I *can't*,' she finally blurted. 'I can't, Steve,' she implored.

'Come on, come here.' Steve drew her gently to him. 'Breathe. Speak slowly and you'll be fine,' he encouraged her, reminding her of the management techniques her speech therapist had taught her.

Laura nodded into his shoulder and pulled air slowly into her lungs. Her intuition about him hadn't been wrong. She'd known he was the kind of man who wouldn't ridicule her.

'Okay?' he asked after a second.

She answered with another small nod.

'So, do you want to tell me what you're worrying about?' he coaxed her.

'I'll *mmm*ess it up.' She forced the words out. 'She'll think I'm a b-b-bad influence.'

'No she won't.' Steve laughed kindly. 'Sarah's okay, I promise. She's not looking for reasons not to like you. If I know her, she'll be wanting to find out a bit about you so she can prepare Ollie before he meets you. She'll be looking to make friends with you for his sake. She's a kind person, Laura. She won't be judging you.'

Laura felt a sliver of relief, but still she was troubled. The woman obviously wanted to meet her on her own precisely because she did want to assess her. Laura would do the same in her shoes. Steve might think Sarah was kindness itself, but Laura couldn't see how she wouldn't be measuring up the new woman in his life. He was the father of her child, after all. She couldn't bear for it all to go wrong after all her planning and preparation. She'd worked so hard to make this happen.

'We can organise for Ollie to come over once you've met Sarah,' Steve went on. 'You want to meet him as soon as possible, don't you?'

Laura looked up at him. 'Yes.' She managed a small smile.

Steve looked relieved. 'He's a great kid,' he said, his eyes filled with pride. 'A handsome little fella too. Sorry I haven't been able to show you anything but baby photos. Sarah tended to take most of them, and she's wary of posting pictures of him online.'

'He takes after his father then?' Laura teased.

'Obviously.' Smiling bashfully, Steve squeezed her closer. 'I just know you're going to love him.'

Laura had no doubt she would. She already did. He was a beautiful child. He'd stolen her heart the second she saw him.

CHAPTER FIVE

Sarah

Sarah was beginning to wonder if she'd been stood up. Checking her watch and noting that Laura was now fifteen minutes late, she glanced around, avoiding the gaze of the two men at the bar, who'd been eyeing her curiously. They obviously thought she'd been stood up too. Deciding to give her another five minutes, she selected her Kindle app on her phone, attempting to appear laid-back as she tried to make her drink last.

Ten minutes later, she'd had enough. How ridiculous was it to be sitting in a pub drinking Coke while waiting for her ex-partner's girlfriend, who'd demonstrably indicated how reliable she was by not showing up? Sarah really didn't like confrontations – arguing rarely solved anything – but she was going to have firm words with Steve.

Grabbing her bag, she got to her feet ready to leave just as a woman flew through the pub entrance, looking hurriedly around before rushing towards her. 'S-s-s …' she started, and then stopped, her cheeks flushing furiously as she glanced at the ceiling. 'I'm sorry I'm late,' she said, clearly flustered as she looked back at Sarah. 'There was a crisis at work. A p-p-patient …'

She had a stammer. Sarah was surprised. Steve hadn't mentioned it, though she supposed there was no reason why he should have done. Her gaze travelled over the other woman. Small and delicate-featured, she seemed fragile, a vulnerable quality about her that would make you instinctively want to protect her. Yet there was a determination beyond the nervousness she could see in her eyes; feline eyes, she thought, almond-shaped and the true striking green of a cat. With her rich auburn hair tied messily on top of her head, she was open-faced and undeniably pretty, in an imperfect way. Sarah didn't know her, but she could see why Steve had been so easily attracted to her.

'It's okay,' she said charitably. 'I was beginning to wonder whether you were coming, but I haven't got to rush off anywhere.' Joe had offered to look after Ollie. She still hadn't told Steve that they were sort of together. It was early days yet. She wasn't sure what the future might hold for them, but still she was aware that she might possibly have been practising double standards, wanting to know all there was to know about Laura whilst neglecting to mention that Joe had become part of Ollie's life. She knew Joe, but Steve didn't, after all.

'S-s-sorry,' Laura said again.

Noting the two bright spots on her cheeks turning crimson, Sarah couldn't help feeling sympathetic. She was clearly terribly self-conscious. 'It's fine,' she assured her again. 'Shall I get us a drink while you catch your breath?' They probably looked a bit obvious standing in the middle of the pub. The two guys at the bar were now openly eyeing them both, one of them clearly liking what he saw as he looked Laura up and down. Evidently he was into nurses' uniforms, which was what Laura appeared to be wearing.

'Thanks.' Laura began to ferret in her bag – for her purse, presumably.

'I'll get them,' Sarah offered. 'Why don't you grab a seat before someone else takes the table?' She indicated the one she'd just vacated. 'What do you fancy?'

'White wine, please.' Laura squeezed her eyes closed as she said it, making it obvious she was concentrating hard to get the words out.

Minutes later, Sarah returned with white wines for them both, having given the guys who'd started talking to her at the bar short shrift on Laura's behalf. The woman looked as if she might die of embarrassment should one of them approach her. 'Here you go. I got us large ones. I thought you could use it,' she said, placing the drinks on the table and slipping around it to slide in next to Laura on the bench seat, rather than sitting opposite her, which she thought might seem confrontational.

Laura smiled gratefully. 'I could,' she assured her with a weary roll of her eyes, and took a sip.

Sarah did likewise. 'I noticed your uniform. What is it you do?' she asked. It didn't appear to be a regular NHS uniform, the sort Sarah's mother wore.

'I, um … I'm a p-p-palliative nurse at a hospice,' Laura provided haltingly.

The hospice where Steve's father had died, Sarah gleaned, thinking that trying to improve the quality of life for people with serious illnesses was a commendable thing to do. She couldn't help admiring her for it. She assumed that that was where Steve had met her. Had he become involved with her then, she wondered, while he was visiting his father? He'd stayed at the hospice for endless long hours on his own as his father had deteriorated. He'd been devastated the night he'd slipped quietly away. He would have needed a shoulder. Had Laura been the one to offer it, while Sarah had been at home with their child? The pang of jealousy she felt at that realisation surprised her, along with hurt that Steve might have been seeing someone else before they'd made the decision to part, though that would have happened sooner or later, she supposed. Their relationship had already been floundering.

'Have you worked there long?' she asked.

'*Nnn …*' Laura started, and stopped, clearly embarrassed. 'Just over a year,' she said with a weak smile.

'You have a stammer,' Sarah said carefully, aware of how she must be feeling.

Laura's gaze shot to hers. Her eyes were so large she looked like a frightened kitten.

'It's nothing to be ashamed of.' Sarah smiled kindly. 'I had a friend at school who stuttered. She got stuck on certain letters. Her lips touched, she said, and she couldn't get the words out. She tried to use alternative ways to start a sentence, but she used to get really frustrated. She hated it when people wouldn't give her time to speak, or finished her sentences for her. I think what really hurt, though, was when people avoided talking to her out of embarrassment or ignorance or whatever.'

Laura blinked uncertainly, as if she wasn't quite sure what the catch was. Sarah supposed she was bound to be wary. There was probably nothing more daunting for a woman than meeting her boyfriend's ex-partner. She'd have come prepared for bitchiness and bitter accusations. Sarah did feel bitter to a degree, suspecting what she now did about how they'd met. She didn't feel any malevolence towards Laura, though. There didn't seem much point.

'I told her that friends like that weren't worth having anyway,' she added, hoping to relax her a little.

Laura glanced down again. Her eyes were glassy with tears when she looked back up, and Sarah felt for her. 'Thanks.' She smiled, more readily. 'It is embarrassing,' she admitted, pausing for thought. 'The mental gymnastics I have to do to come up with synonyms is so draining sometimes I give up before I've started.'

'Well, that came out okay,' Sarah assured her, with a surprised smile back.

'Because I was taking it slowly,' Laura pointed out. 'You were right about people getting impatient. You can see their eyes glazing over sometimes, or else they get irritated, and you sense they're itching to check their watches.'

Sarah nodded, thinking of her school friend, who'd said she wanted to give people a fat lip sometimes so they could see what it felt like to struggle to speak. 'Have you always stammered?' she asked gently.

Taking a sip of her wine, Laura thought about it. 'A bit. It really kicked in when I was in my teens, though. I didn't dare open my mouth for a while,' she said, a small furrow forming in her brow.

'Did you not get some support?' Sarah asked, aware that there were various therapies and support groups available.

'Eventually.' Laura looked pensive as she placed her glass back on the table. 'Not at first, though. I think my mother thought I would just grow out of it. We don't get on that well, I'm afraid.'

'That's a shame.' Sarah really did feel for her now. She would have needed all the help she could get at such a sensitive age. 'What about your father? Do you get on with him okay?' she probed, hoping she wasn't venturing too far onto sensitive ground.

'Stepfather. And no, I don't.' A shadow crossed Laura's face. 'He's loaded, old money, you know, inherited from his parents; imagines himself entitled because of it. He didn't want to marry my mother, but she managed to manipulate him into it.' She paused, drawing in a long breath. 'You can see why I ran scared of marriage, can't you?' She sighed amusedly.

'You've never been married then?' Sarah enquired, casually she hoped.

Laura shook her head. 'My job always took up too much of my time. I just never met the right person. I lived with my last boyfriend for a while, but it didn't last.'

'Do you mind if I ask why?' Sarah didn't want to appear to be grilling her. She hoped Laura would understand that she just wanted to know her better.

Laura hesitated. 'He was impossibly controlling,' she said quietly, 'so …' Stopping, she shrugged as if it wasn't a big deal.

Sarah noted the hurriedly downcast gaze again and guessed it *was* a big deal. It certainly would be to her. She could understand Laura's discomfort. No doubt she would be thinking that people might judge her. Sarah's mum had been in a controlling relationship with her father, who'd constantly undermined her until she'd lost faith in herself, as she'd confided once Sarah was old enough to understand. She'd felt worthless, she told her. Eventually, with the help of a friend, she'd found an exit strategy. It hadn't been easy to explain to a child, she'd said sadly.

Sarah understood now what the attraction to Steve would be. Perhaps that was why she'd felt safe with him herself. He was anything but controlling. He just didn't see that in allowing her to make all the decisions in their relationship – about where they lived, household maintenance, arrangements for Ollie – he was also leaving her with all the responsibility. Steve hadn't been her Mr Right. He might be Laura's, though. The woman had her own house, so she was obviously a doer. They could actually be good for each other, in an opposites-attract sort of way. She might even shake him out of his commitment-phobic tendencies. And if there had to be someone involved in the joint parenting of Ollie, Laura seemed capable, sensible. Nice, she thought, albeit a bit reluctantly.

'But that's all history now,' Laura went on, smiling brightly – for her sake, Sarah guessed. 'I'd much rather talk about little Oliver and … um …' There was a flicker of doubt in her eyes. 'If that's all right with you, that is?'

'Ollie.' Sarah smiled. 'And yes, it is.' She'd come here to find out more about Laura. To fish around for any deep, dark secrets she might have. Once she'd started talking more fluently, though, Laura had seemed fine sharing information with her. Sarah had come expecting not to like her, but she found she actually did, perhaps because of her vulnerability. She was nothing like she'd expected her to be. She had a naturalness about her, an openness, which was surprising, considering she too might have had her guard up. It could all be a ploy to win Sarah over, of course, but she felt it was genuine.

'He's three, isn't he?' Laura asked. 'Up to all sorts of mischief, I bet.'

'Almost four, and definitely.' Sarah rolled her eyes. 'Don't get me wrong, he's not a naughty child, but I won't pretend he's not full-on.'

'He's obviously an intelligent little boy.' Laura smiled reassuringly.

'Oh, he's definitely that. He's usually one step ahead of me.' Sarah smiled tolerantly. 'I struggle to keep him entertained sometimes. He gets bored with his toys so easily, apart from his Lego, which keeps him occupied for hours. Mind you, I think I've found the perfect thing for his birthday. It's part of the Geometric Magicube range, which are fun, hands-on toys designed to help develop motor skills and, hopefully, stretch the imagination. I thought the dinosaur set would be perfect, as he's big into them.'

'Sounds brilliant,' Laura enthused. 'He obviously needs a mental challenge. I can't wait to meet him. Does he look like his mummy or his daddy?'

It was an innocent question, a perfectly understandable question – Steve was blonde, Sarah was dark – but even so ... 'Has Steve not shown you a photograph of him?'

'He only has baby photographs. He said you were the photographer,' Laura said with an amused smile. 'He was going to ask you to send him some, but he's been really busy with work ...'

He'd obviously forgotten. That was typical Steve. Clearly Laura knew what he was like, always working late, determined to make his building business successful – in his dad's memory. He was so tired sometimes, though, he said himself he would forget his head if it was loose.

'I think Ollie takes after Steve more than me.' Sarah reached into her bag for her phone. 'He has blonde hair – which Steve says was the bane of his life when he was little, because people kept mistaking him for a girl – and huge, beguiling baby-blue eyes, though don't let those fool you. Here you go.' She flicked to one of the photos she'd taken in the pub garden and passed the phone over.

'Oh my gosh.' Laura swallowed as she studied it. 'He's just perfect,' she whispered, her eyes glassy again, but this time with wonderment.

CHAPTER SIX

Due to pick Ollie up for his first weekend visit at Laura's, Steve rang to say he was a few minutes away, throwing Sarah, who was still in her pyjamas, into a complete flap as she tried to get their son dressed and ready to go. He was early and she was nowhere near ready.

'Is Daddy coming soon?' Ollie asked, his eyes wide with excitement as his head popped through the neck hole of his jumper.

'Very soon.' Sarah gave him a bright smile, whilst inwardly cursing herself for getting up so late. She'd intended to be up and organised, even though it was her Saturday off. She'd wanted Ollie to wear his new tiger hoodie and jogger set but found it wasn't in his wardrobe when she looked for it. Finally remembering it was in the wash, she'd ended up grabbing the first things that came to hand, his Spider-Man T-shirt and monster jeans, both of which she realised, too late, had grass stains on them she hadn't been able to shift. It was no big deal, children got dirty, but despite telling herself she was being silly, she'd wanted to make a good impression. She would hate Laura to think she wasn't meticulous about cleanliness.

She doubted Steve would be very impressed when he spotted Joe's car on the drive. Sure Joe would understand why, she'd been going to ask him to leave before Steve arrived, but then events had overtaken her. She hadn't wanted to shove him out of the door and now she felt immensely guilty that he was obviously here, with no idea why she should. There was no reason she should be defensive about him staying over – Steve hadn't wasted much time before embarking on another relationship, after all. Wasn't it hypocritical of her, though, not to have mentioned Joe, given her reaction to Steve's news about Laura? She really should have said something.

Tugging Ollie's jeans on as the doorbell rang, she hoisted him up, grabbed the bag she'd packed with any essentials he might need and headed for the landing. As he seemed to be growing heavier by the day and insisted he was a big boy now, she didn't generally carry him down the stairs, but even with her holding onto him, she doubted he would negotiate them carefully with his daddy at the front door.

Setting him down in the hall, she took hold of his hand, tugged in a breath and pulled the front door open. 'Morning,' she said cheerfully, though she felt far from cheerful, knowing she was going to have to say goodbye to her little boy for a whole weekend.

Clearly noting her pyjamas, Steve arched an eyebrow curiously, and then bent to sweep Ollie up as he launched himself at his legs. 'Hiya, Batman,' he said, hoisting him high in his arms. 'How you doing, hey?'

'I'm not Batman, I'm Spider-Man,' Ollie pointed out, plucking his shirt away from his chest, showing off the grass stain as he did so, to Sarah's dismay.

Ah well, she doubted he would stay clean for very long anyway. 'Sorry I'm not dressed yet,' she said, moving back to allow Steve in. 'You caught me by surprise.'

'I gathered,' Steve said, stepping into the hall. 'I take it you've got company?'

Hesitating, Sarah was debating how to answer when Ollie piped up, 'It's Joe. He's Mummy's friend and he's having a shower.'

'Is he?' Steve glanced at Sarah, his expression somewhere between troubled and puzzled. 'Well, that's nice, isn't it?'

'Uh-huh. He's my friend as well,' Ollie went on excitedly. 'He plays football with me. And Duplo. He made me a subma ...' Pausing, he knitted his brow.

'Submarine,' Sarah reminded him.

'Submarine,' Ollie repeated with a satisfied nod.

'Did he now? That *was* nice of him, wasn't it?' Steve arranged his face into a smile. The flinty look in his eyes, though, told Sarah he was less than pleased.

'He made some superheroes too. Do you want to see?' Ollie asked.

'You bet,' Steve said enthusiastically. 'Tell you what, why don't you go and get them, and pack your Duplo set up while you're at it. I could have a go at making some superheroes too. See if I can make them as good as Mummy's friend does.'

'Okay, but you might have to practise,' Ollie said innocently.

'Bound to. I'm obviously not as accomplished as *Joe*,' Steve replied, a definite hint of sarcasm in his tone, Sarah noted, as he lowered Ollie to the floor.

'So, this Joe.' Straightening up, he met Sarah's gaze, his own quizzical. 'Is he someone you've been seeing long?'

Standing in the hall in her pyjamas while Joe was upstairs in the shower, Sarah felt immediately wrong-footed. 'No, not very long,' she answered, hoping to God he wasn't imagining she might have been seeing him before they'd split up.

'Oh. Right,' Steve said flatly. 'About the same time I've been seeing Laura, perhaps? Just wondering, out of curiosity.'

Shit. Realising she'd put her foot squarely in it, having demanded to meet Laura and then telling Steve nothing about a man who was clearly spending a considerable amount of time here, Sarah groped for a way to backtrack. 'I've known him a while, though. We went out together once before.'

Steve didn't look appeased. 'Right,' he repeated with a short nod.

God, could she not just think before opening her mouth? 'Years ago,' she clarified, thinking his imagination would now be on a roll. 'Before you and I met. I think I mentioned him. We went to—'

'No explanations necessary, Sarah.' Steve cut across her, a flash of palpable anger now in his eyes. 'Who you sleep with is your business. I was wondering how it is, though, that you get to vet my girlfriend – which, incidentally, Laura found pretty bloody traumatic – but this Joe character gets full access to *my* son while *I* know nothing about him.'

'Steve …' Sarah looked at him, astonished. He hardly ever swore. She'd never known him to use bad language with Ollie in the house. Laura evidently *had* brought out his protective gene. But he was right. And he had every right to be angry. 'Look, Steve, I'm really sorry. I—'

'Did you *have* to give her such a hard time?' he growled over her.

'I did no such thing.' Sarah was flabbergasted. 'I only wanted to meet her out of concern for Ollie. I would have told you about Joe, but we weren't actually properly together then. And I know I should have said something once we *were* seeing each other, but … Well, I didn't, and I'm sorry.'

'Gets better, doesn't it?' Steve smiled cynically. 'You're concerned for Ollie, yet you let a bloke you've been going out with for five minutes spend the night? Several nights, judging by how well Ollie appears to be getting on with him.'

'But I *know* him, I've said.' Sarah tried to justify herself, but knew she couldn't. 'He's all right, Steve, I promise. He's a policeman. And he's only ever stayed a couple of—'

'I don't care if he's the bloody *Chief* of Police.' Steve stared at her, disbelieving. 'You never even *mentioned* him. You can't set out ground rules and then completely ignore them yourself. Do you know how uncomfortable you made Laura feel, thinking she might be a danger to Ollie? This is someone who works in a hospice, for Christ's sake; she's obviously caring. Would you have climbed down if I'd told you what her job was? If *I'd* said, she's all right?'

'But you didn't.' Sarah felt her eyes filling up. 'And I *didn't* make her feel uncomfortable. Or at least I didn't think I had. She didn't seem …' Seeing Joe descending the stairs, she stopped, not sure whether to be relieved or wary.

'Sorry to interrupt,' he said, reaching the hall. His hair was wet from the shower. Sarah noted Steve's agitated expression as he noticed it too. 'I thought I should probably introduce myself, as I appear to be the subject under discussion.' Smiling, he walked towards Steve. 'Joe Sartini. Pleased to meet you.'

Steve looked warily down at the hand Joe was offering him, and then, grudgingly, shook it. 'Likewise,' he managed, looking anything but. 'Steve,' he said. 'Ollie's father.'

'I gathered. Ollie's mentioned you a couple of thousand times.' Joe nodded to where Ollie was standing in the lounge doorway with his Duplo, looking uncertainly between them. 'He's a great kid.'

Steve followed his gaze and then squeezed his eyes closed. Clearly he'd realised, as Sarah had, that they'd been bordering on an argument in front of their child. 'Yeah, he is.' Giving Joe a tight smile, he swung around to pick Ollie up. 'If a little confused right now,' he added acerbically.

'Come on, trooper,' he said cheerfully to Ollie. 'Let's get going, shall we, since it's getting a bit late.' Having imparted that pointed comment, he moved past Joe and Sarah and headed for the front door. 'I'll call you this evening. Let you know how he is.'

'Steve, wait.' Sarah followed him. 'His coat.' Unhooking Ollie's coat from the peg, she handed it to him and picked up the overnight bag she'd packed. 'He has a change of clothes in here, and his PJs and bedtime story book. He's into the "Never Ask" stories now. Oh, and his blue bunny soft toy. He won't go to sleep without it,' she reminded him. 'Laura said she'd bought him some toys, so I didn't pack too many.'

Steve glanced briefly at her. 'She has. She got him a few things to make him feel settled, including the Magicube dinosaur set, by the way. I thought I should let you know, as you mentioned you might be getting him one for his birthday.'

'Oh.' Sarah knitted her brow. 'Yes, I was.' She'd also mentioned it to Laura, so why would she have …?

'Dinosaurs?' Ollie said excitedly, his big blue eyes like saucers.

'Yup.' Steve chuckled and gave him a squeeze. 'We'll have a whale of a time, won't we?'

Obviously she'd already bought it when Sarah had mentioned it, but hadn't wanted to say anything for fear of upsetting her – hence the reason Steve was telling her now. Swallowing back her huge disappointment and trying hard not to mind, she leaned in to kiss Ollie's cheek before Steve disappeared with him. 'Be good for Daddy and Laura,' she said, blinking back the tears she didn't want her little man to see.

'I will,' Ollie promised, flinging his arms around her neck. God, she was going to miss him.

'Bye, Joe.' Ollie gave him a wave.

'See you soon, mate.' Joe waved back, at which Steve looked po-faced, making Sarah feel even more guilty, if that were possible.

Turning away, Steve hit his key fob, and Sarah followed him to his car to drop Ollie's bag into the boot while Steve strapped him into his seat.

Giving Ollie an enthusiastic smile, she waited for Steve to close the door before she spoke. 'We're not where we're at because of me, Steve. It was a mutual decision for us to part,' she pointed out, still feeling guilty, but also angry that he was so furious with her. He'd said he hadn't got together with Laura until after they'd broken up, but given what she now knew about where Laura worked, there was no way she could believe the attraction hadn't been there, even if they hadn't done anything about it. If they had been having an affair, Steve wasn't likely to admit it, and she wasn't about to ask him now. He really had no right to stand in judgement on her, though.

He sighed apologetically. 'I know. It's just … Look, I'll give you a call later. We'll have a chat then,' he said, obviously reluctant to discuss it here on the drive with their son already in the car.

Knowing he was right – Ollie had already overheard more than he should have – Sarah nodded. 'I'll get him the Wheelybug,' she said, attempting some kind of truce. 'In place of the Magicube. You know, the ride-on animals that go round and round as well as forwards and backwards? He's wanted one for ages, so …'

Steve nodded in turn, and managed a less loaded smile. 'Talk soon.'

Offering him a small smile back, Sarah blew Ollie a kiss through the window, and then trailed back to the front door. As she watched them go, her heart squeezed painfully. She had to get used to this, saying goodbye to the little boy who'd never stayed away from home until now. Seeing his empty bed at night was going to be unbearable.

'Okay?' Joe asked softly, walking up behind her and giving her shoulders a gentle squeeze.

Sarah wiped the back of her hand across her cheeks and turned towards him. 'No, not really,' she admitted. 'I feel like I'm missing a limb suddenly.'

'You're bound to.' Joe eased her towards him. 'Just try to take some time out and gather your resources.'

'Resources?' Sarah glanced curiously at him. Despite their intention to end things amicably, to always put Ollie first, were she and Steve going to be constantly arguing now? Joe obviously thought they were. She couldn't bear to imagine how that would affect Ollie.

'For parenthood,' Joe clarified. 'I haven't got kids, but I can see it's not easy.'

'It's not,' Sarah admitted with a small smile. 'Kids don't come with an instruction manual. Nor do relationships, unfortunately.'

'No,' Joe empathised. 'It would be a hell of a lot easier if they did.'

Needing his arms around her, Sarah leaned back into him. 'Do you think he'll be okay?'

'Of course he will.' Joe held her close. 'It's pretty obvious he loves his dad, and vice versa.'

Sarah nodded, but still she couldn't shake the uneasiness that had crept through her when Steve had said that Laura had found meeting her traumatic. 'Why do you think she said that?' she asked. 'That I'd given her a hard time?'

She'd thought they'd got along well, all things considered. Why on earth would Laura tell Steve that they hadn't?

CHAPTER SEVEN

Laura

'All done?' Laura asked, turning from the dishwasher as Steve came down after bathing Ollie.

'All done – and I think I'm just about done in.' Steve rolled his eyes good-naturedly as he came across to her. 'We had a pillow fight. Ollie won.'

Noting his hair was damp and in complete disarray, Laura laughed. 'You look it. He's a bundle of energy, isn't he?'

'Definitely that.' Steve smiled fondly. 'He's a good kid, though.'

Laura reached to smooth his fringe from his forehead. 'You've missed him, haven't you?'

'And some,' he admitted gruffly. 'Thanks for doing this, Laura.'

'What?' She widened her eyes in surprise. 'I haven't done much, apart from feeding him.'

'Playing with him, making time for him.' Steve pulled her into his arms. 'Having him here. It means a lot.'

'How could a girl resist when he's a little replica of his father?' She brushed his lips softly with hers.

'But cuter.' Steve smiled and kissed her nose.

'Obviously.' Laura had to agree with that. Ollie had that cheeky little-boy smile that could melt hearts. He'd melted hers as soon as she'd set eyes on him. She hadn't quite been able to believe her eyes as she'd watched Steve, whom she'd only ever spoken to in passing, walking from his car to the hospice with him. She'd guessed he was his son immediately. With his blonde colouring, the boy had been a little replica of him.

After she'd seen Ollie that first time, she'd begun to visit Annie more often, growing as fond of the old woman as Annie had become of her. The window of Annie's room, where she'd positioned her armchairs, looked out onto the street, allowing them to indulge in Annie's favourite pastime of people-watching. Laura's visits would conveniently coincide with Steve and Ollie's arrival. When she'd heard that Steve's father had deteriorated and that he'd made the decision not to bring Ollie again, she'd summoned up her courage and made an effort to speak to him. She'd soon learned his marriage was in trouble, and a kernel of panic had begun to take root inside her. The child would be a casualty. How could he not be? As she'd come to know Steve better, realising that he was steadfast and reliable, that he had a certain degree of humility, it had been easy to envisage a relationship with him. She felt safe with him. In turn, she vowed that she would keep his child safe, that she would be there for Ollie, provide him with the love and affection she herself had never had. It was as if fate had played a hand in bringing him to her. She wouldn't let him down.

Holding Steve's gaze, she smiled warmly. 'Have you read him his bedtime story?'

'Shoot!' He looked alarmed. 'No, I forgot. I'd better go back up. He'll never settle otherwise.'

'Did you remember to put the night light I bought him in his room?' she asked as he about-faced. 'I left it on our dressing table.'

'Damn.' Steve stopped in his tracks. 'No. I forgot that as well.'

'Too busy pillow-fighting,' Laura chastised him playfully. 'Would you like me to read him his story? You could pour us a well-earned drink while I do. I bought us a nice Cabernet Sauvignon as a treat.' Closing the dishwasher, she headed across the kitchen.

'He'd like that,' Steve said as she selected a bottle from the wine rack. 'You're obviously a hit.'

'Well, that's a relief.' Laura handed him the wine. 'Hopefully he'll report favourably back to Sarah.'

'Yeah ... sorry about all that.' Steve shrugged apologetically. 'She was only looking out for Ollie, but if I'd known she was going to give you the third degree ... I still can't believe she did that while she's letting some bloke I know nothing about come and go as he pleases.'

'It's not a problem,' Laura assured him. 'I would never have told you about it if I'd known you would worry. It's true she did give me a bit of a hard time, but Ollie's here, that's all that matters. And I'm sure Sarah wouldn't let anyone she didn't trust implicitly be around him. Having met her, I imagine she'll know everything there is to know about the man.'

'Yeah, probably,' Steve agreed with a sigh. 'I suppose she was just doing what mothers naturally do.'

'You can't blame her for that.' Giving him another reassuring smile, Laura turned to the door.

Steve caught her hand. 'Dinner was a hit, too.' He smiled appreciatively back and pressed her fingers to his lips. 'I've never seen him clean his plate before. I think he's going to love coming here.'

'I hope so,' Laura said, meaning it. She was desperate for Ollie to look forward to coming to see her, to learn to love her. 'As long as Sarah doesn't think I'm trying to outdo her.' She'd already made Ollie promise not to mention the extra home-made cookie she'd slipped him. Bearing in mind his sugar intake, she probably shouldn't have done, but how was she to resist those huge beguiling eyes?

'I think she might,' Steve warned her jokingly. 'Ollie's not normally big into his veggies.'

'You just have to make them fun,' Laura said, pecking his cheek and heading for the hall. 'I have lots more ideas.'

Heading up the stairs, she felt a moment's fleeting guilt about claiming the BBC Good Food home-made pizza veggie faces as her own idea, but then it was only a little sin in the scheme of things. She needed Steve to have complete faith in her competency as a mother. She longed for Ollie to accept her in that role.

Grabbing the night light from the main bedroom – a magical rotating one that projected an ocean theme she was sure he would love – she peered around the door to the small room, now clearly signed *Ollie's Room*.

'Hey, sweetheart, did you have a nice bath?' she asked, pleased when she saw him sitting on his bed playing with his Magicube dinosaur set. Sarah was right about it being a fun hands-on toy that would help develop his motor skills. Ollie loved it. Laura was so glad she'd immediately found one on Amazon.

'Yes.' Ollie's eyes flicked to hers as she came in, and then back to his building blocks, his tongue protruding as he concentrated on trying to attach the dinosaur's tail. 'Daddy got wet.'

'I noticed. His hair's damp.' Laura smiled, then, popping the lamp on his bedside table, she sat down on the edge of his bed and smoothed his fringe back. It was too long. She would give it a little trim in the morning. Sarah was obviously so busy with her job she didn't have time to take him for a haircut.

'I hear you played pillow fights too,' she said, reaching to help him turn one of the building blocks around so that the dinosaur's tail would fit.

Slotting the block into place and clearly satisfied as he surveyed his completed construction, Ollie looked up at her. 'Uh-huh,' he said, smiling mischievously. 'Daddy cried because he lost.'

'Oh no.' Laura feigned wide-eyed alarm.

'But he was only joking,' Ollie added worriedly.

'I know he was, darling.' She gave his shoulders a reassuring squeeze. 'He's definitely worn out from the battle, though. I think he might need to build up his muscles for next time, don't you?'

'He can do the superhero workout with me and Mummy!' Ollie looked delighted.

'Yes.' Laura was less so. 'Or you could show Daddy and me how to do it here,' she suggested, making a mental note to check out the YouTube video. 'Do you fancy it?'

Ollie closed one eye and thought about it. 'Yes.' He nodded happily.

'Brilliant.' Laura beamed him another smile. 'I'll make sure we have some refreshments handy. Meanwhile, how about I read you your bedtime story while Daddy has a little rest?'

'*Never Ask a Dragon*!' As Ollie scrambled to tuck himself under his duvet, Laura reached out a hand to save his dinosaur tower from tumbling from the bed.

'Ooh, okay, but I'm not sure where your book is.' She frowned thoughtfully. 'How about I tell you a story about a special super-hero, one nobody else knows exists?'

His interest pricked up at that. 'Will he be *my* special superhero?' He looked hopefully up at her.

'Definitely.' Smiling, she turned on his night light and snuggled down next to him. 'So … Once upon a time there was a little boy—'

'Like me?' Ollie whispered, as they both gazed up at an ocean brought to life by the softly rotating light.

'Yes, just like you.' Laura snuggled closer, badly wanting to curl her body around him and hold him until his breath slowed to a deep, contented sleep. 'If you look up there and concentrate really hard,' she pointed to the fish on the ceiling weaving sinuously through the seaweed, 'you might glimpse him.'

CHAPTER EIGHT

Sarah

Sarah unfurled herself from the sofa. She and Joe were supposed to be having a relaxing evening catching up on a thriller series on Netflix, but her attention kept wandering. She couldn't stop dwelling on Laura and what she'd told Steve. No matter how many times she went over it, it simply wasn't right. In her recollection, they'd got along fine. Laura had even managed not to stammer. She wouldn't have done that if she'd been stressed or uncomfortable in Sarah's company.

'Need more wine?' Pausing the TV, Joe half rose from his seat.

'Oh.' Sarah glanced at the wine glass she'd absent-mindedly picked up as she'd got to her feet. 'Thanks,' she managed a small smile, 'but I'm feeling a bit too tired to watch TV, to be honest. Do you mind if I pop up and have a quick soak in the bath?' She actually wanted to text Steve and make sure Ollie was okay. He'd called her earlier, but she needed to know her little boy was safely tucked up in bed and that Steve had given him a goodnight kiss for her. She'd suggested he put him on the phone before he settled down for the night, but Steve said he thought that might make him homesick. Sarah had supposed he was right. But she missed him already, so very much. She really did feel as if part of her was missing.

'No problem. Give me a shout once you're in,' Joe said. 'I'll come and help you ease some of that tension.'

Was it so obvious that she was wound up like a watch spring? 'No, you carry on watching,' she insisted. 'I'll feel bad if I drag you away from it.'

'We'll be out of sync then. In any case, I'd rather watch you soaking in the bath.' His mouth curved into a suggestive smile.

Sarah gave him a mock scowl. 'You're insatiable,' she scolded him. She was glad he was here. She wasn't sure what she would have done otherwise, rattling around the empty house on her own, and he did her flagging ego the world of good. He'd already hinted she was worrying too much, though, and she didn't want him thinking she was checking up on Steve, which she supposed she was.

'Says the woman who practically jumped me while I was distracted making coffee,' Joe called after her as she reached the hall.

Sarah laughed. 'I didn't hear you protesting very loudly,' she called back.

'Because my mouth was otherwise engaged,' Joe replied smartly. 'Let me know when you want your back scrubbed. I'll bring your wine up.'

'That would be lovely. Thanks.' Sarah headed quickly up the stairs.

Turning on the taps and treating herself to a generous amount of Wild Argan Oil Bubbling Bath, she went back to the bedroom to text Steve. It took her a while to get the wording right; she wasn't sure what to say that didn't sound like she was questioning his parenting skills. *Did he settle down okay?* she finally sent.

He took forever to answer. The bath was almost full when she heard her phone ping a reply: *Laura says he's happily tucked up with Mr Whale.*

Mr ... who? Sarah squinted at the text, confused. *Did he not go to bed with Bunny?* she sent back worriedly. Ollie never went to bed without Bunny. If he woke in the night and couldn't see him, he would fret about him. And they'd just gone and swapped him for some brand-new toy? Or rather, Laura had, it seemed.

She'd barely shot off the first text before she keyed in another. *Didn't you read him his bedtime story?*

Growing agitated when Steve took his time replying again, she twirled the taps off before the bath overflowed, then jumped on her phone as it rang.

'What the hell is this all about, Sarah?' Steve asked tersely before she had a chance to speak.

'What?' Sarah laughed, disbelieving. Was he actually annoyed that she would be concerned about her son? 'Nothing, I—'

'It doesn't sound like nothing.' He spoke over her, his voice low – from which she gathered he was talking out of earshot of his girlfriend. To spare Laura's feelings, she also gathered, rather than hers. 'Are you seriously telling me you're going to vet who tells him his bedtime story now?'

'No,' Sarah denied. 'I'm concerned, that's all, for Ollie. I just thought that as he's in a strange environment, you would want to settle him into bed yourself. It's not a big deal, Steve.'

'It sounds like it is to me,' he growled.

'Only because you're making it one,' she countered. 'I'm just worried for my son. I think I've every right to be, don't you?'

'Meaning what, precisely?' Steve asked, plainly working to restrain his anger.

But why was he angry? 'I don't mean anything, Steve.' Sarah sighed despairingly. Was it really so unreasonable of her to want Ollie not to feel lonely or disorientated by his new surroundings? Surely Steve could see that familiarity was important? That however insignificant Laura thought his comfort toy seemed, it wasn't. The woman wasn't a mother. How could she know? Sarah was Ollie's mother and she knew her child. 'I just wanted to know he went to bed contentedly. He's never been away from me before. Don't you think I'm bound to be worried?'

Steve didn't reply for an interminably long minute. Then, 'You've really decided not to like her, haven't you?' he asked, knocking her sideways.

What utter rubbish. She hadn't decided anything of the sort. 'That's not true, Steve,' she retorted tearfully. 'I made a big effort to get on with—'

'Why? Is it because you're jealous?'

'That's bloody ridiculous,' she snapped, swallowing back a mixture of anger and humiliation. Where was this coming from? She'd moved on. He'd *clearly* moved on. The only reason she was contacting him was out of concern for their son.

'I'm going,' she said, cutting the call before she was tempted to ask him whether it was his girlfriend and her motives he should be questioning. Fuming at what he'd implied, that she was actually jealous of the woman, she was too busy trying to digest his words as she trailed back to the bedroom to realise that Joe had come in.

'Problem?' he asked.

'No.' She ran a hand quickly under her nose. Then, 'Yes,' she blurted. 'They've taken his bunny off him.'

'What?' Joe looked taken aback.

'His bedtime comfort toy,' she tried to explain, cursing the tears that plopped from her eyes. Cursing Steve for reducing her to tears. 'He's had it since he was six months old. I got it specially personalised for him. It has his name embroidered on its ear. It's his absolute favourite. He *never* goes to bed without it.'

'Ah.' Now looking concerned, Joe placed the wine he'd brought her on the dresser and walked across to her.

'Why would they do that?' she asked him as he wrapped his arms around her, easing her to him. 'Why would Steve let her do that?'

'Hey, hey.' Joe stroked her hair as she cried into his shoulder. 'Perhaps he's just outgrown it?'

'No, he hasn't. He hadn't last night,' Sarah assured him.

'It might just be that he took a shine to one of the toys Steve said they'd bought him,' he suggested. 'No more than that. Did you ask Steve?'

'I didn't get a chance. He thought I was making a fuss about nothing.' Sarah looked up at him. She was probably a complete mess, but she didn't care. 'He even accused me of being determined not to like Laura when I asked him why he let her read Ollie his bedtime story.'

Joe looked perplexed at that. 'Does it matter who reads it? I mean, as long as they haven't just shoved him to bed with no story at all?'

'Of course it matters.' Sarah's frustration grew as it became apparent that Joe didn't think it was a big deal either. 'This is all new to him, leaving me, sleeping in a strange bed in a strange house. He'll be bewildered. He needs familiar things around him, his comfort toy, his daddy tucking him in, not some strange bloody woman he's only just met.'

Joe nodded slowly. His eyes were still flecked with concern, but Sarah guessed from his puzzled expression that he didn't really understand how important this was, that routine was paramount to a child's development. 'You're upset,' he said. 'You're bound to be a bit.'

'Of course I'm upset.' She moved away from him. 'I just … I don't trust her, Joe.'

He furrowed his brow, his expression growing serious. 'Why?' he asked, probably worried now in a professional capacity, and Sarah almost wished she hadn't said it. The fact was, though, she didn't trust Laura. How could she?

'Because of the things she told Steve,' she reminded him.

Joe's expression was back to confused.

'She said she was traumatised by our meeting. Why would she say that? That she felt uncomfortable, when I saw she was struggling and did my best to make her feel relaxed?'

'Struggling how?' He looked at her as if *he* were struggling – to keep up.

'She has a stutter, though I'm beginning to wonder if she actually does.'

'Right.' Joe nodded again pensively and drew in a breath. 'Sarah, are you sure you're not getting this a little out of perspective?'

'No I am *not*. It's *her* who's getting things out of perspective,' Sarah retaliated, her frustration mounting. Could no one see what was happening here but her? 'I just don't understand why she would have told Steve what she did unless it was to make me look bad.'

Shoving his hands in his pockets, he tipped his head to one side and squinted curiously at her for a long, contemplative moment. Then, 'Why would you care what Steve thinks, though?' he asked her.

Her heart plummeted. 'What's that supposed to mean?' she asked, though she knew from the flash of humiliation in his eyes exactly what he meant. He too clearly thought she was jealous of Laura.

'Nothing.' He ran a hand over his neck, looking now as frustrated as she felt. 'I can't see why you would be so upset about what might well be a simple miscommunication, that's all.'

Miscommunication? Sarah stared at him. The problem here was that there *was* no communication. Steve and his new girlfriend were changing Ollie's routine without consulting her and with no thought about the consequences. 'Whose side are you on?' she asked, biting back her tears.

'Jesus.' Joe shook his head and eyed the ceiling. 'I'm on *your* side, Sarah, obviously. It's just—'

'Me being neurotic,' she finished flatly.

'I don't think that. The thing is, though …' He hesitated. 'I didn't want to interrupt so I waited on the landing before coming down. I didn't hear Steve saying that Laura had said those things after meeting you. What I heard was him telling you how she felt.'

Sarah laughed, incredulous. 'She said I'd given her a hard time.'

'That wasn't my interpretation,' Joe disagreed. 'From where I was, it sounded as if it was Steve asking you why you'd given her such a hard time.'

She looked at him, confused. 'It's the same thing.'

'Is it? She probably did feel uncomfortable before you two spoke; with good reason, since she has a stutter and her boyfriend's ex-partner was demanding to meet her on her own, to weigh her up, no doubt. Think about it: wouldn't you feel anxious? From what you say, the meeting went well, though, so …'

Sarah's stomach knotted. 'You mean you don't think she was reporting back.'

Joe shrugged. 'I think I'd probably talk to her before jumping to too many conclusions.'

Meaning he *did* think she was being neurotic – out of jealousy. Was it possible she was, because she thought Laura might replace her in Ollie's affections as well as Steve's?

CHAPTER NINE

Ollie's feet had barely touched the pavement before he was racing towards Sarah to throw himself into her arms, his little face beaming and obviously excited to see her. Swooping him up, she squeezed him close, peppering his cheeks with sloppy kisses and nuzzling his neck, which had him in a fit of giggles in an instant. His fringe had been cut, she noticed, her tummy flipping. Had Steve done that? Or had Laura? Quashing her immediate agitation, she made herself smile, for her little boy's sake. 'Did you have a lovely time?' she asked him.

'Uh-huh.' Ollie nodded enthusiastically. 'Mr Whale did too.' He waggled the new soft toy he was clutching, which Sarah had been sure would be a bone of contention between her and Laura. Now, after Joe had pointed out that she might have got things out of proportion, she was realising that she might be being overprotective simply because Ollie was her child. Everything he was, everything he thought and did had come from her. She knew she was struggling to share him, but she had no choice. Whoever Steve was with, she could never bring herself to alienate him from his child, to rob Ollie of his father. She hoped they'd think to consult her in future, though, before making major decisions such as changing his comfort toys. And cutting his hair – she couldn't help feeling Laura was making a point, hinting that Sarah wasn't taking proper care of him.

Pushing her irritation aside rather than creating more animosity between her and Steve, she concentrated on Ollie. 'Ooh, he's a lovely bright blue, isn't he? Is he your new snuggle friend?' she asked, wanting to gauge how he felt about losing Bunny.

'Yes,' Ollie said with a nod. 'Because Bunny has a portant job to do.'

'Does he?' Sarah looked at him, surprised.

'Uh-huh.' Ollie gave her another firm nod. 'He's guarding my new toy box.'

'Oh, well, that is an important job.' Dismissing the pang of sadness she felt at the thought of Bunny being in a strange house – which was a bit silly, even if it was the first toy her little boy had loved – she injected some cheeriness into her voice.

'Laura's going to feed him pizza faces if he gets hungry,' Ollie informed her assuredly.

'Yummy. They sound delicious.' Sarah supposed they must have been if Ollie had remembered them.

'Can I go inside and play, Mummy?' he asked, now wearing his best beguiling eyes – and knowing full well Sarah couldn't resist.

'Go on then,' she said indulgently. 'You can have twenty minutes before bath time, but that's all.' Lowering her wriggling son to the ground – he was obviously keen to bolt off and no doubt upend his toy box – she made sure he was through the front door before turning back to Steve, who was retrieving Ollie's bag from the boot of his car. Placing it on the pavement, he stayed where he was – a safe distance off, it appeared – and looked her over warily.

He had every right to be peeved. Sarah's concerns had been for Ollie, but the truth was, she had judged Laura before even meeting her, which must have communicated to Steve that she was going to make his life difficult whoever he was with. She hadn't meant to do that. She hadn't meant to communicate what she must have to Joe either. He hadn't said anything, but she'd seen the uncertainty in his eyes, the obvious hurt as he'd undoubtedly considered whether, like his wife, she was still stuck on her ex.

'How did it go?' she asked, walking towards the car.

'Fine.' Steve's expression was guarded. 'I'd have let you know if there were any problems, not that there would be any I couldn't handle. I have been part of Ollie's life since he was born, after all.'

'I know.' Sarah felt contrite. 'Look, Steve—'

'We went out for lunch today,' Steve said, fetching Ollie's coat from the boot. 'He had mini chicken nuggets and vanilla ice cream. He didn't eat a massive amount, so Laura made him some toast with peanut butter and cream cheese for tea. He had a home-made kiwi fruit lolly too. He wolfed that down. He's obviously keen on those.'

'Oh, right.' Sarah was surprised. She'd tried him with kiwi fruit once. He hadn't been that enamoured. She hadn't thought of making lollies. Laura was plainly making a huge effort to ensure he ate properly. 'That's brilliant,' she said, now feeling even more guilty. 'I was wondering whether to give him a bedtime snack, but he obviously won't need one.'

'No.' Steve smiled shortly. 'Laura's been great with him.'

'I gathered.' Sarah paused, and then braced herself to broach the subject of Ollie's hair, which she couldn't pretend she hadn't noticed. 'I see you've cut his fringe,' she said carefully.

'Laura did.' Steve studied her cautiously. 'It was tickling his eyelashes. It's not a problem, is it?'

'No,' Sarah said quickly, thinking better of pointing out that it might have been nice to check with her first. 'It's just … I had him an appointment booked, but I can easily cancel it. It will save me some money.'

'Great.' Steve nodded and walked to the driver's-side door.

'Steve …' She stopped him as he pulled it open. 'About the argument we had, the way you said I made Laura feel. I didn't mean to. I really was thinking about Ollie's welfare, but … Anyway, if I did make her feel uncomfortable, I'm sorry.' She waited, hoping he would accept her apology and they could get back to being friends, as they'd promised they would be.

He appeared to debate with himself, then, 'It's okay, no harm done,' he said with a shrug. 'Laura said you got along all right in the end.'

Sarah felt a huge surge of relief. Joe had been right. She should have listened to him, been less defensive. She would have to apologise to him too, and try to reassure him. She hoped he wasn't regretting getting involved with her.

'I don't think it's me you should be apologising to, though,' Steve suggested, smiling more easily, which was at least something. 'I'll call you about having Ollie the weekend after next,' he said. 'Meanwhile, try not to worry so much, hey? We'll work things out. I'm one hundred per cent with you in regard to what's best for Ollie.'

Nodding, Sarah gave him an appreciative smile in return, then waved him off and hurried into the house to check on Ollie. Finding him whirling Mr Whale around, Spider-Man hitching an undulating ride on the creature's back, she smiled and went to run his bath.

Half an hour later, she encouraged a still far too excited little boy into bed. 'So did you like Laura, sweetheart?' she asked. It was obvious he had got along with her, but still, she just wanted to check.

'Yes.' Ollie nodded happily. 'She told me a story,' he said as Sarah reluctantly tucked Mr Whale in with him. He did seem to love the cuddly toy.

'I gathered.' She reached to smooth her fingers through his fringe, which wasn't too bad, she supposed, if a little bit lopsided. 'About dragons, I bet.' She smiled, assuming Laura had read to him from his bedtime story book.

'Uh, uh. *Super*heroes.' Widening his eyes animatedly, Ollie stretched out his arms superhero style.

Not his bedtime story book then. Sarah tried very hard not to mind. Stipulating which stories Laura should read really would be bordering on neurotic. She hoped she realised that overstimulating his mind at bedtime wasn't a good idea, though.

'Was it indeed? We'll have to see if we can find you some bedtime superhero books, then, won't we? Meanwhile, under the duvet, little man.'

'But I'm not tired, Mummy.' Ollie angled for a reprieve.

'You've had a busy day. You'll be tired in the morning. Come on, chop, chop, or no sweeties tomorrow.' Wearing her best stern face, she reached quickly to tickle him into submission.

He wriggled and giggled, and eventually gave in, burrowing under his duvet before she could get him again.

'I have a secret,' he announced as he finally settled his head on his pillow.

'Oh yes?' Sarah looked at him curiously. 'And is it a secret you can share with me?'

He scanned her eyes, a reluctant look in his own. 'Laura told me I can't tell you.'

CHAPTER TEN

Sarah had to psych herself up to call Laura. She'd been going to suggest they meet up so she could offer her an apology, as Steve had suggested, though she wasn't sure an apology was actually in order. Now, though, she was perturbed. Planting ideas in Ollie's head about keeping secrets from his own mother wasn't on. Then there was the issue of his bunny. In Sarah's mind, Laura really should have consulted her about taking away his comfort toy. He might have been fine for one night, excited and tired out enough to go off to sleep, but what about if he woke in the night here, and Bunny wasn't home where he should be?

'Hi, Laura. It's Sarah,' she said when Laura picked up. 'I know it's early, but I wondered if we could have a quick word?'

'Yes, of course. Is everything all right? It's not Ollie, is it?' Laura asked, with a panicky edge to her voice that threw Sarah a bit.

'No, he's fine,' she assured her. 'It's just ... Well, to be honest, Laura, I'm a little miffed. Ollie tells me you've been telling him to keep things from me. I know it probably looks like I'm nit-picking, but I had to say something. Encouraging him to keep secrets from his own mother is sending out the wrong signals, don't you think?'

'Oh no ... God, I'm so sorry, Sarah. I didn't mean to do that,' Laura said, clearly contrite. 'I gave him an extra cookie and told him it was our secret and not to tell anyone. I was just joking with him, but I should have realised that at his age he would take me seriously. I'm really sorry.'

Sarah immediately felt bad. Telling him to keep an extra biscuit a secret was fairly innocuous, even if she would rather he didn't have too many. 'It's okay.' She climbed down, feeling awkward. 'I was a bit concerned, that's all. Ollie's normally such an open little boy, and I ...' She trailed off, not sure what to say that wouldn't sound as if she were imagining Laura capable of all sorts of things.

'You were worried. Obviously you would be,' Laura picked up sympathetically. 'You can never be too careful where children are concerned. I do understand, Sarah. Really I do.'

'Thanks,' Sarah said, feeling guilty again. Wasn't it her who was supposed to have been doing the apologising? 'I, um ... I was going to call you anyway,' she went on, wondering how many wrong feet it was possible to have. 'I wondered whether we could perhaps meet up for a quick chat about things generally. I thought we might do better to talk to each other rather than through Steve. I mean, he's bound to feel a bit like piggy in the middle, isn't he? What do you think?'

'Oh, right.' Laura hesitated. 'Yes, okay. I'm good with that. I think Steve will be relieved for Ollie's sake if he knows the two of us are getting on.'

'Brilliant. Tonight, possibly? I could pop round to you if you like?' Sarah offered, thinking it might give her an opportunity to see Ollie's new home from home for herself. She couldn't help but worry about what kind of place Laura had, though she didn't dare say that to Steve, which rankled. Wouldn't Steve want to know what kind of place Joe lived in if Ollie were to spend any time there? As it happened, Joe was living in a rented room until he'd got his affairs sorted out, so Ollie wouldn't be going there, but still it seemed as if she had to be on the defensive. She wasn't quite sure how that had happened.

'Sure. No problem.' Laura seemed keen. 'Steve's working late. It will be nice to have company.'

'Fab. How about six thirty?'

'Perfect. I'll pop some wine in the fridge. See you then.'

As Sarah finished the call, her fears about Laura were allayed somewhat. She couldn't ignore a new sense of apprehension creeping through her, though. Where had the stutter gone? she wondered.

At bang on 6.30, having left Ollie with Joe, Sarah pulled up in front of Laura's terraced house on the outskirts of Stratford-upon-Avon. It was only a small property, but still, she wondered how Laura had afforded it. She'd googled the address in her lunch hour, also how much similar properties in the area were selling for. They weren't cheap. Laura would be on a fair income as a palliative nurse, though, she supposed. Steve presumably helped out now too, so ...

She pulled herself up. It was none of her business. She'd already caused enough upset, and then compounded it this morning by overreacting to Ollie supposedly keeping secrets from her. She hadn't come here this evening to make things worse. She'd come to smooth things over. Ollie would have ongoing contact with his father, and she wanted things to be as amicable between them all as it could be.

Grabbing her bag, she climbed determinedly out of her car and headed for the front door. She was poised to ring the bell when Laura swung the door open. 'Hi.' She smiled nervously. 'Come on in.'

Noting her obvious apprehension, Sarah felt awful. She really hadn't meant to upset her by asking to meet her on her own. She'd just wanted to get to know her. She'd thought Laura might be more open with her if it was just the two of them. Yes, she'd been testing the waters, wondering whether she would like her. More importantly, whether Ollie would. She actually had liked her, which was why she herself had been so upset by what Steve had said.

'You'll have to excuse the mess.' Laura indicated several boxes and bags in the hall as Sarah stepped inside. 'Steve's still moving his things in and they tend to get stored in the hall en route to wherever they're going.'

That was Steve. Sarah couldn't help but smile. He wasn't lazy, far from it; he'd never been workshy – he wouldn't be running his own building company if he was – but when it came to household chores, he simply didn't see jobs that needed doing unless he was pointed in the right direction. 'You might have to give him a few subtle hints,' she said indulgently. 'He tends to get sidetracked.'

'I have, don't worry.' Laura rolled her eyes knowingly. 'I've warned him I'm not going to move his stuff for him when Ollie wants to ride his Wheelybug down the hall. I've ordered him the Wheelybug tiger. I hope that's okay?'

'You've ordered it?' Sarah eyed her quizzically. 'But didn't Steve mention I was going to get him one?'

'Oh no. You weren't, were you? I'm so sorry.' Laura looked mortified. 'Typical Steve, he forgot, obviously.'

Had he? Sarah scanned her eyes guardedly.

'I can always cancel it,' Laura offered quickly. 'I can do it now if you—'

'No, don't do that.' Sarah reprimanded herself. Her suspicion was going into overdrive. Knowing Steve, he probably had forgotten to mention it. Presumably he wasn't aware that Laura had decided to get one. She was trying to buy Ollie's affections, that was what this was. Sarah couldn't blame her for that, but she would have to have a word with her at some point about what toys she did buy Ollie. He would end up being spoilt otherwise, which wouldn't endear him to other children. Perhaps today wouldn't be the best time to mention it, though. 'I can always get him something else,' she assured her. 'I'll let you know what,' she added, trying not to sound as if she were making a point.

'I probably should have asked you first, shouldn't I?' Laura's expression was a mixture of apologetic and guilty, telling Sarah she'd got the point nevertheless. 'I'll make sure to next time.'

'That might be an idea. He could end up with two of everything otherwise.' Sarah relaxed a little, then, noting Laura's downcast eyes, felt even more guilty. After their conversation earlier, Laura probably thought she was here to give her a list of do's and don'ts. 'He really enjoyed his visit,' she said, attempting to put her at her ease.

'Good.' Laura brightened. 'I want him to be happy here, obviously, but I'd hate it if I'd done anything that might have upset you.'

'You haven't.' Sarah couldn't help but feel for her. She was plainly trying hard to get things right, possibly trying too hard, bearing in mind her abundant purchase of toys, but her heart was clearly in the right place. 'Although ...' She hesitated, reluctant now to bring it up. On the other hand, it was something she felt strongly about. 'I was a bit perturbed when I heard you'd swapped his bedtime bunny for a new snuggle toy.'

Laura's face fell.

'But when I saw how thrilled he was with Mr Whale, I realised it didn't really matter that much,' Sarah backtracked, though quietly she despaired of herself. If she really did have an issue she needed to tackle with Laura or Steve, she would have to be a bit more assertive.

'He loves it, insisted on taking it to bed with him.' Laura looked pleased as she turned to lead the way down the hall.

'I can see he does. It looks like Bunny will have to bow out gracefully.'

In the kitchen, Sarah glanced around, taking in the decor. There was a high-tech coffee machine, and a breadmaker, a freshly baked loaf filling the air with mouth-watering aromas on a cooling rack next to it. The kitchen itself was light and airy, with patio doors onto a small terrace, white cupboards with apple-green splashbacks. It was bold, bright and cheerful. Was this who Laura was under the anxiety? Someone she was striving to be maybe? It was likely the kitchen had come with the house, but still, it was definitely warm and homey, which was reassuring. 'Where is he?' she asked.

Laura knitted her brow. 'At work,' she said, clearly misinterpreting Sarah's distracted question. 'He has to finish a plumbing job on the Redwood estate. The carpenters are going in tomorrow, so—'

'No, sorry. I didn't mean Steve. I meant Bunny,' Sarah clarified. 'It's just that Ollie's had him since he was six months old, and … Well, he means a lot to me and I'd like to keep him.'

'God, of course. I should have thought.' Laura squeezed her eyes closed. 'He's upstairs, guarding Ollie's toy box. I'll go and fetch him.'

'No, don't worry.' Sarah stopped her as she headed back to the hall. 'Ollie's obviously happy with him being on guard, and he'll probably feel more secure with him here when he stays over. Could you make sure to let me have him eventually, though? I'd rather he didn't just end up languishing in the bottom of the toy box.'

'Absolutely. I understand completely. It would be like giving away his first tooth or a precious lock of his baby hair. I'll make sure to keep him safe,' Laura promised.

'Thanks.' Noting her earnest expression, her eagerness to please, Sarah smiled, now definitely feeling more at ease.

'No need to thank me. I would feel exactly the same,' Laura assured her. 'Take a seat, and I'll grab us some wine … assuming it's not too early for you?'

'I'd love one.' Sarah thought she actually would. It might be just what she needed to unwind. 'It's been a full-on day. We had three dogs returned before lunchtime,' she explained. 'I do wish people would understand that many rescue dogs need a lot of input. We try to educate them, but too many adopters imagine that once the dog has a nice comfy home, it will be so grateful at being rescued that it'll turn into the perfect pet. Sadly, it often takes more time and a lot more patience than new owners have. Then there was a half-starved puppy-farm dog brought in by the dog warden. It took me ages to settle her down. I think I've just about won her confidence, though, poor thing.'

Nodding her towards the small table and chairs, Laura headed for the fridge. 'I don't know how you do it. I'd be tempted to bring them all home. I'm not sure I'd do very well working outdoors in all sorts of weather either. At least I get to keep warm and dry, even if my job can sometimes be heartbreaking.'

'Yes, it must be.' Sarah looked her over thoughtfully as she turned from the fridge. 'I honestly don't think I could do what you do either.'

She'd been horribly wrong about Laura, assuming that because she didn't have children of her own, she wouldn't be up to the task of looking after Ollie. She hated to admit it, but there was possibly a part of her that had been hoping her worries might be justified, because she couldn't bear for Ollie to bond with Laura and end up seeing her as a mother figure. Taking a breath, she steeled herself to do what she'd come for. Laura obviously was a caring person, and clearly Sarah had made her feel uncomfortable, insisting on scrutinising her before allowing her to even meet Ollie.

'I know you're wondering why I'm here,' she started awkwardly. 'It's just … Well, I felt I owed you an apology.'

Fetching glasses from one of the cupboards, Laura glanced back at her, surprised. 'An apology? What on earth for?' she asked, her expression communicating to Sarah that she hadn't come home in floods of tears, telling Steve his ex-girlfriend was the biggest bitch she'd ever met.

'Judging you. Pre-judging you,' she admitted. 'I shouldn't have asked to meet up with you on your own. It was really pointed, and you must have found it stressful.'

Laura nodded. 'I did a bit,' she confessed. 'I thought you'd think I was a complete idiot, stumbling and stuttering over my words – I do that when I get nervous – but I understand why you wanted to get to know me before allowing Ollie to come and stay. It's only natural. Sensible, too. I was a complete stranger, after all, and as I said before, you never know, do you?'

Sarah felt a huge wave of relief sweep through her. Laura knew why she would be worried. Of course she did. You couldn't work in a hospice without being sensitive to people's feelings. It seemed to Sarah that it was Steve who was perhaps being overprotective of her. Being as slim and delicate as she was, Laura might look vulnerable, but she would have to have a certain amount of strength of character to do the job she did. 'No, you don't. Thanks for understanding, Laura,' she said, giving her a warm smile.

Passing her a filled glass, Laura smiled back. 'Here's to us being friends, for Jacob's sake.'

Sarah stopped, the glass halfway to her mouth. 'Who?'

'God, sorry.' Laura winced and pressed the heel of her hand to her forehead. 'Me and my muddled mind. He's my friend's little boy. I babysit for her sometimes. To Ollie and his future happiness,' she said, settling down at the table and raising her glass.

Scanning her face, Sarah hesitated for a second, then pulled herself up. It was a slip of the tongue, that was all. Perfectly understandable. Even she forgot Ollie's name when he was up to something that made her heart somersault. She'd called him Steve by mistake numerous times. She'd even called him Spot once – the name of one of the rescue dogs she'd been thinking about – when he'd charged from the bathroom behind her, heading for the stairs. She'd been so paralysed with shock she'd been completely unable to spit his actual name from her mouth.

'To Ollie,' she said, clinking her glass against Laura's.

Laura had barely taken a sip when the doorbell rang. Frowning, she glanced towards the hall. 'It will be a salesperson probably. We get loads at this time in the evening. Even when I tell them I'm renting, they don't get that I don't want my garden landscaped, or new windows. Hopefully they'll go away if I ignore it.'

Renting? Sarah had got the impression she owned the property. Hadn't Steve said she had her own place? She'd misinterpreted, obviously.

'Or possibly not.' Laura sighed, getting to her feet as the doorbell rang for a second time. 'I'd better go and see who it is. Won't be a tick.'

'Actually, do you mind if I use the loo?' Sarah asked, pushing her chair back.

'No problem.' Laura led the way back into the hall. 'It's that one.' She indicated the door under the stairs and Sarah slipped inside.

She couldn't help overhearing the exchange as Laura answered the front door. 'You're still alive then,' said an unfamiliar voice, sounding peeved. 'I'm assuming you've changed your phone number, since the old one's suddenly no longer in service?' The voice was now directly outside the loo door.

'No,' Laura answered. 'I *mmm*ean, yes, ages ago. I … M-M-Mum, where are you going?'

'To make a cup of tea, darling,' replied the woman – Laura's mother. 'I swear I'll die of thirst if I don't have one soon.'

'But M-M-Mum, I have *company*,' Laura protested.

'And what company would this be that's more important than the mother you haven't seen in months?' The woman now sounded hurt.

'A friend,' Laura said, her tone agitated. 'You can't just turn up when you feel like it. I—'

'But I've been worried to death about you, Laura. I've taken a taxi all the way here from the airport. You might at least look as if you're pleased to see me.'

Oh dear. It sounded as if the mother/daughter relationship really was strained. Inching the loo door open, Sarah glanced towards the kitchen. The kitchen door had been pushed to, and she hesitated, wondering what she should do. Her gaze flicking to the stairs, she hovered in the hall for a second, and then took a tentative step towards them. She shouldn't, but … Curiosity got the better of her. No one could blame her for wanting to check where her little boy slept when he was here, could they? She would just poke her head around the bedroom door, that was all. She'd been going to ask Laura to show her anyway, but with her mother arriving unannounced and Laura clearly otherwise engaged, she might as well utilise the time to have a quick peek now. She would be up and down again in a flash.

Climbing the stairs quickly, she gathered which was Ollie's room from the dinosaur-themed name plaque on the door, which was remarkably similar to the one he had at home, she realised, somewhat disconcerted. Had Steve chosen it? But … he hadn't long moved in. Surely they hadn't been planning the theme for Ollie's room before that? Pushing the partially open door wider, she glanced inside, feeling somewhat reassured as she noted the high-sided toddler bed in the shape of a racing car, which had undoubtedly been Steve's choice. He'd chosen the similar bed at home, which was one of the all-important 'boys and their toys' decisions he'd made. Perhaps he was trying to replicate Ollie's bedroom? He had mentioned he was concerned about him being homesick.

She was less reassured when she glanced towards the dinosaur toy box – also similar to the one Ollie had at home – on top of which Bunny was noticeable by his absence. Listening to make sure Laura hadn't emerged from the kitchen, she tiptoed across to the box and lifted the lid. Bunny didn't appear to be in there either. Her heart lifted a little as it occurred to her he might be tucked under the duvet where he belonged. She was about to close the lid when she spotted a familiar tuft of baby-blue fur peeking up between a playtime bus and a fire truck. Moving the toys aside, she extracted Bunny – who was lying face down, obviously already languishing in the toy box – and her heart skipped a beat.

He was missing an ear, the one that had been personalised with Ollie's name. The hairs rose on Sarah's skin as she examined him more closely to find that the ear didn't appear to have been accidentally torn. It had been cut off.

CHAPTER ELEVEN

Laura

'I'm really sorry about this,' Laura said, showing Sarah out. 'She's been abroad for a while. She's a fashion columnist and tends to travel a lot. And then turns up when she feels like it, unfortunately.'

'It's fine,' Sarah assured her. 'I wasn't going to stay long anyway. Joe's on duty this evening, so I have to get back.' Smiling, she turned for the door.

Something behind her eyes had shifted, though, Laura perceived. She was sure Sarah had warmed to her. That she'd decided she could trust her. Now, there was a wariness about her. She'd probably heard her exchange with her mother as she'd barged her way in. Laura had told her that they were estranged, but there was no way to explain that she lived in a constant state of emotional flux where her mother was concerned. That she dreaded her breezing back into her life whenever she deemed it necessary, dreaded more the ghosts from her past that would sweep icily in with her. She was also angry with herself for not being assertive with her mother, as she always vowed she would be, especially after the last time she'd turned up and her world had fallen apart.

Closing the door behind Sarah, she walked determinedly back to the kitchen. *Just do it. Tell her no*, she willed herself. *It's not that hard a word. Tell her to go; that you don't want her here. Not now, not ever.*

'Tea, sweetheart?' her mother asked over her shoulder as she waited for the kettle to boil – as if everything were perfectly normal. As if it ever had been or ever could be.

'*Mmm*um …' Laura started.

'Do call me Sherry, darling,' her mother interrupted. 'You know you struggle with the word Mum.'

Laura's chest constricted with anger. She did struggle to address her mum. Not because of her difficulties enunciating the 'm', but because the woman didn't have a maternal bone in her body. After the unbearable tragedy that had ripped Laura's damaged heart from her chest, she'd begun to address her as Sherry, the name her mother had adopted, deeming Sharon too ordinary for a fashion columnist who travelled in the social circles she did. She was a fake. Everything about her mother was false.

Turning from the work surface, Sherry frowned as she surveyed Laura critically. 'Really, Laura … grey?' Taking in her M&S cashmere sweater and tracksuit bottoms, she shook her head disparagingly. 'You know neutral colours don't flatter your pale skin tone, darling. If you wore that outfit to the hospice, you'd probably be mistaken for a corpse. And that *hair* …'

Leaving that one hanging, and Laura tugging on a lock of hair she'd refused to cut, no matter how many times her mother, out of jealousy and insecurity, had suggested she should, Sherry strode past her, her heels clicking on the ceramic kitchen tiles as she headed to the hall.

'Despite my busy schedule, I managed to squeeze in a bit of retail therapy, you'll be pleased to hear,' she called enthusiastically back from where she was retrieving the bags she'd dropped beside the front door.

Laura's irritation escalated. Her mother would have been shopping for her – again – selecting clothes that were horrendously expensive and tasteless. She just wanted to be seen to be doing the things normal mothers might. Laura had no doubt this was all for

Steve's benefit, and that whilst appearing to be concerned for her, Sherry would slowly but surely turn him against her. If she were to forge a relationship with someone she could trust implicitly, long-held secrets might surface, after all, and her mother couldn't possibly have that, could she?

How dearly Laura wished Steve hadn't answered her phone that fateful day her mother had called from the spring fashion show in Milan – which was what had prompted her to immediately change her number. Once her mother realised she was in a new relationship, Laura had known she would materialise, embroiling herself in her life, making it impossible for her to have the only thing she craved: a normal family, the child she desperately wanted. Now it was within her grasp, and here was Sherry like a bad omen about to spoil it.

'How did you know my address?' she asked, following her mother to the hall.

Straightening up with her bags, Sherry blinked at her in surprise. 'Your young man told me, darling,' she said, as if wondering why on earth she would ask.

Laura guessed that he would have. Steve was far too easily taken in, and she hadn't asked him not to. She'd only ever given him scant detail about her past, as much as she thought it was necessary for him to know.

'I'll just take these straight up, shall I?' Sherry asked, her Dior-painted mouth curving into that brittle sweet smile Laura had seen so many times. It was as fake as the rest of her. Behind the facade, she was scared, living in fear that her world would come tumbling down. 'You do have a spare room, don't you, darling? You did say it was a little three-bedroomed house you'd rented?'

Laura picked up on the word 'little'. It stung, reminding her of everything her mother had ever valued above her: the grand Georgian farmhouse set in two acres of rolling Warwickshire countryside, with its paddocks, tennis courts and gym. And its pool, of course. They loved that pool. Laura couldn't stand the sight of it.

Sherry was in her element there. She would never give it up, or the prestige she imagined it afforded her in the tiny village of Stepton, where she was 'respected by the community'. She even helped out in the parish church nowadays, laughably; trying to assuage her conscience, Laura would bet. The house was a living, breathing part of her, she often said. She'd refurbished it with sweat and blood, making it the desirable residence it was. Or rather, with Grant's money, once she'd got her fingernails firmly dug into him.

Sherry – or Sharon as she still was then – had been a stable hand there originally, Laura had learned from local gossip when she'd emerged from her bedroom – her self-made tomb – determined to breathe again. She'd lost her job at the local biscuit factory and had apparently been working at the house, grandly renamed 'Stepton Manor', when she'd met Grant, the son of the wealthy owners. The place had been neglected, but Sherry had loved it; convinced Grant they should stay there and restore it to its former glory. She'd had a plan, a plan that had included making sure Grant's mother went to a nice rest home shortly after his father had died. She'd entrenched herself in his life, become part of his world. He'd been her passport to a better future, her way to extract herself from her roots, which were firmly embedded in the council estate she'd been brought up in. She had been determined to marry him: she would never go back to a life of poverty. Her grim determination now was to hold on to it all by whatever emotionally manipulative means she had to employ, caring nothing for the impact on her own daughter.

She knew Laura suffered because of it. Unbelievably, she made light of it. Told her that events in the past were nothing but the imaginings of her subconscious. 'The things you see when you sleepwalk aren't real, darling,' she would say to placate her. How could she have remembered things she saw while she'd been sleepwalking, though? Laura had asked her. Amnesia was part of the condition – her mother knew that. If she'd been asleep, she wouldn't have been able to recall anything.

'It's not a bad little property, is it?' Sherry observed now, slightly breathless as she heaved her bags up the stairs.

God. Laura's stomach churned. She couldn't do this. She just *couldn't.* 'There is no spare room!' she shouted.

Sherry stopped, blinking down at her in surprise from where she was balanced precariously near the top of the stairs. Of course she would be surprised. Laura almost laughed. Her timid little daughter had never stood up to her. She'd always accommodated her, because she'd had to, trying to forestall the inevitable tales Sherry would tell. Not this time. This was her chance at a future. She'd worked so hard to make it happen, to be with Steve. She wouldn't let her mother scare him off. 'The spare room has no furniture in it and the small room is Ollie's,' she said, holding her gaze defiantly.

'Ollie's?' Sherry's eyes widened, a flicker of apprehension visible. 'And who is Ollie, sweetheart?' she asked, manufacturing a smile.

'Steve's little boy. He stays here at weekends,' Laura informed her firmly.

Sherry's face blanched. 'Oh, I see,' she said, glancing down and back. 'How lovely. And he's how old?' she enquired sweetly.

'Almost four,' Laura said. 'I won't let you spoil this for me,' she warned her.

Sherry looked shocked. 'Spoil it? Why on earth would you imagine I would do that? Honestly, Laura, you have to stop this, darling, blaming other people for things that go wrong in your life. I'm only here to help, as I always am. To make sure everything is all right with you. You know how you're prone to restlessness at night when you're—'

'Everything is *fine* with me.' Laura's voice rose. 'Or at least it *was.* So you can just go on back to your bloody mansion now, can't you?'

'Don't be like that, Laura,' Sherry said, her eyes filling up. 'I'm here now.' She smiled again, tremulously. 'I might as well stay overnight. I'm quite happy with the sofa. Grant will be back from London tomorrow and he can—'

'No! I don't want him coming here.' Laura felt her blood boil. 'I don't want either of you here, *ever*.' Did she honestly think she would want to spend time with Grant, smiling charmingly in that unbelievable way he did, defending her bloody mother, as he was bound to?

Sherry's expression changed to one of alarm. 'Laura, please, don't do this,' she beseeched, a hand fluttering to her chest, as if she might have a heart attack. As if. The woman had a heart of stone. 'Grant only wants to help you, as I do. He loves you as if you were his own. You're confused about what happened, my lovely. I suspect you might always be. I know it's difficult to accept, but you really were very muddled then, prone to all sorts of imaginings. Weren't you?'

Now her look was one of sympathy. False sympathy. False. False. *False!*

CHAPTER TWELVE

Sarah

'Did he go off to sleep all right?' Sarah asked, glancing anxiously up the stairs as she came through the front door.

'Out like a light, despite the absence of Bunny,' Joe assured her, meeting her in the hall. 'How did it go with Laura?'

'Fine.' Aware that Bunny – whom she'd guiltily taken from the toy box – was stuffed in her shoulder bag, Sarah gave him a small smile. 'I think.'

Joe moved to help her off with her coat, which she was getting in a tangle with as she tugged at it. 'You don't sound very certain.' Hooking it on a peg, he looked back at her, his brow furrowed in that way it did whenever she voiced her doubts about Laura.

'I am. Sort of,' Sarah said, wondering how much to tell him. She knew he thought she was getting things out of perspective because she was jealous of Laura's relationship with Steve, which was utterly ridiculous.

He arched his eyebrows. 'Sort of?'

Trying not to notice the wary look in his eyes, Sarah headed for the kitchen. 'I mean, Laura was fine. We got along quite well. It's just …'

'Just?' Joe followed her.

Sarah hesitated, but then wondered why she was worrying about what other people thought. She wasn't jealous of Laura. She wished Steve nothing but luck in his relationship. If it impacted badly on Ollie, however, then she had every right to voice her concerns. She should be able to, in fact, especially to the man *she* was in a relationship with. 'Something was a bit … odd,' she said carefully.

'Odd how?' Joe asked over his shoulder as he extracted the wine from the fridge. Grabbing a glass from the cupboard, he poured her a large one and walked across to her. Sarah accepted it gratefully. She'd hardly touched the wine she'd had at Laura's, and now she could definitely use one.

'I don't know. I can't quite put my finger on it.' She pondered. She couldn't escape the nagging feeling in the pit of her stomach that something wasn't right, no matter how hard she tried. 'She seems to be replicating Ollie's room.'

'Well, that's hardly odd.' Joe eyed her quizzically. 'It sounds as if they're just trying to make sure he doesn't feel homesick.'

'Yes, but … how did she know? About the detail, I mean?' Sarah frowned pensively. 'She has the same toy box. The bed could be Ollie's own. It's almost identical to the one he has upstairs. Even the name plate on the door is the same.'

Joe looked wryly amused at that. 'Er, because his father might have had some input?' he suggested.

'I suppose.' Sarah wasn't convinced, though. They would have had to furnish that room pretty damn quickly. 'But what about the presents?'

The bemused furrow in Joe's brow deepened.

'Twice she's bought the same present I was going to get him. I told her I was getting him a Magicube dinosaur set for his birthday, and coincidentally she gets him the very same thing. Then I find out she's bought him a Wheelybug, which I'd decided to get him instead. We looked at them in John Lewis, remember? I told Steve I was getting one and then she goes and orders one. She said Steve forgot to tell her, but ...' She knitted her brow. 'Don't you think it's odd that she would choose the exact same toys?'

'Sounds to me as if it's definitely a case of miscommunication.' Joe checked his watch. 'They're popular toys, right? Steve probably did forget to tell her.'

'So you think it was just a coincidence then? *Twice?*' Sarah forced the point, because it did all seem bloody odd – and this was without finding Ollie's maimed bunny.

He emitted a sigh. 'I don't know, Sarah. Maybe you should be asking Steve.'

He looked as if he'd rather be gone, making Sarah feel she couldn't talk to him about her concerns for her son. What kind of future did they have if that was the case?

'Her mother turned up,' she said, willing him to realise that she needed him to listen and try to understand. She couldn't compromise where Ollie was concerned. Joe had to be every bit as caring about him and his welfare as she was, or it simply wouldn't work between them.

'And?' he asked patiently.

'They don't get on. It was obvious immediately. Laura had already told me they didn't. Yet she still let her in.'

He nodded and massaged his forehead. 'She is her mother, though, Sarah. She could hardly have left her standing on the doorstep, could she?'

'Yes. No. I ...' Sarah was confusing herself now. Was it such a big deal that Laura didn't get on with her mother? Lots of people had parent issues, after all. 'She started stuttering,' she tried to explain, but how did you explain something that was nothing more than intuition, a feeling that whatever issues there were between them *were* a big deal? 'As soon as her mother arrived, she started stammering.'

'Because she was nervous?' Joe suggested.

'Precisely.' She latched onto that. 'It's a bit odd to be nervous around you own mother, isn't it?'

'So now you've decided you don't like her because she doesn't get on with her mother?' He shook his head in obvious despair. 'Don't you think this might be a bit—'

'No!' Sarah snapped, before he accused her of getting things out of perspective again. 'It's nothing to do with whether I like her or not.' She groped for a way to make Joe see that she wasn't being neurotic. 'She said she'd left his bunny guarding his toy box, and when I slipped up there—'

'Slipped up there?' He narrowed his eyes. 'You mean you went up to Ollie's room without being invited?'

'Yes,' she admitted, her cheeks heating up. 'Laura and her mother were talking in the kitchen. It was obvious the situation between them was awkward, so I waited in the hall. I wondered whether I should just let myself out, but I wanted to see where Ollie slept. I thought it wouldn't hurt to pop up while—' She stopped as Joe's phone rang.

He pulled it from his pocket and checked the number. 'It's work. I have to get it,' he said, frowning as he took the call. 'Yep, on my way … Sorry. Car trouble.'

He was lying, because he was late, because she'd made him late. Sarah swallowed back another lump of guilt.

'I have to get going,' he said, pocketing the phone.

'You're annoyed, aren't you?' She noted the agitated tic playing at his cheek.

He hesitated. 'I'm not annoyed, Sarah,' he said contemplatively. 'Why would I be? I'm just concerned, that's all. I hear what you're saying, but if you want my honest opinion, it seems as if you're looking for reasons not to like her.'

What? Was that what he thought too? Suddenly Sarah felt as if the whole world were against her.

'I really have to go.' He hesitated, and then leaned to give her a cursory kiss on the cheek. 'I'll call you.'

Stunned, she stared after him as he turned and headed up the hall. The front door opening galvanised her into action. She was *not* looking for reasons. She was *not* being neurotic. She was *not* jealous of Laura! Had he not heard a word she'd said? He should be concerned *for* her, not about her.

'She cut his ear off!' she shouted as Joe neared his car. 'Bunny, she cut his ear off!'

Opening the car door, Joe stopped and turned around. Even under the glow of the street lamp, Sarah could see that his look was deeply troubled.

'Sarah …' He sucked in a breath, blew it out slowly. 'Listen to what you're saying, will you? You're becoming *obsessed* with her.'

'I am *not*!' she argued tearfully. 'I'm concerned! For my son. With damn good reason it appears only *I* can see.'

Joe dropped his gaze. 'I have to go,' he said, his tone flat. 'I'll ring you. We'll talk tomorrow.'

Sarah's heart dropped. Would he? she wondered, tears pricking her eyes. Would any man bother to ring a woman he believed was obsessing about her ex's new girlfriend, and was therefore clearly obsessed with her ex?

CHAPTER THIRTEEN

Laura

'So stupid of me not to have taken my house keys. I was in such a rush when I left,' Sherry sighed melodramatically from the bedroom. Laura was well aware that she was pretending despair at herself. Her keys were probably in her bag. She really was a master manipulator. Recalling how she'd coerced Grant into marrying her, how she continued to mercilessly control her daughter, Laura felt a shudder run through her.

'Any good, darling?' Sherry enquired as, attempting to keep the peace until her mother had gone, Laura struggled into a top that was supposed to be on trend: a gaudy apple-green thing with bat wings. There was a similar one in fuchsia pink, another colour Laura detested. She'd always preferred subtle, calming colours.

'Yes, fine, thanks. I'll try them on with my leggings later,' she called from the bathroom. Best not to get into an argument about why Sherry insisted on bringing her clothes that were shapeless and unflattering, she decided, pulling her own clothes back on. That was bound to stress her out.

'So how's the job going?' Sherry asked as she emerged, with her usual nuance of interest.

'Fine,' Laura replied shortly. 'I love it there.'

'I gathered you must. I mean, you'd have to be keen to work somewhere like that, wouldn't you? With all those poor old people dying around you, I mean.'

And kind, and dedicated, Laura didn't bother to add. It was rare that her mother recognised her attributes. 'They're not all old,' she remarked, for what it was worth. Steve's father hadn't been old. Sixty-five was no age. She'd felt for Steve, been glad she'd been there for him.

'I still think you could have done so much more with your life than become a care-giver at a hospice, though, darling.' Sherry sighed with exasperation, causing Laura to bite hard on her tongue. 'Something that required some kind of qualification at least. You would be a little better off financially then, wouldn't you? I mean, Grant and I don't mind helping you out here and there – we're always happy to, you know that – but it would be nice to know you were secure.'

Don't rise to the bait, Laura warned herself. Her mother was doing what she always did: making her feel like a failure, undermining her. As if she'd stood any chance of finishing her education when her mind and body had basically stopped functioning. She'd stayed ensconced in her room, watching the press mass like a pack of hungry wolves outside, the police coming and going, answering questions when she'd had to. She hadn't told them anything more than her mother had already told them: that she'd taken a sedative, that she'd been sleeping. Sherry had taken her aside once the police had left that first time, told her she *had* been sleepwalking. She hadn't informed the police, she'd said, wringing her hands, her eyes fraught with worry, lest they think Laura might have been involved in some way.

When the walls had closed in on her until she was silently screaming, she'd rebelled, nightclubbing and partying, anaesthetising herself with alcohol and drugs until she couldn't smell the chlorine any more, couldn't hear the lap of the water, couldn't remember the events of the day before, or the night before. She'd changed her name when she left, managed to stay hidden until, shaking and twitching, desperation had forced her to use her debit card. She'd woken at the squat to find her mother looming over her. 'Don't be angry, darling.' She'd smiled her brittle sweet smile as Laura had shuffled away from her, screamed at her to get out of her head. 'I'm just here to help,' she'd said, gathering her up and taking her home. She'd turned up several times since, oozing sympathy as Laura's life had fallen apart, taking her back to the place where her nightmares had started. If the memories haunted her, her mother haunted her more. She would never let go of her. Laura thought she would probably follow her to the grave.

She wouldn't let her. She *would* have her life back, if only she could find the courage to confront her, tell her she didn't believe that she had been sleepwalking on the darkest night of her life; that when she'd woken, she'd experienced the kind of hangover she'd later come to recognise as drug-induced. Her mother claimed she was trying to protect her. She wasn't. She was protecting herself. Her lifestyle. That was all Sherry had ever held dear.

'I do wonder why you didn't think about going to university, Laura,' she went on now. 'You were always so good at English. It seems such a terrible waste.'

Because I wanted to teach, but I might have found it a bit of a challenge when I was struggling to speak, you insensitive cow. Fuming inside, Laura braced herself to walk back into the bedroom, then stopped, and baulked, as she realised Sherry was poking around in her wardrobe. 'M-M-Mu …' she started, and then paused and forced the word out. 'Mum! What are you *doing*?'

Her back towards her, her mother didn't answer for a second. Then, 'Why have you kept this?' she asked, her face drained of all colour as she turned around.

Laura's stomach tightened, her gaze going from her mother's shocked expression to the photograph she held in her hand, one of the few precious photographs she had, which she'd printed and also scaled down for her locket. She found the physical photo of him brought him closer somehow.

Stand up to her. Her heart boomed. There was no reason she shouldn't have a photograph. He'd gone, leaving nothing but the memory of him, but he'd existed. Existed still. Laura could see him in the eyes of the children who miraculously came into her life; she could hear his melodic laugh when they laughed. Destroying photographs of him couldn't eradicate him. 'There's no harm in keeping it,' she said, notching her chin up, trying to look braver than she felt.

Sherry's mouth dropped open, and then her expression darkened. 'You *know* how painful the memories are for me,' she hissed, her voice hoarse with disbelief. 'How hard I've worked to protect you. Burying my *own* grief in the process.' She slapped the flat of her hand against her chest, as if she were capable of feeling.

Laura felt anger well up like corrosive acid inside her. 'Are you sure it's me you've been protecting?' she asked, finally finding the courage to challenge her. She had nothing to back up her challenge with, nothing but fleeting images that floated tauntingly away before she could catch them. She'd heard him sobbing. She *had*. In her dreams and her waking nightmares, she *still* heard him sobbing. Sometimes, as she walked the fine line between sleep and wakefulness, she heard him calling plaintively, 'Mummy, *Mummy!*' – a tiny child alone and frightened in the night.

Her mother and Grant had been arguing. About *her*. It came to her with blinding clarity. She'd heard *them*. High-pitched screaming, a male voice growling, glass breaking, doors slamming, the patio doors. He *had* been crying! It hadn't been the imaginings of her bloody *subconscious*.

'Do you want to rake this all up again?' Her mother snatched her back to the present. 'Have people digging into your past?'

Your past. Laura's blood pumped.

'Reporters raking it all over, pointing fingers at his grieving family? Asking you questions you'll stutter and stumble over answering?'

Fear pierced Laura's heart like an icicle. Knowing she would be incapable of making the word 'no' spill from her mouth, she shook her head hard. She didn't want that. She couldn't have it. Not now. She wanted her mother to leave her alone. For everyone to leave her alone. All she wanted to do was to care for the little boy who'd come into her life. She couldn't let him down. She had to keep him safe.

'For God's sake, Laura.' Sherry fixed her with a reproachful glare. 'Hasn't this family been through enough?'

'It's painful for me too!' Laura cried as her mother swept past her to the landing. '*Mmm*uch more p-p-painful …' Her voice trailed to a whisper as she heard Sherry descending the stairs, muttering, 'Selfish, *selfish* girl,' as she went.

She'd found her house keys then. Fifteen minutes later, Laura watched from the landing, hatred burning inside her, as her mother strode to the front door, heaving her luggage along with her. Her heart stalled when Steve opened it from the outside just as Sherry reached it. She'd guessed he would have to meet her mother at some point, but she'd hoped it would be under circumstances that wouldn't require her to explain away her mother's interference in her life.

'Evening,' Steve said, looking Sherry over, bemused, as she bustled past.

She didn't answer him. Didn't even so much as acknowledge him, marching onwards instead towards the waiting taxi she'd called.

Steve watched her go, then closed the door with a shake of his head and turned his puzzled gaze to Laura.

'My *mmm*other,' she enlightened him. 'We had a row and, um …' The words catching in her throat, she stopped, turned her gaze to the ceiling and blinked hard.

'Hey, hey.' Seeing she was upset, Steve bounded up the stairs. 'It wasn't that bad, surely?' he said, pulling her into his arms.

Strong arms. Tanned and toned from working largely outdoors. Protective arms. He was a good man. A fundamentally nice man, if a little too trusting. Laura relaxed into him, rested her head on his shoulder and allowed herself to feel safe, just for a second. She wished she could stay in his embrace forever, but it was impossible. Her mother would make sure it was. She shook herself mentally. It would be different this time. She would stop her. She had to. She couldn't lose him. She *wouldn't* lose Ollie.

'It was,' she said, easing away from him. 'She can be a bit … dictatorial sometimes.' With no way to tell him why she was so distraught, she improvised. 'It drives me mad.'

'I'm sure she's just trying to look out for you.' Steve followed her to the bedroom.

Control me, Laura thought.

'My mum was always telling me I should do this and do that,' Steve went on good-humouredly. 'Course, I thought I knew better. Turns out she was right, more often than not.'

He'd obviously had a normal child/parent relationship. He'd certainly loved his father. She envied him that. He wouldn't be quite so charitable about Sherry if he knew why Laura could never feel that way about her.

'She'll be back,' he said reassuringly.

'I'm sure she will,' Laura muttered, and set about looking for the photograph her mother had discarded somewhere. She didn't want Steve seeing it.

'You sure you're all right?' he asked as she plucked the discarded clothes Sherry had brought her from the bed, hoping the photograph was underneath. It wasn't there.

'Yes, fine, honestly.' Scouring the floor around her, she gave him a distracted smile. 'She just rubs me up the wrong way sometimes, that's all.'

'Yep, my mother did that, too.' Steve sighed. 'She meant well, though.'

If only. Laura decided she'd rather not get into that conversation.

'I'll just have a quick shower,' Steve said, 'and then I'll grab something out of the freezer for dinner. Unless you fancy takeaway or a pub meal? Might cheer you up a bit.'

'Takeaway would be lovely.' Laura managed a proper smile. 'Thanks for being so thoughtful, Steve.'

'No problem. I think I'd rather have that than my cooking.' He gave her a warm smile in return and then headed for the bed, dropping down on it to take off shoes.

Laura willed him to hurry up as he bent to unlace them, and then scrunched her eyes closed as he delved under the divan, clearly having spotted something. Her heart leapt into her mouth as he drew out what she'd known he inevitably would.

'Is this what you're looking for?' he asked.

'Yes. Thanks,' she said, her voice strained. She stepped towards him, her hand outstretched to retrieve the photo, but he held onto to it, a frown crossing his face as he studied it.

After a blood-freezing moment, he looked up at her. 'Someone you know?'

CHAPTER FOURTEEN

Sarah

Up early the next morning, having not slept a wink, Sarah made herself a coffee and then keyed in a text to Joe. Hesitating before sending it, she reread it: *I know you think I'm being paranoid, but I'm not, I promise. There's such a thing as a mother's instinct, Joe, and mine is screaming at me that something is off. If I can't talk to you about it, then I'm wondering if we have a future.*

Agonising for a second longer, she braced herself and then hit send.

She hadn't been angry with Steve when they'd split. They'd limped along for a while, but she'd known it was inevitable. They'd grown apart, fallen out of love. She was beginning to feel angry with him now, though, his being so stridently defensive of Laura. How much did he really know about her, at the end of the day?

Checking her phone and finding no reply from Joe, she shrugged, as if it wouldn't hurt unbearably losing someone she cared deeply about and who she'd thought cared for her, then gathered herself and went back upstairs, careful not to make a sound in case she woke Ollie.

Hearing him already awake and chatting – to one of his toys, presumably – she paused, smiling, outside his bedroom door. She loved listening to how his imagination worked. Part of her hoped he wasn't talking to Mr Whale, though, who she saw as a bit of an intruder, which she supposed could be deemed neurotic. She hadn't yet spoken to Ollie about Bunny. She would have to – she needed to establish whether he'd somehow got hold of scissors and cut the ear off – but she wasn't sure how to broach the subject. He might be distraught if he knew nothing about it. She would fish a little, she decided. Refer casually to Bunny and gauge his reaction.

Talking of fish … She leaned closer to the door. 'Did Mummy starfish give you some sweeties when you took little starfish home?' he was saying, his voice filled with awe.

Sarah hadn't even realised he knew what a starfish was. It had obviously come from Laura. Perhaps they'd had a conversation around Mr Whale's habitat?

'Uh-huh,' Ollie went on, as if he really were having a conversation with someone. An invisible friend, perhaps?

'When I'm four, I'm going to be a superhero too,' he continued chattily, 'and I'm going to help save all the fishes, just like—' He stopped abruptly as the alarm on Sarah's phone sounded, almost giving her heart failure – and probably making Ollie jump out of his jim-jams, since she was standing right outside his door.

Pushing the door open, she went in to find him peering worriedly over his duvet, which he'd pulled up to his chin. Poor thing, he obviously had been startled. 'Hi, munchkin,' she said, giving him a bright smile. 'Sorry about that. Mummy woke up early and forgot to turn her phone off. Did it frighten you?'

'No.' Ollie shook his head adamantly. 'Superheroes don't get frightened,' he assured her, his little face serious.

'Course they don't.' Sitting on the edge of his bed, Sarah matched his expression with a serious one of her own. 'Except maybe for the people they're going to save?' she suggested.

'And the fishes. They save them too,' Ollie added, his big eyes widening with excitement.

'And the fishes.' Sarah glanced at him curiously. 'Who were you talking to?' she asked, giving his hair a ruffle. A sudden chill prickled her skin as she wondered whether Laura had used the same scissors she'd cut his fringe with to chop his bunny's ear off.

Ollie immediately glanced down without answering, which was unusual. He was normally such a chatterbox once they got on to the subject of superheroes.

'Ollie?' she prompted him.

Still no answer. In fact, shrinking back down under his duvet, he looked reluctant to talk to her.

'Mummy asked you a question, sweetheart,' Sarah said softly. 'Do you not want to tell me?'

Ollie's eyes flicked to hers. 'It's a secret,' he whispered, dropping his gaze again.

'Oh, I see.' She felt a knot of apprehension tighten inside her. Was this yet another secret, despite the conversation she'd had with Laura? If it was the same one Ollie had imagined he should keep before, it seemed to have made much more of an impression on him than being passed a surreptitious extra cookie would. 'Is it a big secret or a little secret?' she asked cautiously.

He furrowed his brow. 'A big one,' he told her, his gaze flicking again to hers.

Sarah's heart flipped, but she tried to keep things in perspective. It might have nothing to do with Laura. It could simply be that Ollie had invented a secret friend and he wanted to keep him just that: secret. 'I think you might have a friend. One I can't see.' She narrowed her eyes playfully. 'Am I right?'

Noting that he now looked guilty, her apprehension quadrupled. What on earth …? Whatever this was, he shouldn't be feeling guilty, for goodness' sake. 'I had one when I was your age,' she told him – a little white lie in hopes of reassuring him and winning his trust, which clearly she needed to. 'I think it's okay as long as they're nice friends. Is your friend a nice friend, Ollie?'

He glanced up from under his eyelashes, his eyes wary. 'Yes,' he said in a small voice.

'Well, that's good, isn't it?' Sarah smiled encouragingly. 'So, is it a boy or a girl?' she asked, her heart pounding as she imagined all sorts of nauseating scenarios.

'A boy,' Ollie replied at length.

'And how old is he?' she probed gently.

'He's small, like me.' He sounded uncertain.

Thank God. She felt relief crash through her. 'Is he now?' Her frenetic heartbeat abating a little, she forced a smile.

'Uh-huh.' Ollie nodded. 'I saw him in a photo.'

'What, an actual real photo?' She widened her eyes in surprise.

'Yes. A little one.' He made a tiny 'o' shape with his thumb and forefinger.

Sarah studied him, puzzled. 'Really?' she said. 'Did someone show you the photo?'

His gaze flicked down again.

'Who is the photo of, Ollie?' she pressed him. 'Does he have a name?'

'Yes.' Ollie looked uncomfortably back at her. 'But I'm not supposed to tell you, Mummy.'

Unbelievable! Bloody Laura! She'd been lying to her. She'd told Ollie specifically not to tell Sarah about this – and it was definitely nothing to do with an extra bloody biscuit. Ollie might have a vivid imagination, but there was no way he would invent all this, *or* the fact that Laura had stressed it was something he should keep secret, quite obviously. She scanned his face, trying not to let her growing anger show in her own. His big blue eyes looked nervously back at her. He was struggling with his conscience, a child his age, for goodness' sake. She had no idea what game Laura was playing here, but one thing she did know was that she was *not* getting things out of perspective.

'You can tell me his name, can't you? You trust me, don't you? I cross my heart I won't tell anyone,' she cajoled him, and felt terrible for emotionally compromising her child.

'Jacob,' Ollie finally disclosed, his forehead set in a worried frown. 'He's a superhero and he helps all the fishes, but Laura's lost him and I want to help him find his way home,' he said, his little face earnest.

CHAPTER FIFTEEN

Relieved that Ollie seemed back to his normal self, charging off to play with the other children at the nursery only to charge back again when he remembered he hadn't said goodbye to her, Sarah crouched to squeeze him into a firm hug. 'Bye, gorgeous little man. See you later,' she said, breathing in the smell of him. 'Be good for Melanie.'

'I will.' Hugging her back, he slapped a kiss on her cheek and scooted off again, keen to catch up with his real-life friends.

'He'll be fine. He always settles down as good as gold,' Melanie, the nursery manager, assured her, clearly thinking that the tear that had escaped Sarah's eye was because she didn't want to leave him. She was right. Suddenly she felt she didn't want him out of her sight. She'd almost convinced herself she *was* being paranoid, that she'd overreacted to Joe pointing out that she was, until this morning's discovery. Did Steve know Laura was encouraging Ollie to keep secrets? Worrying secrets? She should talk to him. But she wanted to talk to Laura first.

'I know he will.' Giving the woman a smile, she pulled herself together. 'I think I'm just getting overemotional because he seems to be growing up so fast. I'm wondering when he will stop wanting to give his mum a hug.'

'Not for a while yet.' Melanie laughed, waving her off as she skidded across the hall to short-circuit an imminent fracas between two toddlers who were claiming first dibs on the soft-play crocodile.

Sarah left her to it and headed back to her car. Climbing in, she took a calming breath, glad that her temper had had time to cool down, warning herself not to dive in and make accusations until she'd established the facts, then selected Laura's number on her mobile.

'Hi, Sarah. Is everything all right?' Laura asked in her usual nervous way when she picked up.

'I'm not sure,' Sarah said, wondering how to tackle it and then deciding to take the bull by the horns. 'Ollie is insistent that you've shared something with him and told him specifically not to tell me.'

'Really?' Laura sounded puzzled. As she would, meaning she was obviously about to deny it.

'Before you say anything, yes, I am sure, and no, it doesn't have anything to do with extra cookies.'

Laura went quiet. 'I can't think what else it would be.'

'Something about a little boy,' Sarah provided carefully. 'He was reluctant to tell me at first; I had to prise it out of him. I was annoyed when he said he wasn't supposed to tell me, as you can imagine.'

'A little boy?' Laura repeated, now sounding confused. 'We never had a conversation about … Oh, wait … his *story*, of course. I told him a story about a little boy who rescued a lost starfish. I was trying to make him see that superheroes didn't necessarily need to have superpowers. You know, that they could just be ordinary people? Would that be it?'

Sarah considered. It sounded perfectly feasible, perfectly innocent, but … 'Possibly,' she said. Then, 'Did you show him a photo?' she asked bluntly.

Laura took a second. 'No,' she said. 'Not that I can remember. Do you think he might have imagined it?'

No, Sarah did *not* think that, or at least she hadn't. She'd been on the verge of calling the woman a liar, but now she felt herself backsliding in the face of her plausible explanations. Ollie had said he wasn't supposed to tell, not that Laura had told him categorically not to. Had Sarah misinterpreted what he'd said, jumped to the wrong conclusion? 'He's imagining the little boy is his invisible friend,' she admitted, somewhat reluctantly, 'so yes, I suppose he might have.'

'Do you think that might be why he wants to keep him a secret? Because he might be a bit embarrassed, I mean?' Laura suggested tentatively.

'Possibly,' Sarah agreed, with some effort. Might she be reading too much into this? It was possible her protective gene had gone into overdrive because she felt very much a single parent right now, therefore needing to try twice as hard. Might she be losing her perspective because she felt threatened by Laura's involvement in Ollie's life? She had an awful feeling she might be.

'Actually, now you've called …' Laura paused, causing a fresh prickle of apprehension to run the length of Sarah's spine. 'It doesn't matter if you have other plans,' she went on, 'but we were wondering …'

What? Spit it out, for goodness' sake. Aware of her growing agitation, Sarah now felt guilty about that too.

'Do you mind if we have Ollie this weekend rather than next?' Laura finally asked. 'It's just that Steve has a job on next Saturday, and … Well, to be honest, I'd rather he was here while everything is still so new to Ollie.'

So would Sarah. She didn't like the idea of Ollie completely on his own with Laura, and had no idea why she felt that way either, other than the nagging feeling that something just wasn't right.

'I suppose,' she said with a sigh. She would be at work, therefore she could hardly claim she had other arrangements. She could be awkward, she supposed, say that she preferred Ollie to have a regular routine, but that would just be unreasonable. 'As long as it's not a regular occurrence,' she added, feeling the need to at least set a precedent for future visits.

'Brilliant,' Laura said, sounding pleased. 'We thought we might take him to the zoo – if that's all right with you?'

Sarah's heart sank. Her little boy's first trip to the zoo and it would be without her. 'Yes, fine,' she agreed reluctantly.

'You're sure?' Laura clearly picked up on her tone.

'Positive, as long as it's just this once.' A deep loneliness was opening up inside her already at the thought of another whole weekend with Ollie not there. Splitting up with Joe, which it looked like she had, would exacerbate that loneliness. Why had she shot that text off in a fit of pique? She'd said she felt she couldn't talk to Joe, but she *had* talked to him. In response to which he'd offered his opinion, and she'd as good as dumped him for it. He wouldn't want a future with her on that basis.

'Fab. See you then. I'll get a lovely packed lunch organised for us to take. I thought star sandwiches with cream cheese and pesto – I have this star-shape cutter, Ollie loved it when I made his toast star-shaped,' Laura informed her enthusiastically, extolling her own culinary skills. 'I thought I'd do a BLT pasta salad to go with them, and maybe choco-dipped tangerines for afters. What do you think?'

That you have stars on the brain. 'Lovely,' Sarah said wanly. What she actually thought, with a jerk, was that she *was* jealous, because Laura seemed to be having all the fun with Ollie, organising lovely things for him to do, while she got stuck with the mundane, everyday tasks. She was so tired in the evenings and at weekends that she hadn't been doing very much with him other than trips to the park, playing at home and reading. With Laura and Steve he was having lots of excitement and the attention of two parents, whereas with her he was probably growing bored, and possibly lonely too – hence the invention of his invisible friend. 'I'd better get to work,' she said, her throat tightening. 'See you Saturday.'

Ending the call, she checked her messages, harbouring a tiny sliver of hope that Joe might have contacted her. He hadn't. Why would he? She'd blown it, blown everything out of proportion. Swallowing back the bitter taste of regret, she plopped her phone on the passenger seat, started the engine and headed for work, where she doubted she would find comfort even in her furry companions today.

She'd barely pulled away when the phone rang.

Joe. Seeing his name pop up on her hands-free, her heart leapt. It was as if he'd been reading her mind. He was possibly calling to tell her he hadn't thought there was much of a future for them anyway, but she had to talk to him, apologise. With some trepidation, she accepted the call. 'Joe, I—'

'Look, Sarah, I'm sorry,' he said before she could say any more. 'Can we talk?'

'Yes.' She felt a surge of relief run through her. 'Yes please. Give me a second, I'll just pull over.' Seeing a garage up ahead, she swung into it and found a space in one of the shopping bays.

'Safely parked?' Joe asked, because he did care about her. She knew he did.

'Safely parked,' she assured him, praying he wasn't about to agree that they call it a day, because she cared about him too, deeply, and she hadn't really communicated how much.

'You were right,' he continued with an audible intake of breath. 'There can't be any future for us if you feel you can't talk about your worries. Ollie is your number one priority, as he should be. I understand that, Sarah. Really I do. I just …' He faltered.

'Thought I was jealous?' she finished as he searched for the right thing to say.

'Yes,' he admitted after a second. 'Though I accept that that might have something to do with my own insecurities.'

He was talking about his former wife. A woman he'd loved who'd still been in love with her ex. That must have been so painful for him. Sarah braced herself. She had to be honest; there was no future without that either. 'I think you were right,' she confessed.

'I am jealous of Laura. But because of her involvement in Ollie's life, not Steve's.'

Joe paused. 'I get that too,' he said softly. 'I'm not completely insensitive … even if I did act like an insensitive prat.'

'You didn't.' Sarah jumped to his defence, though she had thought he was being insensitive.

'I think I probably did, and I apologise,' Joe said with another intake of breath. 'The thing is … You know my parents split when I was a kid, right?'

Of course they had. She hadn't really thought about that.

'You know what that's like. You've been there. Stuff happens, you get over it. The worst part for me, though, wasn't them separating,' he went on, 'it was the acrimony afterwards. The arguing didn't stop, it bloody well escalated. I don't want Ollie caught up in the middle of that scenario, Sarah. I care about him too.'

Recalling how his parents had never really been there for him – for his sister either, who'd eventually lost her way and taken her own life, which had almost crucified him – Sarah swallowed hard. 'I know you do,' she said emotionally. He was too natural with him for it ever to be considered forced.

'So can we work on it, do you think? Our future?' he asked hopefully.

'Yes.' She smiled, and the gloom she'd felt descending on her at the thought of rattling around the empty house on her own lifted. She felt comfortable with Joe, as if she didn't have to make massive efforts to be anything but who she was, and a huge part of her identity was being Ollie's mum. Joe was hands-on with him. She'd seen how much he cared about him. He'd accepted without question that they came as a package, that more often than not when they went out together it would be the three of them. Thinking she might have lost him, she'd realised she didn't want a future without him.

'Great,' he breathed, relieved. 'I promise I'll try to be more supportive.'

'And I'll try to be less reactive,' Sarah promised too.

'Unless you have to be,' Joe suggested, letting her know that he also got that sometimes she might have to react, for her son's sake. 'So, how's it going this morning?'

'Okay … ish. I've just spoken to Laura, actually.' Sarah tried to sound matter-of-fact. 'I, um …' Pausing, she blew out a sigh, realising she couldn't tell it any different to how it was. 'To be honest, I think I might have overreacted a teeny bit,' she admitted.

'Ah.' Joe sounded amused. 'How so?'

'I heard Ollie chatting to himself earlier. He has an invisible friend, it seems. A superhero who rescues starfish.'

'Right,' he processed. 'That's not a problem, is it?'

'No,' she assured him. 'It's just … he said he was a lost little boy, that Laura had lost him and that he was trying to find him and take him home. He also said he'd seen him in a photograph. He was worried about telling me. Said he wasn't supposed to, and I thought …'

'That Laura had told him not to?' Joe picked up.

'Yes. Exactly.' Sarah breathed out another sigh, one of relief that Joe did appear to understand. 'I was really concerned, to be honest. I mean, it didn't sound like something Ollie would invent.'

'So what did Laura say? You asked her about it, I take it?'

'I did. I felt I had to.'

'And?' Joe sounded wary, but hopefully for the same reasons she did this time.

'She said she'd told him a story about a lost little boy, wanting to impress on him that superheroes didn't all have to have super-powers, or something like that, but that she hadn't told him not to tell me.'

'Sounds feasible,' he said.

It did. Also a good life lesson for Ollie, teaching him that ordinary people could be heroes, but still something was niggling away at her.

'And the photo?' he asked.

'I suppose it's possible that he dreamed it up, or else saw a photo at Laura's house.' The way he'd described it, though ... he'd seemed so specific. Sarah just wasn't sure.

'Could be,' he agreed. 'Children's imaginations tend to embellish the facts, don't they?'

'I suppose,' she mused, but still she wasn't convinced. Ollie had never kept things from her in the past, yet he'd seemed positive he shouldn't tell her. And would he really invent a photograph?

CHAPTER SIXTEEN

Laura

Noting Ollie's startled face as a lorikeet swooped down, landing on Steve's hand to peck at the nectar in the cup he was holding, Laura quickly crouched to reassure him. 'It's okay, Ollie,' she said, looking into his eyes, which were flecked with worry. 'It's just a parrot. See its pretty rainbow colours?'

Ollie nodded uncertainly, glancing up at the bird and then back to Laura. He stepped swiftly into her arms as the lorikeet took off again with a raucous screech.

A man next to them chuckled as Ollie followed the bird's progress across the top of the foliage. 'Don't you worry, young man,' he said jovially. 'Your mummy will fight them off for you.'

'Course I will.' Laura smiled and gave Ollie a squeeze.

Steve looked at her curiously, she noted, as he bent to pick the little boy up. 'Hey, it's all right, mate,' he assured him. 'These birds are tame. They won't hurt you.' Ollie still looked uncertain, his big blue eyes brimming with tears.

'Shall we?' Laura gestured towards the exit.

'Good idea.' Hoisting Ollie higher in his arms, Steve headed that way. 'He thought you were his mum,' he commented as they walked.

She noticed his questioning glance sideways. He was probably wondering why she hadn't corrected the man. 'That's because we look like a family,' she said, sliding an arm around his waist. 'It's a natural assumption to make. I thought it was easier not to try to explain.'

'I suppose.' He nodded thoughtfully.

'Maybe the Lorikeet Lookout wasn't the best plan after watching the birds of prey display,' she suggested as they emerged.

'Yeah, you're probably right,' he agreed. 'He's only three, after all.'

'Four,' Ollie piped up, trying very hard to put on a brave face now he considered they were safe. Laura had to smile at that.

'Almost.' Steve laughed, chucked him under the chin and set him back down on his feet. 'How about we go and meet the farmyard animals instead?' he asked, taking hold of his hand.

'What kind of animals?' Ollie asked, a concerned furrow forming on his brow.

'Ooh, lots,' Laura said. 'Chickens and geese and cows. They have guinea pigs and rabbits, too.'

'Do they have baby rabbits?' His eyes growing wide, Ollie brightened considerably.

'I believe they do.' She smiled and checked the zoo schedule, and then her watch. 'If we hurry, we'll just make it.'

After meeting all the animals in the Farm and Barn, including an abundance of baby rabbits, with which Ollie was delighted, followed by a visit to Kidzoone, where he was congratulated on his very realistic loo roll model of a baby giraffe, he got to pick their next stop: the adventure playground, inevitably.

Once they'd found their way there, Laura eyed the various apparatus worriedly. 'Do you think he might be a bit too young for some of this?' she whispered sideways to Steve.

'Nah. He's been on most of this stuff at the local park. We have a system, don't we, Ollie?' he assured her. 'He wobbles, I hold him.' Giving her a reassuring wink, he swept up Ollie, who was raring to go, and headed for the monkey bars.

Watching them, Laura almost had palpitations, but Steve was so good with him, never letting him take a step that was beyond his ability and making sure to shadow and support him. She almost had complete heart failure when, once back on the ground, Ollie pointed gleefully to the long green chute attached to one of the wooden climbing frames, shouted, 'Slide next, Daddy,' and made a dash for it.

Steve helped him up, making sure he was steady, and was ready for him as he emerged from the end of it, thank God.

'He can't come to much harm in there.' Laura nodded towards the sandpit Ollie was happily making sandcastles in minutes later. Sitting on the bench, she finally allowed herself to relax as she watched him. 'Unless you want to join him anyway, just in case?' She eyed Steve with wry amusement; he'd obviously enjoyed their adventures in the playground as much as Ollie had.

'No, I'm good.' Giving her a mischievous smile, Steve moved closer, sliding his arm around her. 'It's a tough choice, but I think I'd rather sit here with you than make sandcastles, although I'm red hot at them, obviously, me being a builder.'

'Obviously. You're a big kid, do you know that?' Laughing, Laura turned her face up to him as he leaned towards her.

'About that photograph in the bedroom,' he started, then stopped, his gaze shooting towards Ollie.

'Oh my God!' Her heart leaping into her mouth as Ollie let out a squeal, she shot up and flew to where he'd fallen trying to climb out of the sandpit, Steve close behind her. 'It's all right. It's all right, sweetheart,' she said, dropping down beside him to assess the damage. 'He's cut his knee,' she said, her alarmed gaze going to the blood dripping from his leg and plopping starkly into the sand.

'It hurts.' Pale with shock, his face creased with pain, Ollie was doing his best not to cry, and failing.

Laura hugged him close as the tears rolled wetly down his cheeks. 'It's all right, baby, I've got you,' she whispered. 'I will *never* let anyone hurt you again, I promise.'

CHAPTER SEVENTEEN

'Is he all right?' Laura asked worriedly, as Steve slipped back into bed after climbing out to investigate a bump in the night.

'Fast asleep,' he assured her with a tired yawn. 'His book fell off the bed. He must have been having a sneaky read.'

His new scissor skills workbook. Laura had bought it because, besides teaching children how to use scissors, it had an array of animal patterns and shapes to cut out. He'd been so excited when she'd given it to him after their trip to the zoo, she'd decided to leave it with him. It wouldn't hurt him to browse it under the softly undulating theme of his night light, and he deserved a bit of a treat after being so brave about the injury to his knee, which had turned out to be not as bad as it looked, thank goodness.

Yawning herself, she snuggled into Steve as he wrapped his arm around her. She'd been the tiniest bit annoyed with him for agreeing to let Sarah pick Ollie up early tomorrow. She and Joe wanted to take him out for a meal, she'd said. Ollie would no doubt love it, but Laura was concerned about disrupting his visiting schedule. Steve had an arrangement: Saturday morning to Sunday evening. Yes, Sarah had agreed to swap weekends, but still, Laura didn't want them to take him off early. She didn't want them to take him at all. She loved being with him, getting into his mindset, where the troubles of the world drifted away and everything was magical, and all things were possible.

A smile curved her mouth as she pictured the giraffe he had painted so vividly in her mind. His big blue eyes sparkling, his trip to the zoo fuelling his imagination, he'd told *her* a story at bedtime, in which the superhero had been Mr Giraffe, whose neck 'growed and growed and growed until his head was poking above the clouds', he'd said animatedly, stretching his own neck.

'Grew.' Laura had laughed and gently corrected him. 'Mr Giraffe's neck grew and grew and grew.'

'Grew,' Ollie repeated, his brow furrowed in concentration.

'That's right. Good boy.' She beamed, delighted – and wondered whether Sarah bothered to correct him. She really ought to. Laura would hate to think of him struggling verbally when he started school. 'And then what did Mr Giraffe do?' she'd prompted him.

The furrow in his brow deepened. 'He looked down from the clouds and saw some people were crying.'

'Oh no.' Laura had widened her eyes in pretend alarm. 'Why were they crying?'

'Because they'd lost their friends,' he went on, with a sad shake of his head. 'So he growed … grew … some more and said hello to the little stars.'

Because that was where all the lost people went. Laura had gleaned what he meant. Steve had told him that was where his grandad had gone after he'd died; that he was a twinkling star, looking down on him from the night sky. She'd thought Ollie's story was quite lovely. Snuggling closer to Steve, she forgave him for not being as assertive as he should be. She couldn't stay angry with him for feeling compromised. How could she when he'd brought her Ollie?

Hearing Steve's breaths slow, she listened for a while to make absolutely sure Ollie had settled, and then, her eyes growing heavy, her thoughts drifted. His small hand in hers, she was walking with Ollie through a pleasant woodland, where bees buzzed happily pollinating wild flowers and big red butterflies fluttered breathtakingly from petal to petal.

And then her mind shifted. The dream grew darker. Woods turned to bricks and mortar. His hand had slipped from hers. He was no longer with her. Nowhere to be seen. Not *safe*. Her throat caught as she heard them twisting and grinding, wild vines as thick as giraffe's necks, snaking their way up the walls as she moved silently around the objects that were there, yet not. Through the house that was familiar, yet not. Her dream hazily superimposed over reality, she negotiated the stairs, her tread soft, determined, unfaltering. She didn't flinch as a spider as big as the palm of her hand scurried across the wall a hair's breadth from her cheek. It was huge, hunch-legged, obviously escaped from the zoo, but there was none of the petrifying fear she'd felt as a child when faced with such threats, no thudding heartbeat, nothing but the urge that drove her, placing her feet blindly, steadily, one in front of the other as the voice in her head persisted. *You have to find him. You have to save him.*

The lounge was her lounge, but different; brighter, like an overexposed photo. The furniture was solid, yet ill-defined; blurry, jagged edges, like the memories that floated on the periphery of her mind, day and night, night and day. Her one abiding recollection was that of his trusting little face, his wide eyes, the truest sky blue and crystal clear with the innocence of childhood. Trust broken. Innocence lost. She had to find him.

The patio doors – her eyes travelled towards them, refocusing … click … the lens of a camera, shutter closing, shutter opening. She found them locked. She knew they would be, to keep her in, keep the memories out. She moved instinctively, releasing the catch, sliding them open. Wind whipped her hair as she stepped quietly onto the patio, whispering through the leaves on the trees, imploring her more urgently, *Hurry, hurry.* Her gaze moved to the pool. Sunk into the lawn, it wasn't there, yet it was, its surface rippling; fracturing like broken glass as the wind stirred it.

'Oh my *God*, what have you done?' She heard her behind her, the woman who'd paraded herself as their mother, who was no mother at all. 'What have you *done?*'

No! Laura tried to say it out loud, but though her head screamed it, her lips jammed together and wouldn't let the sound out.

'Laura …' A male voice spoke, snatching her away. Steve. He shouldn't be here. He didn't belong here in this time and this place, which was another time, another place.

Futilely, she stretched out a hand, trying to hold onto the memory her mother claimed wasn't a memory as it slipped from her mind back into the water.

'Come inside, sweetheart. It's wet out here.' She sensed him approach her, his tone cautious as she watched the soil fall from the sky to rain down on the soul that would always be lost.

Disorientated, she fixed her gaze on the water as it receded. Soon it would be gone, fading from her mind like an ebbing tide. 'I have to *sss*ave him,' she stammered uncertainly.

'It's okay, Laura.' He held her as she took a stumbling step forward, needing to follow him to the place where his spirit never rested. How else would she find him? 'He's safe. I promise,' he said softly, steering her around to face him.

Laura blinked, her focus shifting from the pictures in her mind to Steve's face, a kind face. She could see under the glow of the floodlight that his gentle features were etched with deep concern.

'We saved him, Laura,' he said softly. 'Do you remember?'

She searched his eyes. He was trying to placate her, but she knew they hadn't saved him. *She* hadn't. She might have, if only she'd known where to find him.

'Let's go inside, shall we?' His voice strained, Steve drew her to him. 'Ollie's woken up. We don't want to scare him, do we?'

Laura frowned. Little Ollie. He was here, upstairs. No, she didn't want that. Walking falteringly, she allowed Steve to guide her back to the house. But still she heard the leaves whispering over and over, *You have to save him.*

CHAPTER EIGHTEEN

Steve

The rain was lashing down relentlessly as Steve led Laura back to the house. 'Almost there,' he said, and then, 'Step,' he warned her, aware that she might be unsteady on her feet. When she was in a deep sleep phase, she seemed to be able to negotiate everything in front of her. When she started to come out of it, though, she would become less sure-footed.

'Here we go.' Guiding her from the patio doors through the lounge, he steered her towards the stairs. 'Let's get you tucked back up in bed where it's nice and warm, shall we?' He noted the small nod of her head and guessed she was on the cusp of waking. Having spoken to her GP for advice, he knew that she was now caught between wakefulness and sleep; that waking her vigorously might disorientate or shock her, causing her to lash out or even attack him. He couldn't just leave her, though, when she could so easily fall down the stairs or do something else to injure herself.

Though it still petrified him when he found her sleepwalking, he was determined not to let it affect their relationship. Her previous boyfriend would apparently scream at her to wake up, telling her she was a mental case and a danger to everyone around her. She wasn't. She walked in her sleep, that was all. Yes, it was scary sometimes, but it just made Steve more protective of her.

She'd seemed so nervous when she'd approached him at the hospice, he couldn't help but feel for her. She'd been sympathetic to his situation with his father, joining him in the communal kitchen whenever he'd taken a break from sitting with him. He'd felt bad about spending time with her, albeit innocently at first, but he and Sarah seemed to have drifted so far apart. He'd wanted to fix things in their relationship. Throwing himself into his work, determined to make his business viable, to clear off their debts, wasn't going to fix anything, though, was it? It was Laura who'd pointed that out. Sarah would just want him to open up to her, she'd told him. She was right, he knew she was, but by then it was too late. The gap was too wide. He'd felt that Sarah didn't want him there. Maybe her feelings for him had changed before then – this bloke Joe being so fast on the scene once they'd split up had made him wonder. Truthfully, though, the more he'd seen of Laura, the more he'd realised his own feelings had changed, which only compounded the guilt he carried around. He'd been gutted when he and Sarah had decided to split, but quietly thanked God that Laura had been there for him. It was his turn to be there for her now.

'I have to find him,' she mumbled as he guided her towards the bed.

'We will,' he assured her, his heart hurting for her. He'd realised she'd been searching for someone the first time he'd found her sleepwalking. She never had any recollection of what she said or did, though, which left him wondering who it was.

Helping her into bed, he eased the duvet up over her and, checking she was still asleep, went quietly out of the room and back downstairs. Wide awake himself, he made a coffee, pondering what had happened when Ollie had fallen climbing out of the sandpit. Laura had been great with him, comforting and reassuring him. She'd promised not to let anyone hurt him again. She'd whispered it, but Steve had heard it. Earlier, she'd got choked up when she'd tried to tell him more about the photograph he'd seen. He hadn't pushed it, figuring she would tell him when she was ready. She hadn't. She hadn't told him much about her family either, other than that her parents lived in a grand house somewhere in Stratford-upon-Avon and that she didn't get on with them.

Checking the clock, he went to retrieve Laura's phone from her bag in the hall. He felt bad sneaking around behind her back, but he'd decided he had no choice but to talk to her mother. This rift between them couldn't be good for her. It was still early, but since the woman had turned up here only for her and Laura to end up arguing, he suspected calling her while Laura was around might not be prudent.

He was relieved when he eventually found her mother's number – a landline it looked like. He wouldn't have had a clue how to contact her otherwise. It was listed under 'Sherry', rather than 'Mum', which baffled him slightly. Why would she list her under her Christian name?

Realising he'd left his own mobile in the bedroom, he glanced up the stairs and then went into the lounge to call from their own landline, rather than use Laura's phone or risk waking her. Hoping he was doing the right thing, he let the call ring out for a while. Thinking they might still be in bed, he was about to ring off and try again later when someone picked up.

'Grant Caldwell,' a male voice said.

Caldwell? Steve hesitated. 'Sorry, I think I might have the wrong number. I was looking for Sherry Collins.'

'And you are?' the man enquired.

'Steve. Steven Lewis. I'm Laura's partner.'

There was silence for a second. Then, 'Sherry's not up and about yet,' the man said. 'Can I give her a message?'

'Er, no. I'll …'

Call back, Steve was about to say, when a voice in the background said, 'Who is it, darling?'

CHAPTER NINETEEN

Sherry

'Hi. It's Steve, Laura's partner,' the young man introduced himself once Sherry came to the phone. 'We met when you came to see Laura. Briefly.'

He sounded nice, as he had when she'd first spoken to him while trying to contact Laura. He was obviously concerned for her daughter, happy to give her her address when she'd explained she'd been abroad and hadn't got her details to hand. He clearly hadn't been aware of their troubled history. He might not have offered the information so readily had he been.

'Yes,' she said. 'Please accept my apologies for rushing past you the way I did. You must have thought me very rude. Laura and I had had a few words. I imagine she's told you why.'

'Not really, no. She was upset after you left, not making much sense, to be honest. She mentioned something about a long-ago incident and the police being involved, no more than that. The thing is …' he paused, taking an audible breath, 'she seems reluctant to reveal much about her family history. Scared, even, and I can't help wondering why, and whether it's something she's still struggling to deal with.'

Sherry drew in a sharp breath of her own. She'd guessed he would ask, eventually, it being so obvious that Laura *was* struggling.

'I'm not trying to poke my nose in where it's not wanted, or to upset anyone,' he went on as she debated how to answer, how much she should tell him, 'but I'm concerned for her. I want to try and help her, but without the facts …'

'Yes, I imagine you do,' Sherry said at length. 'We all do, but Laura's so determined she doesn't need our help.' She paused, a combination of long-suppressed grief and anger sweeping through her as she recalled how Laura had retreated into herself after the 'incident', as her daughter had termed it. Would that it was just that, something that had occurred that had a beginning and an end. It seemed to Sherry that it would never be over, that the nightmare would never end. She'd felt so powerless to help Laura afterwards. The girl had barely spoken, unless to mumble and stammer. Barely ate, staying shut in her room, no matter how much she and Grant had tried to persuade her to come out. When she had finally emerged, it was to tear their world further apart, traumatising them all over again with her nightclubbing, drinking and drug-taking. Sherry had almost been glad when she'd left. She'd soon realised she couldn't lose contact with her daughter, though, that she would always have to keep tabs on her, know where she was, how she was, what she was doing and thinking.

Taking another breath, she attempted to compose herself. She doubted this young man would be easily fobbed off. 'You know she sleepwalks?' she asked, guessing that by now, he would.

'That's partly why I've called,' he said, his tone cautious. 'Also to ask why you two have fallen out so badly. You obviously care about her, or you wouldn't have sought her out.'

'I do, very much. I want to be there for her, but …' She faltered. It was too complicated to explain how impossible it was to be there for Laura when the girl had steadfastly accused her of *never* being there for her. Sherry had given birth to her at eighteen years old, for goodness' sake; a dreadfully difficult birth – Laura had been a difficult child since the day she was conceived. Before she'd met Grant, she had worked her fingers to the bone to feed and clothe her daughter and keep a roof over her head when she realised the man she'd stupidly moved in with had only one skill in life: collecting debts to fund his drinking habit. Her days – depressing, dark, lonely days – had been filled with soiled nappies and endless crying, her nights spent on the production line at the biscuit factory. She'd lost her second baby there – she swallowed back the hurt and humiliation fresh in her throat – right there on the factory floor. And Laura had the nerve to say she'd never cared for her? Of course she had. She would always care, if only the stubborn girl would realise it. Could she not understand that she was simply trying to protect her? That she was scared for her? She didn't know how long she could go on like this, though. She pressed a hand to her badly palpitating chest. The stress really was too much. Her blood pressure was rising so rapidly she was sure she could feel the blood pumping.

'She seems to be searching for someone,' the man continued carefully. 'When she sleepwalks, she appears to be trying to find someone. She had another episode last night. I found her in the garden.'

'But she doesn't remember anything?' Sherry checked.

'I doubt it,' he said, sighing tiredly. 'I haven't spoken to her yet, she's still sleeping, but she generally has no recollection whatsoever.'

'She gets confused,' she explained. 'I suspect the sedatives are largely to blame.'

'Benzodiazepines,' he confirmed.

'She's taken them for years, out of necessity.' Sherry sighed expansively. 'They can have side effects, as you may know: confusion, memory problems. Events in her past are skewed, I'm afraid. She imagines certain things happened that didn't.'

'I see,' he said at length.

She doubted he did. 'We fell out years ago, sadly, Laura having convinced herself that Grant and I were to blame for the tragedy that traumatised us all. She went completely off the rails after that,' she revealed, wanting to reinforce how muddled Laura was. 'Drinking, taking drugs. She wouldn't see me. She even changed her name rather than have anything to do with us. That broke my heart. It was as if she were trying to erase me from her life.' She paused, needing him to realise what kind of impact that had had on her. 'It breaks my heart now that she still tortures herself, that she refuses to have any kind of a mother-and-daughter relationship …' She stopped, her throat catching. 'I won't give up, though, Steven,' she went on resolutely, using his name so that he would know she'd taken him into her confidence. 'I intend to try and keep in contact with her, even if she's not that thrilled at the prospect.'

He didn't reply immediately, plainly processing what she'd told him. Then, 'What was it, Mrs Caldwell? This tragedy that's clearly had such a profound effect on all your lives?'

Sherry was silent for a long moment, letting him know how painful this was for her. How selfish it was of her daughter to make her keep reliving it over and over. 'She'd taken sedatives,' she said tearfully. 'On the night it happened. She'd taken more than one, I suspect. She didn't have anything to do with it, though,' she added defensively. 'I'm absolutely sure of it. A mother knows her own daughter, after all. And I suppose it's natural that she looks for someone to blame. It's just …'

'What happened, Sherry?' he urged her, clearly impatient to know.

'Her dear little brother,' she said eventually, her voice cracking. 'He went missing.'

'Her …? Your *son*?' He sounded astounded. As Sherry had guessed he would be.

CHAPTER TWENTY

Sarah

'Here we go. Home sweet home. You can snuggle into your nice comfy bed now. Much better than my bumpy old car, hey?' Joe talked softly to Ollie as he carried him from the car to the house.

He'd fallen asleep on the way back from the pub. As he was stuffed full of toad-in-the-hole and fresh strawberry sundae, Sarah wasn't surprised. She'd only been surprised that Laura hadn't whipped up some culinary masterpiece for lunch, making sure he was too full to enjoy his evening meal. She'd immediately felt guilty for having thought it. Laura had been nothing but smiles when they'd arrived to pick him up, and full of concern said that he'd had a bad dream early that morning. She'd been worried it might have had something to do with his trip to the zoo – he'd been frightened by one of the bird exhibitions apparently. Sarah had reassured her. He did have bad dreams occasionally, she'd said, possibly because of his overactive imagination. She'd had to work at not sounding pointed.

Going into the hall before Joe, she stepped aside, allowing him to negotiate Ollie carefully through the front door. 'Straight up?' he asked, indicating the stairs.

Sarah nodded. He hadn't brushed his teeth, so she would have to persuade him to the bathroom, but she guessed he was worn out enough to go straight back to sleep. With trips to the zoo and pub meals, his weekend had definitely been a full one. Carrying the overnight bag, she followed Joe up, marvelling at how he pressed his hand protectively over the back of Ollie's head as he carried him. He might not have children of his own, but his parenting instincts were intuitive. He'd wanted children, he'd confided that much, but would he want to be a father to another man's child? She was jumping the gun a bit, but assuming they were over the current hiccup and continued to see each other, it was something she had to consider. As would Joe. It would be a huge decision for him, making such a commitment. She'd been concerned about the disruption to Ollie's life when Steve had announced he was moving in with Laura. She was worrying now whether Joe's presence might be far more destabilising if he suddenly disappeared from it.

Watching him lower Ollie gently onto his bed, she couldn't deny the contented glow she felt inside her. Working on the premise that it was better for her child to have one loving parent than two warring ones, she'd told herself she would rather be a single parent, but right now she was so glad Joe was around sharing some of the responsibility. Seeing how he'd been with Ollie today had reminded her how much he really did care about her little boy, making her realise that, as men go, she could do worse. Far worse. She would take her worry head off for tonight, she decided, looking forward to snuggling up in bed with Joe, who'd turned out to be an excellent foot-warmer as well as lover. He was extremely intuitive in that department too.

'Thanks,' she said, looking him over as he straightened up. Broad-shouldered and dark-haired, and with that broody look about him he sometimes had, he was definitely attractive – she felt an undeniable little flip of excitement in the pit of her tummy – in and out of his uniform.

'No problem,' he whispered, a smile curving his mouth as he caught her gaze gliding over him. 'I'll go and make us a coffee. Unless you prefer something stronger?'

'A liqueur coffee might be nice,' she suggested, thinking that would be just what was needed to ensure they relaxed before bed.

'One coffee with Cointreau coming up,' Joe said.

Knowing it was her tipple of choice, he'd brought some with him last time he was here. They hadn't had a chance to open it yet. He was thoughtful too. Yes, she could do a *lot* worse than Joe. She caught his hand as he walked to the door, tugging him back towards her and leaning to plant a kiss on his cheek.

He arched his eyebrows amusedly. 'What was that for?'

She shrugged. 'Just because.'

'Fair enough. As long as it's a promise of more,' he said, giving her a mischievous wink.

Definitely, Sarah thought as he headed on out. He really was lovely. Quite irresistible. She could see what Ollie saw in him.

Sighing happily, she went across to the little boy, who was wriggling onto his side. 'We have to brush your teeth, sweetheart,' she reminded him, easing his thumb away from his mouth. She was almost tempted to leave him, but she really should get him into his jim-jams. 'Come on.' She helped him to sitting. 'Arms up, and let's get this dirty T-shirt off, shall we?' It was spattered with strawberry sundae, not something she would be happy to let him sleep in.

After hitching the shirt over his head, she helped him with his jeans and trainers. Once he was in his pyjamas, she led him to the bathroom, where his teeth-brushing consisted of a lick and a spit – ah well, it would have to do for tonight – and then helped him back to bed and tucked him in. Reminding herself not to be too miffed that his fringe was lopsided, she smoothed it away from his forehead, then leaned to kiss his cheek and breathe in the special smell of him. 'Night, night, little man,' she said, hugging him close.

'Where's Mr Whale?' he asked, craning his neck to glance worriedly around as she straightened up.

Damn, she'd forgotten about the cuddly toy. Wished that Ollie would, she thought, possibly a bit childishly. 'In your bag, I think. Hold on, I'll fetch him.'

Going across to his bag, which she'd dropped by the door, she delved inside to fish for Mr Whale – and froze. 'Ollie …' Her heart leapt into her mouth as she drew out a pair of scissors. 'Where did you get these?' she asked, walking back towards him. They were obviously safety scissors, but what in God's name were Laura and Steve thinking, letting him carry them around?

'Laura gave me them.' Ollie blinked sleepily. 'To cut up the animals.'

The hairs on Sarah's skin rose at the image that conjured up, but she bit hard on her tongue, humming softly to him instead until he'd drifted off, his whale tucked under his arm in place of his maimed bunny. Creeping quietly out, she pulled the door behind her. Her heart was still thumping as she went downstairs, taking the scissors with her. Was she getting *this* out of proportion too? Should she be glibly saying *okey-dokey* to everything Laura did? Even allowing Ollie to carry scissors around in his bag? They were obviously in there so he could bring them home with him, but why would she put them in there without telling Sarah? More worryingly, what on earth was Ollie talking about when he'd said they were 'to cut up the animals'?

'All good?' Joe asked as she went into the lounge to be greeted by the aroma of coffee and Cointreau.

'I'm not sure,' she prevaricated, feeling slightly nauseous now. Whether with nerves at the prospect of what Joe's reaction might be when she voiced her very real concerns, or with worry about a situation that seemed to be growing more ominous, she wasn't sure, but she definitely felt shaky. 'I found these in Ollie's bag,' she said, holding the scissors out.

Joe glanced at them from where he was sitting on the sofa and then pulled himself to his feet. 'Scissors?' he asked, his forehead creasing into a frown as he walked across to her.

'They were right there in his bag, on top of his clothes under that whale toy she bought him. It's as if she wanted me to find them.'

A flicker of doubt crossed Joe's face. Sarah didn't miss it.

'Why would she put them there without telling me?'

'I've no idea.' He took them from her. 'They're children's scissors, I take it.' He studied them, noting the bee motif and the yellow and black striped handles, as Sarah had.

'Yes, but they're still quite sharp,' she pointed out. 'Ollie said they were for cutting up animals.'

'Ah.' Joe nodded thoughtfully. 'That might explain the cut-off bunny ear then.'

'Not that sharp.' Sarah buried a sigh of frustration. 'His bunny's ear was surgically removed. Trust me, Ollie didn't do that. I'm positive he didn't.'

The furrow in Joe's brow deepened. 'And you really think Laura did?'

She splayed her hands. 'Who else?'

'But why would she? Out of spite?' He was looking at her dubiously, Sarah noted.

'Yes!' Her frustration surfaced, despite her best efforts. 'No.' She glanced away, her heart plummeting. He thought she was overreacting – again. It was obvious he did. 'I don't know. I don't know her. And that's the point here. I *don't* know her. You don't. Steve doesn't know her that well; he can't possibly. All I do know is that she appears to be manipulating my son in some way and also managing to come between you and me.'

'Manipulating's a bit harsh, isn't it?' Joe ventured.

Shaking her head, Sarah smiled sardonically. 'I rest my case,' she said. 'You're doing it again, Joe. Accusing me of getting things out of perspective.'

His expression was now one of surprise. 'I didn't say that, Sarah. I just … Look, sit down, have your drink and we'll talk this through. I honestly think your best bet is to leave it until tomorrow and call her. There's bound to—'

'I don't want to sit down. I don't *want* to call her. She'll just lie,' Sarah said exasperatedly. 'Those scissors were planted there. I *know* they were. She's probably realised I discovered his bunny and is trying to convince me that Ollie is responsible. What she's actually doing is convincing everyone around me that I'm mad!'

Joe said nothing, glancing down instead, which spoke volumes.

Sarah swallowed back her hurt. 'You're missing the point here a bit, Joe,' she went on, working hard to speak calmly. 'Ollie shouldn't be carrying scissors around. It's irresponsible to let him. I wouldn't. Would you?'

He looked at her uncomfortably. 'No,' he admitted. 'No, I wouldn't.'

She nodded. That was something, at least. Not enough, though, she thought, her heart aching. She was losing him. Because her natural instinct was to protect her son from threat, no matter how small or how insignificant other people thought it might be, she was losing Joe.

'Whatever her explanation, she shouldn't have put them in his bag without mentioning it,' she said, for clarification's sake. 'They are safety scissors, yes, but to allow a child Ollie's age to use them unsupervised …' She stopped, a tight lump rising in her throat that she couldn't seem to swallow. She'd said enough. Joe was a policeman, for goodness' sake. He knew what the consequences could be.

He ran his hand over his neck. 'I do see what you mean,' he said awkwardly.

'Do you, Joe?' she challenged him. 'Do you really?' He was trying to appease her. She didn't want appeasing. She didn't need appeasing. She simply wanted him on her side.

'I've done it again, haven't I?' Sighing heavily, he glanced at the ceiling.

Sarah didn't answer. She didn't feel she needed to.

'Do you want me to go?' He looked pig-sick as he gazed back at her.

She didn't know. Could they ever have a conversation about Laura that didn't include her being on the defensive? Would they ever be able to spend time together without the topic of Laura coming up? Mr bloody Whale wasn't the intruder. *She* was. 'Do you—' she began, just as the hall phone rang.

God, it would wake Ollie. Tearing her gaze away from Joe, who now looked utterly dejected, she turned to the hall, and then stopped dead as the answerphone picked up.

'Sarah, it's Laura. I couldn't get you on your mobile. I've sent you a text, but just in case, I put Ollie's safety scissors in his bag and completely forgot to mention it. I've put his scissor skills workbook in there too. Hope you had a lovely meal. Speak soon.'

CHAPTER TWENTY-ONE

Joe hadn't gone home, but the evening had ended far differently to the way Sarah had hoped it would. As they'd lain in bed together, he had tentatively wrapped an arm around her, but she'd felt his tension. Any other night she would have snuggled into him. With the issue of Laura wedged between them, though, she hadn't known how to. It was all she could do not to cry. It was her instigating the arguments between them, not Laura magically manipulating them from a distance. If Joe hadn't acknowledged her attempt to bridge the divide and squeezed her close as he normally did, she couldn't have borne it. After being everything he had accused her of, seemingly obsessed with her ex's girlfriend, reacting apparently unreasonably to something that clearly had been a miscommunication – or lack of communication, anyway – she'd felt bitchy and petty. In short, not very good about herself.

Joe had had an early training meeting. As an authorised firearms officer, he qualified to apply for a role at the West Mercia operational policing unit, and had decided to go for it. She'd been worried to death when he'd told her that. She would always worry about him, even if they weren't together. She felt the tears rising, her throat tightening at that thought. She'd hoped he might wake her, or leave a note. He hadn't. She couldn't blame him. No doubt he'd been mulling things over while he'd tossed and turned in the night and was probably desperate to put as much distance between them as he could. He hadn't signed up for this. He was single, child-free. Why would he want this kind of hassle in his life?

Exhausted after lying awake herself most of the night, she forced herself out of bed and dragged herself through the morning routine, smiling for Ollie's sake, chatting to him on the way to nursery about his trip to the zoo and his flipping scissor skills workbook. She'd broached the subject of Bunny, delicately. Ollie had looked upset and said he'd lost him and that he'd asked his invisible superhero friend to help find him. Sarah really didn't think he had cut Bunny's ear off. She was sure he would mention it if he knew anything about it. Someone had, though. It hadn't just dropped off, had it? Then there were the secrets he'd been convinced he should keep from her. No matter how plausible Laura's explanations had been, she still couldn't understand why Ollie would have imagined he shouldn't share information with her unless someone had categorically told him not to.

Laura's relationship with her mother was also bothering her. She wasn't sure why. It just seemed odd. Everything about Laura seemed … off, unless it was her own instincts that were, totally. The fact was, she *was* bothered, out of concern for her son. Perhaps she had been looking for reasons not to like Laura – she was only human, after all, and it was normal, surely, to compare yourself to the new woman in your ex's life and wonder what it was you were lacking. She might have charged in unthinkingly initially. She might have upset Laura, but only inadvertently. In her heart, she didn't think she was any of the things that Joe thought she was, that Steve did: a vindictive, jealous person.

Driving dejectedly to work after dropping Ollie off, she went over it again and again. Try as she might, she simply couldn't ignore the niggling feeling in the pit of her stomach that something about Laura was off kilter. By the time she'd got through her morning 'Welcome to Dog School' training session, she'd decided on a plan. She would be the epitome of friendliness, and would certainly keep any thoughts about the woman to herself, for now. Meanwhile, she would do a little digging. She'd taken Laura at face value. Steve had too. Joe had been won over, smiling readily at her when they'd picked Ollie up; Sarah supposed most people would be, with that air of vulnerability she had about her. Laura had stammered when she'd spoken to him, she recalled. Why would that be? Because she was nervous because he was a policeman? Or because she'd been attracted to him?

She acknowledged that the green-eyed monster might now be rearing its head, but decided not to beat herself up about that either. She wouldn't apologise for being human. Nor would she apologise for wanting to protect her child. She needed to find out all she could about Laura. Some indication of what had caused the rift between her and her mother, for a start. Also whether there was any truth to what Laura had told her about her previous controlling relationship. There was bound to be some hint of who she really was online. And if there wasn't, why not? Everyone had an online profile of some sort, a trail of life events left behind them. Even Steve, who wasn't much into Facebook other than to set up his business page, had an online presence.

After invigilating a meet-and-greet session, where, sadly, the prospective new owners of a Labrador cross were completely overwhelmed by his boisterousness, she went to check on the puppy-farm Jack Russell rescue, who'd been brought in half starved and riddled with ticks, worms and fleas.

'Hey there, little Dot,' she said, going carefully into the dog's kennel. It had taken her ages to gain her trust enough to do that. For days after she'd come to them, the poor thing had shaken uncontrollably and cowered in the corner whenever anyone had gone near her. She would need special owners, people with experience of JRs who had lots of time to devote to her and would understand the amount of care she would need. 'You've put on a little weight, haven't you, gorgeous, hmm?' She spoke to the dog softly, her heart swelling with love for the tiny animal that had probably never known human kindness.

Approaching her cautiously, she bent to gently pet her and was delighted when she was rewarded with a nervous wag of her tail. 'You'll be okay, girl,' she assured her, as the dog lapped at her hand and then looked up at her, her huge chocolate-brown eyes full of uncertain hope. 'I'll make sure you are, I promise.'

Her chest constricting with a mixture of determination and anger at the way little Dot had been treated, she spent another few minutes with her, feeding her nutritious treats. She wasn't a bad person. She was *not* getting things out of perspective, wanting to rubbish Laura out of spitefulness, insecurity or jealousy. It just wasn't who she was. She didn't need to prove that to herself. She did need to prove it to Steve, though, for their son's sake. She also needed to trust her instincts. They were too strong to be ignored.

Fetching her lunch and her PC from her car, she went to the small office set aside for form-filling and paperwork. Ten minutes later, having checked Instagram first, she found what she wanted on FB. There were a few people with the name Laura Collins, but the Laura she was looking for was unmistakable, with her long mane of rich auburn hair. Snatching a bite of her sandwich, she scrolled down. The profile hadn't been updated for over a year. The most recent photos posted were mostly wild flowers and landscapes; impersonal stuff, giving nothing away. Glancing through them, she paused at a photo of an orange sunset dated almost two years ago, with the caption *A New Chapter in My Life*. There were previous chapters, then? Gulping down a mouthful of food she had no taste for, she wiped her fingers and scrolled on, skipping through random reposts and pictures of cute animals – and then froze.

There was no mistaking that the woman looking back at her was Laura, her hair slightly shorter, a smile dancing in her eyes. No mistaking either that the blonde-haired, blue-eyed child she was crouching beside bore an uncanny resemblance to Ollie. Her heart lurching, Sarah stared hard at the photograph.

Who was this child? Her stomach twisted in confusion as she scanned a plethora of photographs, mostly of the little boy – Liam, she learned: Liam on a slide in the park, Liam at Halloween dressed as a devil, Liam smiling gleefully astride a bike with stabilisers. His first two-wheeled bike? There were photographs of Liam on holiday, planting seashells on a sandcastle, one of him laughing as he chased a ball across a lawn in a back garden, a man close behind him; photos of him taking his first baby steps, Laura hovering nervously as he did. Fear pierced her chest like an icicle as she realised that this could almost *be* Ollie; that this could be her own child's life story. These were intimate photographs, capturing milestones; major events in a child's life that Laura would have had to be there to witness.

Her hands trembling, she went further back, and her blood froze in her veins. For a second, she blinked stupefied at the happy couple in the photograph. The man sliding the wedding band onto the woman's finger was the same man chasing the little boy across the lawn. The bride … Sarah's head reeled … was Laura.

The child … this child was *their* child. He *had* to be.

Laura had told her bare-faced lies. Why would she? *Dear God.* Where was the child now?

Jumping up too fast, Sarah spilled her food on the floor. She dropped down and scrambled around after it, lest one of the animals come in and eat it. Did Steve know about any of this? Panic clutched at her chest. If she tried to tell him, would he tell her this was *her* being unreasonable? Anger unfurling inside her, she stuffed her uneaten food into the bin. Would he tell her that she was being jealous and vindictive if she pointed out that the woman had a child from a former marriage who appeared to have disappeared from her life?

She had to talk to him. Closing the PC down, she grabbed her phone. First, though, she needed to know more. This boy had to be somewhere. If anyone could find out where, Joe could, assuming he wanted to, that he cared enough to, that he didn't think she was stuck on her bloody ex. God! Why hadn't she stood her ground? She'd known something wasn't right; her every instinct had been screaming at her that something wasn't right. Yet she'd left her child in the woman's care. Nausea swilling inside her, she selected Joe's number. *Shit!* She cursed when his phone went straight to voicemail, remembering he was on a course.

Flying out of the office, she raced to reception, waving her phone at the staff there and citing an emergency, then ran to her car. Trying Joe again as she drove to the nursery to pick Ollie up, and still getting no answer, she left a message for him to call her. What would she do if he didn't? Suddenly she felt more alone than she'd ever felt in her life. There was nothing she could do about it if he had decided he'd had enough. She had too. She was bloody pissed off with being told that *she* had a problem, when it was obvious that the one with the problems was the woman Steve had leapt into a relationship with. Serious problems. It was becoming abundantly clear that Steve had been manipulated. Laura hadn't come into his life by accident, Sarah was sure of it.

She'd chosen him.

Her heart boomed out a warning.

She'd chosen Ollie.

CHAPTER TWENTY-TWO

Joe

Seeing a stream of missed calls from Sarah, Joe's heart sank. What was he supposed to do? Every time he saw her, the conversation centred around her ex, and every single time, they ended up verging on an argument. He could understand her being cautious about who she allowed to have access to Ollie – he'd thought initially over-cautious – although the thing with the bunny's ear and then the scissors turning up had jarred him. Despite that, he'd managed to open his mouth and put his foot in it, again. The expression on Sarah's face had said it all. He'd disappointed her. She felt he was letting her down. He wanted to support her, be a hundred per cent there for her, but he couldn't escape the fact that she did seem fixated on finding fault with Laura, which begged the question why.

He'd turned a blind eye to his wife continually banging on about her ex, meeting up with him, even though his every instinct had told him she was cheating on him. He'd been a complete idiot, not wanting to believe it – until he'd had to. And now here he was seeing another woman who didn't seem to be able to move on. At least that was how it appeared to him. Was he right, or was it actually *him* who was obsessing because of his own insecurities? He wasn't sure, but he was bloody sure he couldn't go that route again. He'd been there. Done that. So what the hell was he doing here now, about to meet the woman who'd already crucified him? He clearly was the prize prat Courtney had him down as.

Sighing, he glanced towards the bar where she would be waiting. He was late, having at first decided not to come and then wrestling with his conscience. She'd been upset when she'd rung him, barely making any sense, something to do with the dickhead she'd preferred over him, he'd assumed. In the end, he'd been worried enough to show, as she'd undoubtedly known he would. He always had been a sucker for tears.

He supposed he should go in, if only to confirm in his own mind that she wasn't about to do anything stupid. In between the incoherent rambling, she'd said she'd been an idiot. That she'd thrown everything away and had nothing left to live for. As much as he wanted to walk away – knew that that was exactly what he should do, since he owed her nothing – he couldn't. His sister hadn't threatened to take her own life, she'd simply done it. She'd been just sixteen. Joe would never forget it. His whole world had stopped turning when he'd found her, held her, screamed at her, '*Please* … don't do this.' It was too late. He couldn't breathe life back into her body, couldn't bring her back, couldn't help her. He'd failed her. He was her big brother, he should have been there for her, and he hadn't. That was why he was here now, for selfish reasons, he guessed. He didn't think he could ever go through that again.

Feeling bad about how he'd left things with Sarah – without a word, basically – he was about to ring her back when she texted him. His heart, which had been sinking steadily since they'd gone to bed last night with a bad atmosphere still between them, plummeted to the pit of his stomach. *Could you call me, Joe, please?* she'd sent. *Desperately in need of advice about Laura. X*

He shook his head despondently. She'd signed off with a kiss; he supposed that was something. It wasn't enough, though, was it? If he was going to have a relationship with her, it had to be all or nothing. When he'd told her about the disaster his marriage had been, which he'd found bloody difficult, he'd thought she would understand why he would need to know she was fully committed. Clearly, she didn't.

Pocketing his phone with a heavy sigh, he climbed out of the car and made his way into the pub to see what Courtney's latest game was. Christ, he really was a glutton for punishment. She'd liked the fact that he was reliable; she'd told him that when they'd first gone out. That he wasn't the type of man who would let a woman down. Yeah, he wasn't likely to, was he, since it was some bastard letting his little sister down that had screwed her up. He'd told Courtney about it, sharing stuff, as you did early in a relationship. The cynical side of him couldn't help thinking now that she knew damn well that that was exactly why he tried to be reliable.

He saw her immediately. She was on her feet, waving across the room, looking nothing like the broken woman she'd sounded like on the phone. Going across to her, he noted the figure-hugging lacy black dress. He remembered buying it for her when she'd oohed and aahed over it while they were out shopping. It had cost him an arm and a leg. It also showed off a lot of leg. Her long blonde hair was sleek and freshly shampooed; he noticed that too as she threaded an arm around his neck, dragging him towards her to plant a kiss on his cheek. Her make-up? Not an eyelash out of place. He hadn't thought there would be. That was Courtney. Swap the dress for jeans and she hadn't looked much different, despite the crocodile tears, when he'd left.

'You're definitely looking good,' she said, appraising him slowly. 'Policing obviously suits you. I know the uniform does.'

Seeing the suggestive look in her eyes, Joe laughed wryly. 'Yeah, you too, Courtney. But then you always do.'

'Thank you.' She smiled, missing the facetiousness in his voice, or choosing to. 'I got you a drink,' she said, nodding to a pint of beer already on the table. 'Sit.' She dropped to the bench seat, patting the space next to her.

Joe hesitated.

'You are still drinking pints, aren't you?' she asked, a flicker of uncertainty in her eyes.

'Occasionally, but not usually when I'm driving,' Joe said, wondering whether she'd get the hint. He'd never drunk when they were out together. He'd always been the one doing the driving then – and making sure she made it to the car without falling over. Reaching to slide the pint across the table towards him, he sat opposite her.

She looked marginally perturbed, but Joe doubted anything he said would faze her. She'd always been able to wrap him around her finger, until he'd seen the light. He guessed she was up to something now. The question was, what?

'So, are you still seeing that woman I saw you with at the pub?' she asked him.

Joe sipped his drink. Taking his time, he placed the glass back on the table, turned it around, considered his answer. 'We're going out together, yes,' he said, and left it at that. 'How are things with you and the hotshot advertiser?'

Courtney glanced down, and then looked back at him from under her lengthy eyelashes. 'They're not,' she said, her face hardening. 'He's decided to try and make a go of things with his partner.'

Meaning the thrill of illicit sex with Courtney had presumably worn off. Well, well. Had she finally seen him for the wanker he was?

'Right.' Joe nodded. He was hardly going to offer his commiserations. 'And you wanted to see me to tell me this why?' Maybe she did want to discuss the apartment, looking to sell it possibly? Make a clean start? A penthouse apartment at the junction of the Worcester and Birmingham Canal and the River Severn, it would have gone up a fair whack in value since they'd purchased it. She'd paid the bulk of the deposit, but as he had some equity in it, he supposed they should discuss it, though he would much rather have done that by email or over the phone.

Her gaze flicked away again. 'I just wondered how you were doing.' She shrugged, her sharp blue eyes tinged with sadness as they came back to his.

'Fine, as it happens.' Joe picked up a table mat, twirling it between his thumb and forefinger as he studied her. Where was this going?

She nodded slowly and took a breath. Then she reached out, catching him by surprise and taking his hand. 'I never stopped loving you, Joe,' she said, locking her gaze meaningfully on his. 'What happened … it was a mistake. I didn't mean to hurt you. I lost my way. Lost sight of what mattered.'

Ah, now he got it. He would have laughed, had it not been so bloody unfunny. He was the rebound guy. Again. 'That would explain it,' he said. 'I suppose you must have been struggling a bit.'

Knitting her perfectly shaped eyebrows, Courtney looked at him curiously.

'To see the sat nav,' Joe added acerbically. 'Bent over the bonnet of his car as you were.' Stamping down the anger that still simmered inside him every time he thought about it, he kept his gaze locked hard on hers.

'Joe … don't.' She snatched her hand back, her eyes swivelling to the side – lest the people on the next table overhear, presumably. 'That's just crude.'

'Funny, that. That's exactly what I thought.' He took a swig from his pint and got to his feet. 'Sorry,' he said, with a tight smile. 'I have to go. My girlfriend's expecting me.'

'Joe?' Courtney's tone was a mixture of astonished and bewildered as he walked away. He supposed it would be. He'd practically begged her to stop meeting the guy before they'd split. He really hadn't seen her for what she was: a woman who was full of herself, sure of herself; a user.

He was out of the door, heading back to his car, the sudden torrential downpour doing nothing to lighten his mood, when he heard her behind him. 'I was pregnant!' she yelled. 'When you walked out, I was pregnant!'

Joe's stride faltered. His heart skipped a beat. He didn't turn around.

'I tried to tell you,' she went on tearfully, 'but you wouldn't take my calls.'

Massaging his forehead, he tried to assimilate. Was she saying …? They'd been together, just before … Christ, she wasn't, was she? 'Was it mine?' he managed, a hard lump expanding in his chest.

'Yes,' she said emphatically. 'I know you probably won't believe me. I know you have no reason to, but … I needed you, Joe.' She choked back a sob. '*We* needed you.'

Joe sucked in a breath. 'What happened?' he asked, his throat thick.

'I lost it,' she said, more quietly. 'I'd already lost you, I knew that; that there was no going back. I had to tell you, though; talk to you. I felt so lonely. I have nobody. Nothing left in my life. I just … can't see what the point is any more.'

Jesus. Joe closed his eyes, clenched his jaw hard and turned back.

CHAPTER TWENTY-THREE

Sarah

'He'll come around,' Becky tried to reassure her as Sarah trailed back into the kitchen after settling Ollie down. 'It's a lot to take on, after all, and it does sound like you jumped down his throat a bit. I mean, I'm not surprised you did, after all you've told me,' she added quickly. 'You must be beside yourself with worry, but give him some time, hey? He's probably just trying to sort his feelings out.'

Nodding despondently, Sarah seated herself at the table, where Becky was pouring her a large medicinal wine. She *had* jumped down Joe's throat. She'd done nothing but regale him with her problems, and he'd listened patiently, but still she hadn't felt he was behind her. 'That's the problem, though, Becks.' She sighed, and gratefully accepted the glass her friend offered her. 'I don't want him "coming around" if he's too busy judging me to hear a single word I'm saying.'

'Have you told him about what you found online?' Becky asked, topping her own glass up.

'No,' Sarah replied gloomily. 'It's a bit difficult to talk when he's not taking my calls.'

'I suppose.' Becky knitted her brow thoughtfully. 'You said he's on a course, though, right?'

'He was today,' Sarah confirmed, with another hefty sigh. 'I texted him this evening, though. Called him a few times before that too.'

'Still nothing?'

She shook her head. 'I'm probably better off without him if I can't rely on his support, aren't I?' she asked, part of her hoping that Becky would tell her she wasn't. She missed him already.

Diplomatically, Becky didn't answer.

'I can't believe he thinks I'm getting things out of perspective. Do you think I am? Be honest.' Sarah locked her gaze on her friend's, knowing she would tell her the truth, no matter how unpalatable.

'Well …' Becky hesitated. 'To be honest, I did wonder,' she admitted, causing Sarah's heart to drop further than it already was, which was about shoe level. 'But now, having seen Ollie's poor mutilated bunny, and that Facebook profile … You did say she actually said she'd never been married?'

'She said she ran scared of marriage because of her mother and stepfather – neither of whom she apparently gets on with. She said she'd had relationships and that her last partner was impossibly controlling. She never once mentioned anything about a child. I'm not imagining that that's odd, am I?'

Taking a glug of her wine, Becky shook her head. 'No,' she said, after a lengthy swallow. 'You need to talk to Steve about it. And soon. I could come with you, if you like? Moral support and all that. And if loopy Laura causes any problems, I could always scratch her eyes out for you.' She flexed her nail extensions.

Sarah smiled weakly. 'I'm not jealous, Becks,' she assured her. 'I'm worried about Ollie. I can't believe that Joe actually thinks I *am* jealous. I was absolutely staggered when I realised he thought I was some sort of paranoid neurotic.'

Becky baulked. 'He actually said that?'

'No, not as such,' Sarah backtracked, realising that he hadn't. That that was her interpretation of what he'd said. 'It's obvious he does think I'm obsessing, though. I can't understand why he can't see that something is off. I know Steve is probably blinded by love or whatever, but I was sure that Joe would take me seriously. Clearly, he doesn't. He imagines I'm still in love with Steve, unbelievably. I thought that after we …' She stopped, her cheeks heating up at the thought of how intimate Joe and she had been.

'Made love?' Becky coaxed, reaching across the table for her hand.

Nodding, Sarah willed the tears back. Recalling the way he'd kissed her, his hands and his mouth exploring every inch of her body before making sweet, meaningful love to her – it had been meaningful to her, anyway – her heart dipped painfully. He'd held her so close afterwards, as if he would never let her go. And now it seemed he *had* let her go, without even a goodbye, and it hurt, excruciatingly.

Drawing in a shuddery breath, she took another large sip of her wine. She was grateful that Becky had turned up with an ear and a bottle after she'd poured her heart out to her on the phone. She didn't generally drink during the week, but realising that Joe didn't care about her as much as she'd thought he did, she'd decided there were worse things she could do than break her own rules. Sobbing herself to sleep and staying in bed until she got over him wasn't an option with a child to look after. Had Joe considered that when he'd decided to take the coward's way out and not return her calls? That she would still have to drag herself up and keep going for Ollie's sake? Probably. Her soldiering on because she had no other choice would allow him to waltz off with a clear conscience, wouldn't it?

Feeling suddenly desperately lonely, her heart sank another inch. And then jolted when her phone rang right next to her on the table. Even knowing she shouldn't jump to answer it, she snatched it up anyway.

'Joe?' Becky asked, as she checked the number.

'Finally.' Sarah ran a hand under her nose, glad that he couldn't see her, still in her jeans and her rescue centre T-shirt that smelled of dog. She hardly noticed it any more, but she was sure other people might. As for her mad crop of mousy curls, even Becky had looked a bit startled when she'd answered the door. It had clearly turned into an even more unflattering demented frizz after she'd got caught in a torrential summer shower earlier.

'I'll just pop to the loo,' Becky said, giving her hand a squeeze as she got to her feet. She really was a good friend. Sarah smiled appreciatively. Perhaps she should just give up on men, since she seemed to make such a mess of everything.

'Sarah, hi, it's Joe,' he said as she braced herself and took the call.

'I gathered,' she said. 'I also gathered you've been rather busy,' she added, trying to keep the sarcasm from her voice.

'Yes. Sorry about that.' He hesitated. 'Look, Sarah—'

'I won't keep you long,' she cut in quickly, her stomach twisting as she imagined what he was about to say. 'I just needed some advice. A favour, really.'

'As in?' he asked cautiously.

'I found Laura's Facebook profile,' she said, deciding not to beat around the bush, on the basis that he already thought what he thought about her anyway.

'Right,' was his weary response, which succinctly summed up how he felt.

'She's been married.' Sarah pushed on regardless. 'She said she hadn't. She also has a child.'

He went quiet, then, 'A child?' he repeated, his tone incredulous.

'A boy,' she confirmed. 'He has blonde hair, blue eyes – and she's never even mentioned him.'

'I see,' Joe said, and paused.

Did he see? Whether or not he was reassessing his opinion of her didn't matter. What mattered was *did* he see?

'And you think he looks like Ollie?' he asked, after an interminably long moment.

He did. Sarah breathed a huge sigh of relief. 'Remarkably like him. I wondered if you could find out more about him, and about Laura's history? There's not much to go on on her profile, other than the posts. I'm going to speak to Steve, obviously, but the more information I have, the better. He might already know, of course, but you have to wonder why he's never mentioned it. Why neither of them have said anything about the existence of this child.'

Joe hesitated before answering. 'I'd like to help,' he said, after a second. 'The thing is, I'm not sure how I can. The national database will only identify people who've committed a crime, and Facebook is a tricky area. We would need to make a legal request to access data. We can apply directly to Facebook now, but it's still a lengthy process. If there's a risk of serious injury, death, or imminent harm to a child, they might release data, but—'

'There *is* a risk of imminent harm, Joe, to *Ollie*,' Sarah interrupted forcefully. 'And what about the child? Where is he? He could well be …' She stopped, stunned, as she heard a female voice in the background.

'Joe?' the woman called. 'Sorry to be a pain, but do you think you could come and help me with the bath tap? The hot water's not running properly.'

'*Shit*,' Joe muttered, not quite under his breath. 'One minute,' he called back. 'Sorry,' he addressed Sarah. 'I'm at—'

'No explanations necessary,' she said frostily. 'It's none of my business, I'm sure.'

'It's Courtney,' he went on, nevertheless. 'My ex-wife. She was upset, and I—'

'I know who she is,' Sarah replied, remarkably calmly considering her heart felt as if it was fracturing inside her. 'You'd better go and warm her up, hadn't you?'

'Sarah …' Joe groaned. 'She was upset. She needed someone. I—'

'So you offered her a shoulder?' Sarah replied, unable now to keep the biting cynicism from her voice. 'Sounds to me like someone else is obsessed with their ex, Joe.'

CHAPTER TWENTY-FOUR

Joe

Cursing silently, Joe unscrewed the cap on the tap and tightened the nut under it, which had mysteriously come loose. 'All done,' he said, straightening up. 'It's getting a bit late. I'll get off and leave you to it.'

'You're going already?' Courtney asked, sounding surprised.

'I'm due at my girlfriend's.' Joe turned to where she was standing in the bathroom doorway and his heart sank. She was undressed, wearing nothing but a hand towel, which barely covered the essentials. *Christ.* What was she doing?

'Oh,' she said, sounding piqued. 'I thought …'

'Thought what?' Joe asked, trying hard to keep his eyes averted as he squeezed past her.

'Nothing.' She followed him down the short corridor to the lounge area. 'It's just … I didn't think your phone call ended very amicably.'

She'd obviously been listening. He turned, squinting at her semi-amusedly. 'We're fine,' he lied. 'She wondered why I would be in the company of a woman shouting about bath taps, obviously – my bedsit doesn't have a bath,' he reminded her, possibly childishly, 'but she'll be fine when I explain.' He doubted very much that Sarah would be anything of the sort. Would he if the shoe were on the other foot?

Courtney dropped her gaze, her cheeks flushing with embarrassment. Was it genuine? Joe didn't think so. Courtney didn't get embarrassed easily. 'You won't tell her everything, will you?' She looked back at him, tears welling in her eyes, Joe noted, sighing inwardly. 'About the baby, I mean. I know you have to tell her something, but …'

Her hand strayed to her stomach, and Joe felt his heart twist. She might have been lying. The baby might not even have been his. She'd told so many lies when they were together, each one tripping glibly off her tongue and piercing his chest like a knife, he'd struggled to believe anything she said in the end. This vulnerability, though? This was different. Not the Courtney he knew.

'It's just … it still feels so raw.' She dropped her gaze again. 'I know it's all been a shock for you and that you might feel you need someone to talk to, but …'

Joe did. He'd thought he'd found that someone. Now, because of his own stupidity, he'd probably lost her.

'I think I'm still grieving, to be honest.' She looked back at him, her eyes filled with such heartache, Joe couldn't help but feel for her. 'I know how badly you wanted children, and that part of you will probably be grieving too,' she went on, wiping a tear from her cheek. 'I'm probably the last person you feel you could talk to, but … I don't know, I can't bear the thought of you talking to a stranger about him. Can you understand?'

Him? It was a boy? Joe felt something crack inside him. 'Yes,' he said gruffly. 'I get it.' He wasn't sure he did, but he doubted very much he would be talking to anyone about this. It wasn't the sort of thing he would discuss with his colleagues. Who else did he have, apart from Sarah? She was highly unlikely to be in the listening mood.

'I knew you would.' Courtney smiled sadly. 'You're a good man, Joe. I was an idiot to let you go.'

Joe knew how she felt. He was very much the idiot right now, for letting Sarah go. For not being there for her when he should have been. For calling her from the apartment. Why was he here? Would it have been too late for him and Courtney if she had carried the baby full term? Could they have somehow mended their relationship? No, they couldn't; he knew that categorically. They were way past broken; irreparable. He'd been devastated by her infidelity, crushed inside for so long. And then one day he'd woken up to the fact that he'd simply stopped loving her. He could have co-parented, though. Would have, willingly.

'What's she like? Your girlfriend?' Courtney asked. 'I saw her briefly at the pub, as you know. She seemed nice, natural.'

'She is,' Joe said, his heart twisting afresh. 'She's kind …' He was going to say she was a good mother to Ollie, but stopped himself. That would be cruel, given Courtney's circumstances. 'Thoughtful. Genuine, you know?'

He hadn't meant to make the point that Courtney wasn't any of those things, but the fact was, she wasn't. He hadn't been looking for a relationship when he'd bumped into Sarah. When he had, though … she'd felt like a breath of fresh air. She had no hidden side to her, he knew that from when they'd gone out together way back. She hadn't changed. She'd still been the same pretty, shy, caring woman he'd known then. He'd lain awake for hours last night, wondering how it had all gone so wrong, but he knew that too. It was his fault, not Sarah's. He'd been so determined not to be on the receiving end of the kind of crap he'd been through with Courtney, he hadn't stopped to remind himself that Sarah wasn't her. She wasn't the sort of person who would use him. He doubted very much she would have embarked on a physical relationship with him if she hadn't had feelings for him. When she made love with him, it was completely. The way she touched him, the way she kissed him, the way she breathed out his name …

He loved her. In that moment, he realised that part of him always had, if that were possible with the mother of all fucked-up relationships in between. He needed to talk to her, to *listen* to her; stop judging her because of his own paranoia. This new development with Laura she'd mentioned, that wasn't her being neurotic. He needed her to know he was on her side.

He'd call her from the car, he decided. Pray that she would accept his apology – again – and tell her he would do his best to look into Laura's background. If she was going to question Steve about his girlfriend's mysterious past, he would offer to go with her. She might not want him to, but he didn't like the idea of her confronting her ex on her own.

'I should go,' he said, glancing back at Courtney. 'You have my number if you—' He stopped, apprehension knotting his stomach as he noticed that she appeared to be in pain, her face pale and her hands pressed hard to her pelvis. 'Courtney, what's wrong?' He raced back to her as she doubled up. 'What is it?' Panic climbed his chest. 'Tell me.'

'Nothing,' she gasped, and attempted to wave him away. 'Go. I'm fine. I …'

Christ. 'It's okay, I've got you,' he said, sweeping her up as her legs gave way beneath her.

CHAPTER TWENTY-FIVE

Laura

As she came down the stairs, Laura wondered who it was ringing the doorbell so early in the morning. Opening the front door, she was tempted to close it again fast. But for Steve, who appeared from the lounge, she would have done.

'I've come to apologise,' Sherry said, her smile uncertain rather than insincere as it normally was. Laura eyed her mistrustfully. What was she up to? Something, she had to be.

'I visited my mother's grave this morning – it's my thinking space, as you know,' Sherry went on. 'I've been doing some reflecting and I've realised I was being unfair to you, not considering your feelings.'

Considering her …? Laura almost laughed. The woman had never considered her feelings in her life.

'I overreacted last time I was here,' Sherry continued undaunted, her expression contrite. 'I wondered if we could …' She paused and glanced past Laura to the hall. 'Do you think I could come in, darling, rather than discussing things on the doorstep?'

Laura had absolutely nothing she wanted to discuss with her. There was never any discussion between them, only ever Sherry insisting that the story she'd told the police about the night Jacob had disappeared was the truth; that Laura was wrong, that she was muddled. The woman was a liar. She was here because she was terrified of being found out.

Laura *couldn't* allow her into her life. To do that would be to lose all that she had, Steve and dear little Ollie. Steve would never understand why she'd felt drawn to Ollie, who really was the living, breathing image of Jacob. She didn't understand it herself, other than that in having Ollie around, she felt as if she had a little piece of Jacob back. Steve might forgive her that. He might believe that she truly cared about him too. He couldn't possibly understand, though, why she had to keep her mother out of her life now that he and Ollie were part of it. It was too unbelievable. Her mother would twist anything she told him. Cite her sleepwalking and amnesia as reasons for her confusion. She would show him doctors' reports, irrefutable proof that her poor muddled daughter wasn't in possession of her faculties that night, nor would she ever be, given that her condition still existed.

Sherry wasn't here to apologise. No one would ever believe Laura if she tried to tell them that the only reason her mother kept turning up where she wasn't welcome was to destroy her relationship, just as she had before. She wanted to keep Laura close, keep a watchful eye on her; feed her another sedative, keep her quiet. Failing that, she would destroy her. If her mother even imagined that she'd remembered, she would stop at nothing to keep her from telling her secrets, even if that meant having her labelled mad and locked away where she would no longer be 'a danger to children'. If Laura tried to explain all that, people *would* think she was mad. She couldn't let her mother win, not this time. She had to keep Ollie safe. She had to find Jacob.

'Morning, Mrs Caldwell,' Steve said behind her, and Laura's heart stalled. In using the surname that she had abandoned, he was no doubt hinting that he knew her history. But he only knew as much as her mother wanted him to. Earlier, realising he was on the phone, and guessing it was the landline since his mobile was on his bedside table, she'd picked up the phone in the bedroom, heard their conversation. Sherry had painted a distorted picture, hinting that Laura might have had something to do with what had happened to their dear lost little boy on that darkest of nights. She was challenging Laura to paint it differently. And then she would reiterate how much she cared for her, how she was scared for her and wanted to protect her. She was a *liar*, thinking herself safe in the knowledge that Laura had no way to prove it.

'Morning, Steve.' Sherry smiled warmly at him and stepped inside. 'We spoke on the phone,' she informed Laura, looking her over and for once refraining from commenting on her dress. 'Such a lovely man. So understanding.' She leaned towards her then, her voice lowered to a whisper. 'You should forget the past and try to hold onto him, darling.'

Laura would have laughed at such a brazen threat had Steve not been watching her carefully, making Laura wonder whether his mind had been poisoned against her already.

'It's a beautiful day, isn't it?' Sherry went on blithely. Laura could hardly believe she was discussing the *weather*.

'It certainly is.' Steve smiled, but the look in his eyes was wary now, as he glanced between them. He didn't realise that Laura knew he'd been talking to her mother. That she understood why he was here this morning instead of at work. He was trying to facilitate a reconciliation between them, imagining that they would talk together, cry together, embrace and move forward. Poor, kind Steve, he'd been taken in by Sherry completely.

'Why don't you two have a chat in the garden?' he suggested. 'I'll bring you some drinks. And some of Laura's home-made chocolate cake, maybe?' He glanced questioningly at her.

'Oh, that would be lovely, wouldn't it, darling?' Sherry declared, striding towards the kitchen without waiting for Laura to answer.

Laura stared incredulously after her. *She's not here to apologise. She's not trying to protect me. She's protecting herself,* she wanted to scream. But she couldn't.

And her mother knew she wouldn't.

CHAPTER TWENTY-SIX

Sarah

After phoning in sick at work – feeling horribly guilty – Sarah had steeled herself to call Steve. She'd been surprised when, sounding as if he'd expected her to ring, he'd invited her to come to the house. What was he doing there, she wondered, when he would normally be at work? Her hand shook with nerves as she rang the doorbell. She imagined he would be annoyed, realising she'd been digging into Laura's past, whatever he knew or didn't know about her.

'Hi.' He smiled warily as he pulled the front door open, as if he too was nervous. Sarah had to wonder why he would be. 'Laura's in the back garden,' he said. 'We can talk in the kitchen.'

'No.' She quickly declined. She didn't want to see Laura, who might well come in from the garden – was bound to, in fact – if she knew she were here. She wanted to speak to Steve first. 'If it's okay with you, I'd rather talk here. I have something to show you.' She pulled her phone from her pocket, hit the screen-on button and handed it to him with the relevant page already loaded.

Steve looked puzzled as he scanned it.

'It's Laura's Facebook page,' she explained. 'Scroll down.'

He glanced guardedly at her and then did as she asked, his brow furrowing as he studied the various photographs.

'She has a child,' Sarah said. 'Or it looks to me like she does. She's also been married, which she categorically told me she hadn't. Did you know?'

Steve said nothing, but she could see he was troubled. 'He looks like Ollie.' She pointed out the blindingly obvious. 'You must see that?'

Sighing heavily, he looked up at last. 'There are some things you need to know. Come through to the lounge,' he said, his tone weary as he led the way.

Sarah glanced cautiously towards the kitchen and then followed him.

Going to the patio doors, Steve nodded towards the lawn. 'That's Laura's mother,' he said.

Sarah followed his gaze in surprise. Laura had said they didn't get on. From what she had heard when the woman had called unannounced, it was obvious they didn't. They seemed to be getting along now. She watched, confused, as Laura's mother appeared to fuss over her, leaning across the garden table to smooth her hair from her face and then taking hold of her hand.

'They're having a chat,' Steve filled her in. 'They have some issues. I'm hoping they might be able to resolve them. At least start talking to each other.'

Sarah didn't let on that she was aware of the issues. 'About what?' she asked.

Steve took a moment. 'A lost child,' he confided, looking at her cautiously. 'It seems Laura once had a little brother.'

'Had?' Sarah's heart skipped a beat. 'Oh my God. Do you mean …? Is he …?'

Gathering what she was asking, Steve shrugged uncertainly. 'They don't know. He went missing.' His expression was a mixture of compassion and confusion as he glanced out into the garden again. 'I don't have all the details, to be honest. I spoke to Laura's mother. She filled me in on some of it. Laura obviously doesn't find it easy to talk about.'

So Laura had never spoken to Steve about this? Why ever not? Sarah scanned his face. He looked as shocked and bewildered as she felt. 'And the child on her profile?' she asked. 'Did you know about him?'

Steve ran a hand over his neck. 'No ... no, I didn't,' he admitted at length. 'She's never mentioned him. She doesn't have contact with him, as far as I know.'

But surely she would have? Unless there was some terrible reason she couldn't? Sarah was growing more bewildered by the second. 'He looks like Ollie,' she said again, wondering why Steve hadn't commented on it.

He drew in a long breath. 'It's probably just a coincidence,' he said.

Rubbish. He didn't believe that. *She* didn't. It was more than a coincidence, she was sure it was. Her heart ached for Laura and her mother both, but she was struggling to digest this latest revelation. It made no sense that Laura hadn't told Steve any of it. She had to be hiding things from him for a reason.

'Don't you think you *should* have all the details, Steve?' She stared at him, wondering how he couldn't see that something was very wrong here. 'These aren't just trifling things she's overlooked mentioning, are they? They're huge, life-changing things. *Why* wouldn't she have mentioned them?'

He averted his gaze. 'I've told you, they're not things she feels comfortable talking about.'

'Oh, right.' Sarah laughed in disbelief. There was an awful bloody lot the woman didn't feel comfortable talking about, wasn't there? 'And you're okay with that, are you? Quite happy to have her involved in Ollie's—'

'Don't start that again, Sarah.' Turning away from the window, Steve walked away from her.

'Start what?' Not sure she was hearing him right, Sarah followed him. 'You *should* have known about these things, Steve,' she said forcefully. 'Especially about her missing brother; every last detail. How can you possibly contemplate leaving your own child in the care of a woman who was involved in the circumstances surrounding a child's disappearance when you don't know all the facts?'

'Right.' He stopped, his expression agitated as he turned to face her. 'And you know all there is to know about this Joe character you're seeing, do you, who's undoubtedly perfect?'

Unbelievable. What the hell had Joe got to do with any of this? 'Actually, I do,' she countered, her heart squeezing, because it seemed that she *didn't* know everything there was to know about him, like the fact that he'd been continuing to see his ex-wife, fixing her bloody bath taps for her while she was no doubt in a suitable state of undress ready to climb into it. 'As I tried to tell you when you first met him, we were at school together. We went out together. I've known him practically all my life.'

'Not quite all,' he corrected her, with a tight smile. 'There are a few years in between where Joe was presumably living *his* life, therefore he also has a history. Has *he* been married?'

'Yes,' she answered, although it was completely irrelevant. 'And he *told* me he had been. He's never been anything but—'

'Does he have kids?' Steve went on, before she could finish.

'No,' she provided patiently. 'He wanted children, but—'

'Skeletons in cupboards?'

'*No*,' she snapped, her heart wrenching as she wondered now whether he had. 'And he certainly doesn't ask Ollie to keep secrets from *me!*' She eyeballed him with a mixture of pent-up fury and frustration.

Steve pulled in a breath.

Sarah breathed out. This was ridiculous. She was being defensive, and it was getting them nowhere except off the subject. Steve was obviously infatuated with Laura, protective of her. While the latter might be commendable, it was misplaced if it put his son in danger. He couldn't be so blinded by love that he couldn't see that.

'I'm concerned, Steve, about Ollie,' she said, more calmly. 'I'm not on a mission to rubbish Laura. I just need to know that *her* skeletons won't hurt him. Surely you can understand that?'

Steve eyed the ceiling, visibly trying to compose himself. 'I know you're not,' he conceded finally. 'I do understand, of course I do.' He looked back at her, his expression agonised, his emotions obviously in turmoil. 'I would die before letting any harm come to him, you know I would. It's just … I don't want to go in too heavy.'

Sarah arched an eyebrow, but cautioned herself not to say anything.

'She has nightmares about her brother,' he confided. 'Actually, it's more than that.' He hesitated, the troubled look in his eyes causing goosebumps to prickle Sarah's skin. 'She sleepwalks. I've found her a few times in the garden. She seems to be searching for him. She's obviously never come to terms with what happened, and …' He paused and kneaded his temples. 'Could you go easy on her, Sarah? Please? Just hold off tackling her about anything until I've had a chance to talk to her? I promise I'll find out more about the Facebook posts. I just don't want to charge in and do anything that will make things worse for her, emotionally I mean.'

Sarah looked him over, and couldn't help but be concerned for him. He was shaken. Conflicted, clearly. At least now, though, he was aware. 'Okay,' she reluctantly agreed, alarmed though she was by this sleepwalking twist. 'But only on the condition that you do establish the facts. All of them. We need to know under exactly what circumstances her brother disappeared.'

He nodded, his look now one of immense relief. 'I will. I'll call you,' he said.

'Soon, Steve,' she urged him. She didn't want to appear to be issuing gilded threats, though in fact she was. She couldn't countenance Ollie coming here until she knew more.

Seeing he had got the message, she headed for the hall. And then turned back. 'Why aren't there any details online about her brother?' she asked, not caring that Steve would know she'd been doing more than browsing Laura's online profiles. She'd spent some time searching the internet for anything she might find. Nothing had come up under Laura's name with any reference to a missing child.

'Try the name Caldwell,' he suggested. 'She left home not long after it happened. Changed her name, according to her mother.'

Not according to Laura, then? She really hadn't been forthcoming about anything, had she? Whatever excuses Steve might be making for her, the woman was a pathological liar. 'What was his name?' she asked, a chill of trepidation creeping through her.

'Jacob,' Steve replied, and Sarah's breath caught in her throat. This was the name of the superhero in the story she'd told Ollie. Laura had called Ollie Jacob. The first time she'd been here, she'd actually called him by her brother's name. Her blood turned cold as she realised that Laura had been keeping this lost child alive through Sarah's son.

CHAPTER TWENTY-SEVEN

Sarah read the online report feeling sick to her soul:

Missing toddler latest: Jacob Caldwell, who vanished from his bed in July 2003, is believed dead. Despite repeated searches and investigations following the three-year-old's disappearance, no trace of the child has ever been found.

Detectives from West Mercia Police searched extensively for clues around the Warwickshire house from where it was first assumed Jacob had been taken. It is since believed that he may have wandered from the house onto land close by that was being excavated. Officers believe he may have been accidentally killed by one of the construction vehicles on site. To date, his body has not been recovered.

There was a photograph of him, Jacob. A sweet, petite little boy with blonde hair and blue eyes; haunting blue eyes that looked straight back at her, tearing her heart into a thousand pieces. She couldn't believe it. Why had Laura never mentioned this, to Steve if no one else? Despite his tendency to sometimes hide away from emotional things, he would have been supportive. Was that why she'd changed her name, Sarah wondered, to try to forget, to somehow put the tragedy behind her? She would never be able to do that if her name was constantly associated with it. It could conceivably be why she would hide it from Steve – because the memories were just too painful. They must be, if subconsciously she couldn't let go of them.

Feeling devastated for Laura and her mother, who must both have been utterly broken, she wondered whether she should call Laura. She was backtracking majorly – she still had to consider Ollie, whose safety was her absolute priority – but perhaps she should try and reach out to her. If Laura opened up a little, maybe Sarah could persuade her to seek help, which she clearly badly needed. Her heart ached as she thought about Jacob, what the poor mite must have gone through, the fear he would have felt out there in the dark night on his own, the terror when he saw what must have looked like some mechanical monster coming towards him. Please God he hadn't seen it. Please God he might have been sleeping, curled up somewhere and oblivious. Her mind went to Ollie, and her stomach lurched as she felt the fear like a physical thing.

She should call her. Closing her PC, she wiped away the tears she hadn't realised she was crying and went to the work surface for her phone. Deliberating for a second, she selected Laura's number, and then paused, perplexed, as she received a text. *Joe.* A turmoil of conflicting emotions ran through her. She hadn't thought he would have the nerve to contact her after their last conversation. Clearly, he had.

Can we talk? he'd sent, unbelievably. Why? Sarah wondered. Did he want to rub salt in the wounds and end things with her officially? She thought she'd already done that. Perhaps he was about to come up with some excuse as to why he would be in the company of a woman who was about to slip into the bath. Was he going to claim he did a spot of plumbing in his spare time and that Courtney had needed hers attending to?

I don't think there's much point, she typed, and was about to press send when he sent another: *It's about Laura.*

Sarah hesitated, and then, pushing her hurt to one side, braced herself and called him.

'Hi, how are you?' he said, the undeniably masculine timbre of his voice causing her stomach to flutter, despite her determination to remain unaffected by him or any excuses he might have to offer.

'Fine,' she said shortly.

'I'm guessing you don't want to hear my explanation?' he said, sounding despondent. He could never feel as despondent as she'd felt realising he wasn't the man she'd thought he was.

'Was there something you wanted to tell me, Joe?' She avoided answering his question, thus, she hoped, stopping her heart from breaking more than it already was. 'It's just that I have a lot on at the moment.'

'I know. I should have been more supportive,' he said, his tone full of contrition. 'I'm thinking you won't want to hear my apologies either, but I'd at least like to say I'm sorry for not backing you up.'

Sarah's throat tightened. 'You were texting about Laura,' she said, the wobble in her voice belying her attempt at indifference.

'Right.' Joe's tone was flat. 'Yes, I was. I checked out the FB page. Obviously I have no grounds to approach them to release information, but the guy in the wedding photograph, his name's Christopher Jameson. I ran a standard criminal records check. He has a caution. I can't say what for – nothing dodgy,' he added hastily, no doubt guessing she might worry about it. 'Anyway, I have his address. Also a phone number.'

Finally he was supporting her, and Sarah had no idea how to feel. It couldn't unbreak her heart, could it? 'That's helpful,' she said awkwardly. 'Thank you.'

'I could call around and see him if you like?' he offered. 'Not in an official capacity, but I might be able to persuade him to answer a few questions unofficially.'

She was tempted, but she actually thought that might still seem too official. 'No. Thanks, but I think I'd rather call him myself. Play it low-key, you know? Say I'm a friend or something and try to do a little fishing.'

'Probably a good idea,' he said.

'I'd better go. I have some things to do.' Sarah made her excuses, not wanting to prolong the call. She didn't think she could deal with anything emotive right now.

'Okay.' Joe blew out a breath, and then, 'About Steve,' he said quickly. 'You mentioned you were going to see him. I was a bit concerned after hearing the argument you two had. I'd like to offer to come with you, if—'

'It's fine.' Sarah stopped him. Did he realise how painful this strained conversation was? 'I've already spoken to him. I think he's accepted that I'm not waging some vendetta against Laura out of jealousy.'

She hadn't been going to say that, but then why shouldn't she? Joe clearly had thought it. Would that have been his excuse for going to see his ex-wife, she wondered, where the door was clearly still open?

'Right. Good.' He sounded awkward now.

As he should, she thought, with some small satisfaction. It wouldn't make much difference now, but at least he'd known he was wrong. 'Laura's mother was there, at the house,' she said, debating whether to tell him more. She should, she decided. He'd offered to help, and she shouldn't let wounded pride stop her asking for it if she needed to. 'You remember I told you they didn't get on?'

'I do. And?' Joe asked. There was no weary tone to his voice this time. He was taking her seriously. Well, what she had to say anyway, if not their relationship.

'There's a reason they don't,' she went on. 'Her mother had another child, a little boy. He went missing, years ago. It obviously put a massive strain on their relationship.'

'Christ.' Joe sounded winded. 'How? When? I didn't find anything online.'

He had checked then? He clearly *was* taking her seriously. Pity he hadn't before. But would it really have made any difference? Seeing his ex-wife for some plausible reason she could have accepted. But being with her while she was getting ready to take a bath? Never even mentioning he had been in contact with her, which he must have been, since they were clearly so intimate? There were no plausible excuses for that. 'Try checking under the name Caldwell,' she said, working to dismiss the image of the two of them in the bathroom together, but not quite managing to. 'Laura changed her name, possibly to escape her past. It could explain a few things.'

'I'll look into it,' he said. 'See if there's anything that's not general knowledge on file.'

'Okay. Thanks, Joe.' She fell quiet. She didn't know what else to say. What they had to say to each other. More, what he might say that wouldn't hurt. 'I, um, should go. I—'

'Have things to do, I know,' Joe finished quietly. 'I'm sorry, Sarah.'

For what? She swallowed hard. That he was breaking her heart? That they were over? That he was sleeping with his ex?

'She really was upset,' he went on. 'I wouldn't have been with her for any other reason than that, I promise you.'

I don't want to hear it. Sarah squeezed her eyes closed. 'Why?' she asked, and cursed herself. His explanation would be feeble. The woman hadn't been asking him to pop the kettle on. How pathetic was she for desperately willing it not to be?

He hesitated. 'She was pregnant,' he said, shocking her. 'When I left, she was pregnant. She lost the baby – at six months, she says. It was mine, apparently.'

Oh God, no. Sarah's heart constricted. She'd lost a baby at just three months, but she knew how unbearably painful such a loss was, the deep, desolate loneliness, the grief exacerbated by the complete silence you were met with when you returned home empty-handed. Her own devastation had been compounded because she and Steve were already so far apart. Ollie had filled the silence with his childish chatter, but still she'd felt fractured, as if part of her were missing. But … wasn't his wife with someone else? Surely he would have been there for her?

'She's split up with the guy she was seeing.' Joe answered the question she hadn't asked. 'She hasn't been looking after herself. She's been ill, grieving; depressed, I suspect. She had a post-surgical infection after removal of a retained placenta. It seems it's resistant to the antibiotics she's been taking. Her doctor has given her stronger tablets. She should be okay, although the antibiotics themselves might have side effects. I … just needed you to know.'

Because he was grieving too? She knew him well enough to know that he would be.

'There's no going back for us. Even if the child had …' He stopped, and Sarah heard his sharp intake of breath. 'I couldn't just walk away, Sarah. I probably should have done, but …'

She felt her heart bleed for him. For his ex-wife too, though given the way the woman had treated him, she couldn't help wondering why she'd sought Joe out to tell him all this now.

CHAPTER TWENTY-EIGHT

Sarah's heart banged against her chest as she waited for the call to be answered. It was a landline. He might not even be there. She was about to give up when someone picked up.

'Christopher Jameson,' the man said.

Sarah took a deep breath. 'Hi.' She forced a breezy tone. 'You don't know me, but I'm a friend of Laura Collins, and I was wondering—'

'She doesn't live here,' he cut across her tersely. 'Please don't call again. I have no wish to discuss her or anything about her.'

He'd hung up. Stunned, Sarah stared at her phone. Well, that was short and sweet, and spoke volumes. Clearly their separation hadn't been an amicable one. Doubting she would get a warm reception if she called around to his house, she wondered what she should do. She toyed with the idea of asking Joe to make a few unofficial enquiries after all, and then jumped as her phone rang. It was Becky, she realised. Sarah had rung her to fill her in. She'd promised she would call her back about meeting up for lunch today and had forgotten all about it. 'Hi, Becks,' she answered guiltily. 'Sorry I forgot to call. I have so much going on, it completely slipped my mind.'

'No problem,' Becky assured her. 'I have a little girl sick with a tummy bug anyway. I'm just waiting for her mum to collect her. Meanwhile, I have some information regarding the mysterious Laura's past relationship I thought you might want.'

Sarah abandoned her attempts to make coffee one-handed. 'As in?' she asked hopefully.

'The boy in the online photograph you told me about, Liam Jameson. I've contacted a few colleagues and it turns out he goes to West Acre Primary School. I'm not sure how useful it will be, but just to let you know he's healthy and happy according to his teacher.'

Sarah breathed a sigh of relief. 'Extremely useful. Thanks, Becks.'

Waiting in the playground of the West Acre primary at school-out time, Sarah's stomach tied itself in knots. She shouldn't be doing this. It was all sorts of wrong. Becky wouldn't have shared the information if she'd imagined she might turn up here; she hoped to God she didn't get her friend in trouble. Joe would definitely think she was being obsessive.

Watching the children spill from the entrance, she identified Liam immediately. An older version of Ollie with his striking blonde hair, the boy charged across the playground, spinning around and almost running backwards at one point as he waved goodbye to one of his little friends.

Her heart in her mouth, she waited until he approached where she stood just inside the school gates. She hadn't seen any sign of his father. He was obviously running late. It was possible someone else was here to pick him up, but she thought not as she watched the boy slow to a stop and glance searchingly around. Taking a breath, she agonised for a moment, then, 'Liam?' She smiled warmly and walked across to him.

Liam nodded, but his expression was wary.

'I'm Sarah,' she said. 'Ollie's mummy.'

He frowned, seeming to assess her as she stopped in front of him. 'Is he in my class?' he asked after a second.

'Not yet. He's a bit younger than you, but he'll be coming to your school soon.'

Giving her another small nod, Liam appeared to accept this. 'Will he bring his football?'

'Probably.' She laughed. 'Very likely, in fact.'

'We can only bring soft footballs,' he informed her knowledgeably.

'Ah, I'll make sure to tell him,' she said with an appreciative smile. Then, 'Are you waiting for your mummy?' she asked tentatively, praying she didn't upset him.

Liam shook his head this time. 'No,' he said, his face clouding over. 'She doesn't live with me and Daddy any more.'

'Oh dear.' Sarah ached for him. 'You still see her sometimes, though?' she ventured.

His expression unsure, the boy answered with a shrug, which Sarah took to be a no. 'Do you miss—'

She stopped as someone shouted from the gates. 'Oi!' Her stomach flipped over as she guessed who it was.

'What the *hell* do you think you're doing?' Liam's father stormed across to her.

'I spoke to you on the phone,' she said quickly. 'I know Laura.'

'Commiserations,' he retorted, walking around to Liam's side to take hold of his hand.

'She's living with my ex,' Sarah persisted, trailing after him as he ushered the child towards the gates. 'Why doesn't she see him any more?' she asked, assuming he would know what she meant.

The man didn't answer, marching on so swiftly Liam struggled to keep up with him.

Sarah hovered behind him as he urged the child into the car and strapped him into his booster seat. 'It can't be good for him, surely?' she said, once he'd closed the door.

Halfway to the driver's side, he stopped and turned to face her, his eyes filled with palpable fury. 'I will *never* let that woman near my child *ever* again,' he seethed.

'But *why*? Mr Jameson, I need to *know*. I have a son of my own,' Sarah beseeched him as he wrenched the driver's door open.

He faltered, appeared to deliberate, then, 'Keep her away from him,' he said, his voice full of dire warning. 'She's dangerous.'

Sarah's blood froze. 'Dangerous how?'

He held her gaze for a second. 'Ask her about her brother,' he said cryptically.

But she knew about her brother. Unless … Was there something she *didn't* know? Something that wasn't general knowledge, as Joe had said?

'You might also want to ask her about her previous job,' he added, climbing in. 'And why she left it. Whatever you do, just keep her away from your child.'

CHAPTER TWENTY-NINE

'Night, night, munchkin.' Trying to quash the nerves and nausea churning inside her, Sarah smiled as she tucked Ollie in. Clutching his whale, he beamed her a smile in return. Her beautiful boy, innocent and oblivious to all the wicked things in the world. He seemed to have forgotten about Bunny. Sarah hadn't. His severed ear now seemed to be serving as another dire warning. Something was very wrong. She'd known it. Somehow, she'd known it before she'd even met Laura. But could she really be *dangerous*? Might her ex-husband be trying to get back at her for whatever reason their marriage fell apart? No. Her gut instinct told her it wasn't that; that he truly believed she was a danger. He'd been furious – she'd felt it emanating from him – but beyond that, she'd sensed he was frightened, as frightened as she was.

'Mummy, am I going to see Daddy and Laura on my birthday?' Ollie asked as he wriggled down.

Sarah's stomach turned over. She'd been trying to avoid the subject of the birthday garden party Steve and Laura were arranging for him. She'd hoped it might be rained off, but the forecast promised good weather, and Steve had already bought the balloons and bunting. There was no way she could let Ollie go.

'It depends,' she said lightly. Her heart dropped like a stone, though, as Ollie's little face fell. 'We might be going somewhere else,' she added quickly. 'Somewhere exciting.'

Ollie brightened. 'With Joe?'

'Maybe,' she said, her throat catching. 'We'll have to wait and see, won't we?'

'Are we going to the seaside?' His eyes widened with excitement.

'It wouldn't be a surprise if I told you, would it?' Sarah tickled his tummy playfully. She would have to call Joe. Swallow her pride and ask him if he would go out for the day with them. If he wasn't on duty or otherwise engaged, she knew he would agree. He would do that for Ollie. 'Sleep now, little man,' she said, wearing her serious face, 'or you'll be tired in the morning.' She smoothed his fringe back and pressed a soft kiss to his forehead. 'Sleep tight, sweetheart,' she whispered, reaching to turn on his night light.

'Night, Mummy.' He snuggled down. 'Mummy?' He stopped her at the door. 'Can I have a lamp like the one at Laura's?'

For an instant, she couldn't breathe. 'Possibly,' she managed. 'I'll ask her where she got it from.'

Going out, she eased his door and wondered what on earth she was going to do. She felt like crying. Like sitting on the landing and sobbing. She felt so alone, so completely on her own. How could she keep her baby safe from a threat she could feel but not see?

Finding her phone in the hall, she went to the kitchen and closed the door. *Please pick up, Steve*, she willed as she called him. *Please be working late*. If he was in the house in earshot of Laura, he would have to ring her back. And she so needed to talk to him.

'Steve, can we talk?' she said as soon as he answered. 'In private, I mean?'

'I'm good,' he replied, that wary edge to his voice that seemed to be there constantly lately. 'Laura's taking a bath. What was it you wanted to talk about? As if I didn't know.' Now he sounded definitely guarded.

'The boy on her Facebook profile,' Sarah responded, her own tone guarded. She didn't want to argue with him. She never had. She needed him on her side, on Ollie's side, not dead set against her. 'I spoke to him.'

Steve didn't say anything for a second. Then, 'Where?' he asked, as if girding himself up for the very argument she didn't want.

'At his school. Becky asked around and—'

'You went to his school?' he asked, astonished. 'What? Just turned up there?'

'Yes,' she confessed. 'I didn't have any choice. His father wouldn't talk to me on the phone.'

'Christ, Sarah. You can't just approach kids at school. You above all people should know that.'

'I do,' she assured him, growing frustrated. 'Look, Steve, that's not the point. I spoke to his father too. He told me she was dangerous.'

'Dangerous?' Steve laughed, astounded. 'Laura?'

'Yes, Laura.' Sarah suppressed a sigh. 'He meant it. There was something—'

'Dangerous how, exactly?' he interrupted flatly.

His defences were going up. She couldn't quite believe it. Surely knowing what he already did, he couldn't condemn her for wanting to know more? 'I … don't know. He wouldn't tell me,' she admitted. 'But he was worried. Very. I could tell. He—'

'And did he tell you why they'd split up?' he enquired, clearly irritated.

Sarah's heart sank. He *was* siding against her. Why? She wasn't the enemy, out to get Laura. She was his son's mother, for God's sake. 'No,' she replied tightly. 'He was reluctant to say very much. Liam was there, so obviously he would be.'

'I see,' Steve said, and paused. 'So it didn't occur to you that this man might feel that he's the injured party? That he might be bearing some kind of grudge?'

'Of course it did,' she snapped. 'But you weren't there. You didn't see the look in his eyes. *I'm* worried, Steve. I'm scared for Ollie. You must be able to see why I would be.'

Again he went quiet. 'I'm scared, Sarah,' he said after a second, his voice terse.

Thank God. 'You need to talk to her,' she started. 'I can't possibly allow Ollie—'

'For *you*!' he growled.

'What?'

'You'll stop at nothing, will you, trying to discredit her?'

'Steve?' Sarah's heart slid icily into her stomach. 'That's not fair. I'm not—'

'It's *you* who's not being fair. You've just accused her of being *dangerous*, for fuck's sake,' he seethed furiously. '*That's* dangerous, Sarah, slurring someone's character with no basis other than some pathetic comment from some bloke who's clearly bitter for whatever reason.'

'For God's sake, I'm not *slurring* her character,' she tried, a mixture of frustration and desperation climbing inside her. 'I'm just trying to make you see.'

'I do see,' he said, after another loaded pause. 'It's you who has the problem, not Laura. You're turning up and accosting kids in the school *playground*? Trawling her online profiles? It's bloody relentless, bordering on insane. If you want the truth, I'm actually beginning to think you need *help*.'

'Steve!' Sarah stared stunned at her phone, her stomach turning inside out as she realised he'd hung up.

CHAPTER THIRTY

Steve

Steve's heart missed a beat when Laura walked into the kitchen as he ended the call. 'I thought you were in the bath,' he said, offering her a cautious smile.

'I hadn't got in yet.' She looked at him, her eyes flecked with uncertainty, which immediately made him feel bad. He should be talking *to* her, not about her. 'I came down for some wine. Was that Sarah?' She nodded to the phone still in his hand.

His heart dropped. 'You heard?' he asked needlessly. It was obvious she had, but possibly not all of it. The look in her eyes now was one of mistrust, making him feel even worse. Did she really feel that way about him? That *he* was someone she couldn't trust? Why hadn't she felt able to confide in him?

Closing her eyes, she answered with a small nod. 'She's spoken to my ex-husband,' she said, her voice flat, defeated almost.

A visible shudder running through her, she wrapped her arms around herself, and Steve's chest constricted. She looked pale, so small and fragile, like a frightened child. What the hell had gone on in her life that was so terrible it had reduced her to this? Anger on her behalf simmering inside him, he instinctively took a step towards her, but she moved back.

'I need to talk to you; to explain,' she said, lifting her chin as if in defiance. Her eyes, though, were filled with such unbearable anguish it almost tore his heart from inside him. 'I should have told you before,' she went on, scanning his face as she did, as if trying to read his reaction, 'but I didn't know how. I was too ashamed. I …'

He heard her voice catch, and reached out to her, only for her to visibly flinch.

Shit. He sucked in a breath, his anger turning to quiet fury. Something had gone on between her and this bloke Sarah had taken it on herself to seek out. Something Laura was too embarrassed to tell him about. He had a sick feeling in his gut that he knew what it was.

'Come and sit down,' he said, his own voice tight with emotion as he reached gently for her again. She didn't move away this time, though neither did she unclasp her arms from around herself as he guided her towards the table. Her body language was defensive. He could feel her trembling. What had this bastard, who was obviously spreading complete bullshit about her, done to hurt her?

After helping her into a chair, he fetched the wine from the fridge, filled a large glass and placed it on the table. 'Medicinal,' he said, giving her a reassuring smile as he pushed it towards her.

Laura smiled tremulously back, then pressed her hand to her mouth to suppress a sob, which exacerbated his fury.

'I'm listening, Laura.' He went to her, tentatively placing an arm around her shoulders. She didn't flinch this time. He felt relief flood through him. 'I'm here for you,' he assured her softly, 'if you want me to be.'

She answered with a more fervent nod and breathed deeply, trying to hold the tears in, he guessed, his heart plummeting another inch. Carefully he eased away from her, giving her the space he sensed she might need, and seated himself opposite her.

She reached for her wine, her hand shaking as she lifted the glass to her lips, her teeth clinking against it as she tried to sip. Steve watched, feeling a combination of sympathy and impotence as she placed the glass back on the table, wiping away a drip that had spilled from it with her finger and then staring intently at it. Not seeing it, he guessed, her mind on whatever horrors she was struggling to communicate.

He didn't speak, waiting patiently instead until she was ready.

'He was abusive,' she said eventually, her gaze dropping back to her glass, her voice barely a whisper. 'I'm thinking you've probably gathered that.'

Steve nodded, as her gaze flicked back to his, and swallowed. Still he didn't speak. She needed time to gather herself. An aggressive reaction from him wouldn't help her do that.

'He wasn't at first. He was kind and attentive, and I … I was in love with him.' She shrugged sadly and dropped her gaze again.

Falling quiet, she ran a finger around the rim of her glass, and then looked back at him. 'I can't believe I actually agreed to marry him. That I was so naïve when the signs were already there. He wanted to make all the decisions around the wedding – when, where, how many guests we had. I didn't get much of a say in anything.' She faltered, her eyes full of self-recrimination, which shook him. 'He really ramped up the abuse once the "honeymoon" was over,' she went on, with a scornful laugh. 'Psychological abuse turned to physical abuse. I suppose it was inevitable really.'

Inevitable? Jesus. Steve massaged his forehead, held fast to his temper.

'He put a lock on the bedroom door,' she continued after an interminably long pause. 'On the outside.'

He locked her in? Shocked to the core, he snapped his horrified gaze back to her.

'Told people things about me that weren't true,' she went on, her eyes fixed firmly down. 'Lies to explain my bruises. He didn't want people to like me, didn't want me to go out and see people, or for people to see me – for obvious reasons.' She smiled bitterly. 'He was very logical, very cold and clinical. All the while telling me that it was my fault he was the way he was. That I deliberately provoked him. My going out provoked him. Flaunting myself at other men provoked him. Being slovenly provoked him – he liked everything in the house to be pristine and dust-free. He would run his fingers along the skirting boards and picture frames. Woe betide if I hadn't cleaned properly.'

She wavered, reaching shakily for her glass, as Steve forced back the words that badly wanted to spill from his mouth. The man was vermin, a complete and utter cowardly bastard.

'Of course he would tell me every morning before the punishment started how much he cared about me. That he loved me. Couldn't bear to lose me.' She laughed cynically again, a laugh that turned to a sob that caught in her throat.

Steve swallowed back a sharp knot in his own. Enough, he thought. She'd told him enough. His heart banging so violently he thought his chest might explode, he pushed his chair back. If he ever had anything to do with the man, he would be responsible for murder.

'It wasn't your fault,' he said, his tone firm as he crouched down beside her, gently taking hold of her hand. 'You didn't provoke him. The sick bastard who did this is to blame, not you.'

Laura nodded again, half-heartedly. 'The tragedy is that his little boy witnessed it all,' she went on, swiping away a tear. 'I almost took him when I ran. I was so tempted.' She locked her eyes on his, a turmoil of emotion therein, a flash of determination, but mostly humiliation and uncertainty. 'I couldn't, though, could I? I had no money, nowhere to go. He would have stopped at nothing to find me if I'd taken Liam too. Because he was his natural father – and a world-class convincing liar – I knew the police would believe him. I doubt I would have got far.'

'I am so sorry, Laura.' It was all he could offer. 'You did nothing wrong, trust me. There is *nothing* wrong with you. Please don't ever imagine there is. I wish you'd felt able to tell me.'

She swallowed. 'I thought you would think I was weak.'

'Weak?' He studied her incredulously. 'You found the courage to leave him. That's possibly the bravest thing a person in your situation could do, knowing they had nowhere to go. You're not weak, Laura. You're a caring person. You probably gave him the benefit of the doubt in the first place because you are. Being caring is not weak. You're strong.' He squeezed her hand. 'A survivor.'

She squeezed his hand back. 'Will you tell Sarah? She's obviously concerned for Ollie. You can't blame her. I'd rather not go over it all again, though, you know …'

Steve did know: because she was embarrassed, because she thought she'd been weak, for fuck's sake. Tugging in a breath, he composed himself. Then, 'I'll tell her,' he assured her. Exactly what he would tell Sarah he didn't elucidate, which would be to get her facts straight before making defamatory accusations, and to bloody well back off.

CHAPTER THIRTY-ONE

Sarah

Watching TV but seeing nothing, Sarah leapt on her phone when it rang. *Steve.* Apprehension twisting inside her, she accepted the call.

'He was abusive,' he said without ceremony.

She buried a sigh. Laura had obviously spun him the same line as she had her. 'I know,' she answered, trying to hide her exasperation. 'She told me she was in a controlling relationship, but she never mentioned she was married. She never once mentioned—'

'He locked her in their fucking *bedroom*,' Steve growled over her. 'Punished her if there was a speck of dust in the house, if she so much as glanced in the direction of another man. Is that controlling enough, do you think, to justify her getting the hell out?'

Sarah was too shell-shocked to speak for a second. 'What about the boy?' she asked, a whirl of confused emotion running through her: bewilderment, shame, anger … for Laura.

'She wanted to take him. She couldn't though, realistically, could she? He wasn't hers. He told you she was dangerous. *He's* the dangerous fucker,' Steve seethed, his language indicating how furious he was. 'Can you imagine what he might have done if she *had* taken Liam and he'd caught up with her? What he would have told the police?'

'I'm sorry,' Sarah said weakly, feeling terrible, most definitely like the biggest bitch Laura had had the misfortune to meet.

'Why didn't she say …' She stopped herself. She knew why Laura wouldn't have admitted any of this. Because she would have been too embarrassed, ashamed probably that she'd allowed it to happen. If it were all true. A nagging little voice in her head reminded her they couldn't know it was. That they had nothing but Laura's word. But then wasn't she herself doing now what many people did, which was precisely the reason women on the receiving end of such abuse *didn't* say – because they wouldn't be believed? Because the recriminations from their abuser when they spoke out might be so much worse. Christopher Jameson hadn't struck her as a kind man. He hadn't been aggressive towards her, but she had felt his aggression under the surface. She'd thought his anger had been justified, though she hadn't known why.

'She was too ashamed to tell me. She blamed herself.' Steve voiced her thoughts, compounding her guilt, which weighed like a stone in her chest. 'This constant looking for reasons to not let her have anything to do with Ollie, it's way over the top, Sarah. It has to stop. If you don't want Ollie to come to this birthday thing she's worked bloody hard to organise, then you tell him why. Okay?'

'I'm sorry,' she repeated. 'I didn't mean …' Realising that Steve had ended the call, again, she trailed off.

'Shit.' Blinking back her tears, she glanced at the ceiling. She'd leapt to conclusions. She'd been ready to believe whatever Christopher Jameson had told her without question – because she'd wanted to, because she hadn't wanted to like Laura. She'd misjudged her. She guessed she would have been working hard organising the garden party she'd decided to throw for Ollie. She'd probably cooked up all sorts of culinary delights, might even have baked him a cake. Sarah had even doubted her motives for that. Suddenly she didn't feel very good about herself at all. Was she really the horrible, vindictive person Steve seemed to think she was? Ollie would have to go to the party. Of course he would. If he didn't go now, after all that Laura had told Steve – and no doubt she was aware that Steve would pass it on to her – she would be destroyed. Sarah still didn't feel easy about any of it, but she didn't want to damage Laura's confidence any more than it obviously already had been.

Had she badly misjudged Joe, too? she wondered now. She wasn't sure it was possible to feel any more guilty, but she did. *Was* he back with his ex-wife? He seemed to think he needed to be there for her. Perhaps he did. Perhaps she should try being the generous person she'd imagined she was and try to support him while he was dealing with whatever he had to. Should she ring him? She was desperate to talk to him; just hearing his voice, she might not feel as lonely as she felt now. He might not be willing to talk to her, though, unless to tell her she'd been spiteful and judgemental – not that he would do that. She could always use the excuse that she was calling to ask him if he would like to come to Ollie's garden party. She would, she decided, tomorrow. Calling him while she was feeling so emotional might only compromise him. He could only say no, after all. Her heart twisted painfully at the thought that he might.

CHAPTER THIRTY-TWO

Joe

'All good?' Joe asked worriedly as Courtney reappeared from the inner depths of the ultrasound department. He'd debated whether to go in with her – by anyone's standards she'd treated him appallingly, but seeing how pale and worried she was, knowing how ill she'd been, and suffering on her own, he'd decided to leave the past where it belonged and be a friend to her. It wasn't easy – she'd damaged his trust in women; he hadn't quite realised that until he'd acknowledged his own jealousy, imagining that Sarah still had feelings for Steve – but he felt responsible, somehow, since the baby Courtney had lost had been his.

'I'm not sure,' she answered with a troubled frown.

He was immediately perturbed, particularly as he noticed her complexion was a shade paler.

'Here, sit down.' Instinctively he threaded an arm around her, nodding her towards a seat in the waiting area.

'Thanks,' she said weakly, 'but do you mind if we go outside? I think I could do with some air.'

'Of course. No problem.' A sense of trepidation growing inside him, Joe took hold of her arm. She definitely didn't look well. He hoped to God she hadn't had bad news. 'I'm on lates tonight. We could go for some lunch if you like?'

She smiled up at him as he pushed the door to the corridor open. 'I'd like that.'

After helping her into the car, Joe climbed in himself, casting a concerned glance sideways at her as he did. She was quiet, appeared lost in her thoughts. Definitely troubled.

'So,' he said, taking a breath, 'do you want to tell me what happened in there?'

She glanced distractedly at him.

'You're obviously worried about something.'

She answered with a small nod. 'They think I have something called polycystic ovary syndrome,' she said quietly.

Joe felt his heart skip a beat. 'Which is?'

'A condition where the ovaries are larger than normal. Something to do with hormonal problems, the doctor said. It's, um ...' She stopped and fiddled with a ring on her finger. Her wedding ring? His heart missed another beat. 'It's known to be one of the leading causes of infertility apparently,' she went on with a shrug, which belied the wobble he heard in her voice.

'Infertility?' he repeated, confused. 'But ...'

'There's also evidence to suggest it can lead to complications during pregnancy, if the ovaries manage to produce enough eggs for one to get lucky and get fertilised in the first place.' She smiled – heart-wrenchingly sadly.

Joe tried to digest the information. 'Jesus, Courtney. I'm sorry,' he said, feeling gutted for her.

'It's okay.' She drew in a breath and held it. 'The pregnancy might have been managed if I'd known, but... it obviously wasn't meant to be,' she went on after a second, her voice quavering.

He watched helplessly as she drew in another shuddery breath and pressed her hands over her face, trying to hold back the tears, he guessed. He'd hated her a short while ago. Now he felt nothing but sympathy and devastation for her. She hadn't wanted children, then found she was pregnant and realised she did, and now, by some cruel twist, she'd ended up losing the baby. She'd grieved the loss of him, clearly, and now she was grieving all over again.

He hesitated. What was he going to do, sit here and watch her cry? He couldn't do that. Reaching out, he placed an arm around her shoulders and eased her to him.

'You're a good man, Joe,' she said shakily as her sobs slowed. 'I was selfish. I deserve all this after the awful things I did.'

'No you don't,' he assured her, tugging in a tight breath of his own. He'd wished her all sorts – that the hotshot would be every bit the prat he obviously was and dump her – but he would never wish this on her.

'You're obviously very potent.' She emitted a wry laugh as she straightened up and attempted to compose herself.

Joe declined to answer. He preferred not to think about the mechanics, what might have been, had he known.

'I don't suppose you, um …' she started after a second, and then faltered.

'What?' He glanced at her warily.

'Want to try again?' She garbled it out. 'For a child, I mean, you and me.'

Christ. Surely she wasn't serious? There was no way. Joe groaned inside. What the hell was he supposed to say to that?

'You wouldn't have to stay with me if you didn't want to,' she added, as he agonised about how to answer without upsetting her further. 'I've changed, obviously. I'm sure I could make you happy; try harder.' She glanced at him hopefully.

Joe looked away.

'You're right, it's a ludicrous idea.' She laughed, but he could hear the hurt in her voice. 'I thought I'd ask anyway, though, just in case … you know …'

'Courtney …' Joe struggled for something diplomatic to say. Telling her he simply didn't love her, that he couldn't envisage being with her any more than he could bringing a child into the world without being a hands-on father, would be too hurtful after all she'd just been through. 'I've changed too,' he opted for. 'I'm …'

'Seeing someone,' she finished, a fatalistic edge to her tone.

He nodded. She knew he was.

'The woman at the pub,' she said reflectively. 'Do you love her?'

'Yes, I think I do,' he replied honestly. He wished he'd told Sarah he did, that he hadn't been such an unsympathetic idiot, jealous himself because he couldn't seem to have a straightforward relationship without Steve stuck in the middle of it.

'I should have a word with her, tell her you're worth holding on to,' Courtney said, with a hint of irony. 'We should go. We're taking up a car parking space. If you're still on for lunch, that is? Don't worry, I won't try to take advantage and have my wicked way with you,' she added jokingly as Joe wavered.

Wiping at her cheeks, she reached for her bag from the footwell. 'Damn, no tissues,' she cursed, delving into it.

Joe opened the glove box, extracting the wipes he kept in there and handing them to her.

'Baby wipes?' She glanced curiously from the packet to him.

'For Sarah's son. She keeps them there for emergencies,' he explained awkwardly.

'Ah.' Courtney nodded. 'The little boy you were playing football with. Do you love her enough to take him on, Joe? For the rest of his life, I mean. I don't suppose it will be easy.'

'I'm not imagining it will be, but yes, yes, I do.' He wasn't his biological father, but he'd grown to love Ollie too, he realised, if missing him every time he saw a family out with their kids was any indication. He'd been on a call-out yesterday, a domestic. There was a boy around Ollie's age on the premises. Joe's heart had ached for the kid, who'd been cowering in the kitchen, scared witless. It ached now at the thought of not seeing Ollie again.

'Good,' Courtney responded shortly. 'We should go,' she repeated.

Burying a sigh, Joe started the engine. Lunch wasn't going to be easy either, he suspected, given the conversation they'd just had.

He'd driven a short way when his phone rang. His heart sank as Sarah's name flashed up on his hands-free. He'd been waiting for her to call him back. He'd looked into Jacob Caldwell's case and left her a message. He hadn't come up with anything much, apart from the fact that the family were initially suspected of having something to do with his disappearance. That was fairly standard in such cases. The investigation had switched from missing person to possible death by accident when a small footprint had been found. The child had wandered out of the house, they'd concluded. Joe's gut had turned over when he'd imagined him out on his own in the pitch black of the night. He must have been petrified. He'd wanted to talk it through with Sarah. Wanted very much for her to know that he was on her side; to tell her again how sorry he was. And now she was phoning while he was sitting right next to his ex-wife. Talk about bad timing.

'I'll call her back,' he said, guessing that Courtney would have gathered who it was.

'No, don't mind me. She'll only wonder if you don't answer. At least tell her you'll get back to her,' she urged him.

Joe hesitated for a second; then, not wanting Sarah to wonder why he wasn't answering when he wasn't on duty, accepted the call. 'Hi, Sarah,' he said. 'How's things?'

'Reasonable,' she replied vaguely. 'I've just teamed a dog up with what looks like a perfect potential owner, so that's brightened my day.'

'Excellent. Here's hoping it works out.' Joe was pleased for her. Her job meant a lot to her. She was a kind person, no side to her other than the one he'd imagined.

'I spoke to Steve about Laura last night,' she went on. 'Can you talk at the moment?'

'Er, now's not a good time,' he responded.

'Oh. Are you on days now?' she asked.

'No.' Joe took a breath. He was reluctant to tell her why he couldn't talk, but he couldn't lie either. 'I've just collected Courtney from the hospital,' he said, hoping she didn't pick up on the guilt he could hear in his voice.

Plainly she did. 'Oh,' she replied after a pause, a short, flat 'oh' this time. 'I see. Is she all right?'

Unsure what to say, he glanced at Courtney, who shook her head, indicating that she didn't want him disclosing details. 'She's doing okay. It's a bit difficult to talk, though. I'm driving. Can I call you back later?'

'Yes, no problem,' Sarah assured him. 'I might be busy, but you can try,' she added – pointedly? Joe wondered. 'I'm glad your wife is all right. Give her my best. Bye, Joe.'

His heart sank another inch. Did that goodbye sound final?

'There, that was better than ignoring her, wasn't it?' Courtney offered.

Yeah. He ran a hand over his neck. Somehow, he didn't think so.

'She sounds nice. Caring,' Courtney observed.

Glancing at her again, Joe noted that she was smiling. There'd been something in her tone, though. Wistfulness? He felt bad for her, but surely she must see that there could be no going back. She'd almost destroyed him. She'd had no qualms at the time. She seemed vulnerable now – clearly she would be – but he couldn't imagine she'd changed fundamentally.

CHAPTER THIRTY-THREE

Laura

Laura was halfway downstairs with armfuls of the decorating paraphernalia she still had to clear away after decorating Ollie's room as a birthday surprise when she heard her mother's unmistakable tones coming from the lounge. *Oh no.* Squeezing her eyes closed, she gripped the handrail hard. It was the day of his party and she'd been up since the crack of dawn. Despite taking a day off work yesterday, she still had so much to do – she was desperate for everything to be perfect – and Steve had let in the last person on earth she wanted to see without asking her. He'd been lovely when she'd been upset, so caring. What was his thinking here, though? He knew how impossible Sherry was, how pushy; that Laura didn't get on with her and never would, no matter how hard he tried to facilitate a mother-and-daughter reunion. In Laura's eyes, her mother had died the day Jacob had disappeared.

Gritting her teeth, she carried on down and went through to the kitchen to dump her stuff in the utility room. 'Shit!' Realising she'd spilled wallpaper paste on the draining board, she cursed out loud and whirled around to head for the lounge. She really wished Steve would stop interfering. There was too much at stake. He would put Ollie at risk, couldn't he *see* that? But of course he couldn't see. How could he … unless she told him?

Every sinew in her body tensing, she braced herself to push the lounge door open, and then froze as she heard Steve's puzzled voice. 'But surely she would benefit from some kind of therapy?' he was asking, as if Sherry had ever considered anything that wasn't beneficial to herself.

It's not his fault. Laura cautioned herself to stay calm and not lose it with him. He was concerned about her, that was all. She'd had another sleepwalking episode the night before last. He was bound to be worried, but broaching this subject was dangerous. Her mother couldn't have her talking, recalling. Her hope was that she never would.

'But she's had therapy,' Sherry replied, an impatient edge to her voice. 'I'm her *mother*, Steven. Don't you think I would have sought all the help for her that I could?'

Steve sighed heavily. 'Yes, of course. It's just … that was a while ago, wasn't it? I can't help thinking that something like, I don't know, hypnotherapy maybe, might help her. At least to understand why she blames you.'

'Because she *needed* someone to blame,' her mother retorted, her voice loaded with obvious agitation. 'She still does. This is why she's so awful to me – and I understand that. I accept it and I'll always be there for her, no matter how angry she is with me.' She paused, and Laura imagined her eyes filling up. *False tears. It was all false.* If Steve looked hard enough, he would see right through her.

'I'm sorry,' Sherry went on, her tone more subdued, 'but I honestly don't think hypnotherapy will help her. God knows, I'd be the first to suggest it if I thought it would, but as amnesia is a known symptom of sleepwalking, I simply don't see how it could.'

'But it might,' Steve tried. 'Don't you think it might help her to—'

'What? Regress?' Sherry cut stridently across him. 'If you'd seen her after the terrible tragedy that befell *all* of us, Steven, revisiting it would be the last thing you would want for her. And what about if her memories are distorted? Have you thought about the damage that might do? There is such a thing as false memory syndrome, you know, which – as you seem to have researched her condition – I'm sure you will be aware of. No. I won't have it. It could be positively dangerous. Laura is a delicate, confused individual. Her mind's too fragile.'

Enough. Laura shoved the door open. Did either of them consider that she even *had* a mind? What was she, invisible? She had no doubt her mother wished she was. That the daughter she claimed to care for would just disappear too.

'Ah, Laura darling.' Sherry shot her a brittle smile. 'We were just talking about you. I was saying to Steven what a splendid job you've done with the bunting.' She glanced towards the patio doors. 'It all looks very jolly out there.'

Bullshit. She was full of it. 'Were you?' Laura looked accusingly from her mother to Steve, who glanced awkwardly away. 'And now you've finished talking about me, are you *sss*taying …' She stopped, a combination of disbelief and fury mounting inside her as her lips jammed.

Sherry blinked sympathetically at her, which only incensed her further. Every time she was around her mother, her stress levels shot through the roof and her stutter resurfaced. The best therapy for her, she would quite like to tell Steve, would be for her fucking *mother* to disappear.

'I thought I would stay now I'm here.' Sherry smiled beatifically. 'Help out if I can. As long as that's all right with you, of course, darling?'

Laura heard the hidden message: *You could tell me to go, which I know you desperately want to, but then dear naïve Steve will witness first-hand your attempts to thwart my efforts to reach out to you, won't he?* The woman was poisonous, deadly; seeping back into her life, her tentacles creeping out ready to smother her. Her chest tightened as she saw the challenge in her mother's eyes. She couldn't breathe. She could *never* breathe around her.

'Laura?' Steve said curiously as she spun around again, heading back to the hall.

Coming after her, as she'd guessed he would and wished he wouldn't – she was so angry with him right now – he placed a hand gently on her back as Laura held onto the newel post at the bottom of the stairs and attempted to pull air into her lungs. 'Are you okay?'

'Yes, fine,' she snapped, shrugging him off.

Clearly taken aback, Steve furrowed his brow as she turned to glare at him.

'What were you doing, inviting her in without asking me?' she hissed. 'Discussing me with her behind my back? Don't ever do that again, Steve. And never, *ever* lie to me! Do you hear me?'

He stared at her, shocked. 'Loud and clear,' he said after a moment, and then, disappointment clouding his features, he shook his head sadly and walked away.

CHAPTER THIRTY-FOUR

Sarah

Refusing to think about Joe and why he was so heavily involved in his ex-wife's life, Sarah tried to carry on as normal; tried very hard not to constantly check her phone to see if he'd contacted her. He hadn't. But then she'd been so confused and angry after finding he was with his wife again, she'd ignored the spate of calls and texts he'd sent.

Forget him, she told herself, fixing a bright smile in place as she unbuckled Ollie from his car seat. She hadn't got time for these childish games. She felt a moment's fleeting guilt that she might be the one who was behaving childishly, but dismissed it. She could have accepted him being with his wife that first time – although it had required a certain amount of generosity on her part to understand why he was there while she was taking a bath. His glibly telling her he was with her a second time, though … *Collecting her from the hospital,* she reminded herself, with yet another stab of guilt. Had he been telling the truth? Had everything his ex-wife had told him been the truth? Sarah couldn't know, but she was beginning to wonder. What she did know – which Joe appeared oblivious to – was that his ex was clearly angling to get back with him. No doubt he would tell her she was getting things out of perspective if she voiced that particular concern. Perhaps she was. She wasn't sure she could trust her own instincts any more. She needed to stop doing this, trying to analyse everyone and everything, getting things wrong, it seemed. She needed to get on with her life instead, and let Joe do whatever he wanted to do with his. She had a child to care for. A child who might pick up on her maudlin mood if she moped about, which would make him miserable too.

'Out we come,' she said, lifting him from the car.

'Is Joe coming to my party?' Ollie asked as she steadied him on the pavement.

Sarah's heart plummeted. He'd clearly bonded with him. She'd thought Joe had bonded with Ollie. She suspected that was what hurt most of all: that he'd turned out to be the sort of man who would let a child down. She'd left him a message about the party, but he hadn't got back to her. Clearly he was otherwise engaged. 'No, sweetheart.' She took hold of Ollie's hand and gave it a squeeze. 'He's on duty today, remember? I told you.'

'Catching baddies.' Ollie nodded, satisfied, and, charging ahead of her, tugged her on towards Steve and Laura's house.

Or else comforting his wife. Her mind, which clearly couldn't stop dwelling on Joe, conjured up that cosy scenario despite her determination not to go there. 'That's right,' she agreed, sighing inwardly.

Ringing the doorbell, she pulled herself up. This was Ollie's day, and she was going to be cheerful for his sake. After what Steve had told her about Laura, she felt she could relax a little more around her, which was some weight off her mind.

'Hi,' she said, her smile back in place as Laura opened the front door. She was a little taken aback, though, when she noted Laura's pallid complexion. 'Is everything all right?' she asked. 'You look a bit pale.' She actually looked quite poorly. Also tearful, disconcertingly.

'Yes. Sorry.' Appearing to shake herself, Laura smiled and stepped back to allow her in. 'My mother's here, being her usual charming self,' she said, as Sarah glanced past her up the hall.

'Ah.' Sarah nodded, understanding, as Laura indicated the kitchen with a despairing roll of her eyes. 'I gathered you two were having a few problems when she first, um …'

'Invited herself in?' Laura finished, evidently guessing that Sarah had drawn her own conclusions about her mother's bolshie behaviour. 'We are. More than a few, I'm afraid.' She sighed despondently, then bent to address Ollie. 'Hello, birthday boy,' she said more brightly, beaming him a smile. 'Are you looking forward to your garden party?'

'Yes,' Ollie assured her, remembering his manners, bless him. His hesitant expression, though, told Sarah he wasn't quite sure what a garden party was. 'Is Lucas coming?' he asked.

'The little boy next door,' Laura elucidated for Sarah's benefit. 'He is,' she said to Ollie. 'He's looking forward to playing on your lovely new garden toys with you.'

More new toys? Sarah arched an eyebrow. Laura missed it, her attention diverted as Steve appeared from the kitchen. 'Hiya, mate.' He gave Ollie a wink and a smile. 'Ready to get this party started?'

'Yes!' Ollie bolted delightedly in his direction.

'Urgh.' Groaning theatrically, Steve swept him up into his arms. 'You're growing so fast I can hardly lift you.'

'That's 'cos I'm a year bigger,' Ollie informed him importantly.

'You certainly are.' Steve laughed, turning back to the kitchen. 'Don't forget his sunscreen,' Laura called after him.

Steve glanced back over his shoulder. 'I won't,' he said, unsmiling. Sarah couldn't help noticing that Laura's face seemed to be set in a scowl as she glanced after him. It looked as if they might have had words. She immediately felt bad. She hoped it was nothing to do with her seeming to be interfering in their lives.

She was surprised when, hanging back in the hall as Steve headed off, Laura confided in her. 'I found them talking about me,' she said, her expression somewhere between embarrassed and furious. 'Sherry and Steve. I came down from upstairs and heard them colluding together.'

'Colluding?' Sarah blinked at her. Steve wasn't the secretive sort. He'd certainly never been the sort of man who condoned gossip, and would actively avoid a particular mutual friend who loved nothing better than to rubbish other people.

'Well, maybe not colluding so much as arguing.' Laura smiled half-heartedly.

Sarah looked at her askance. 'What on earth about?'

Laura hesitated. 'You know I sleepwalk?'

'Yes. Steve did mention it,' Sarah said, feeling uncomfortable as she realised that she was confessing to colluding behind Laura's back too.

Laura's smile was wry. 'I guessed he might have.' She took a breath. 'They were discussing whether I should have therapy, because of my sleepwalking and my stress levels generally. Steve was for. Sherry was against. Suffice to say they didn't bother to ask what my thoughts were, which is why I'm a bit miffed.'

Hell. Now Sarah could see why they'd had words. Steve meant well, she was sure, but he really should have known better than to be discussing something so personal with Laura's mother. And her mother should surely have thought twice before having such a conversation in earshot of her daughter. But then from the way she'd heard the woman talking *to* Laura, she wasn't surprised to hear she'd been talking *about* her. Somehow Sarah felt that tact wasn't high on her list of attributes.

'The thing is …' Laura faltered. 'You know about my brother?' she asked, that look in her eyes that put Sarah in mind of a frightened kitten.

'Yes. Steve told me about that too,' she admitted, her heart wrenching for her. 'I'm so very sorry, Laura. That must have been awful for you.'

'It was.' Laura's gaze flicked down and back. 'I had therapy back then, after J-J-Jacob …' She stopped, breathing deeply and squeezing her eyes closed.

Sarah waited, allowing her some time.

'I had the lot,' Laura went on, more composed after a second. 'Psychotherapy, counselling, speech therapy – which helped, as you might have gathered.' She laughed self-deprecatingly. 'It couldn't bring him back, though, could it? Could never take the pain away. I don't think I'll ever stop having nightmares, however much I'd like to stop inconveniencing others.'

Did Steve imply she was inconveniencing him? Sarah couldn't quite believe that. He'd been upset for Laura when he'd spoken to her, not for himself.

'I can't change who I am, Sarah.' Laura looked so downcast, Sarah felt dreadful for her.

'Oh Laura, I'm sure Steve didn't mean—' she started, only to be interrupted.

'Laura? Do hurry up, darling,' her mother shouted through from the kitchen. 'Steve's doing a marvellous juggling act out here, but he does only have one pair of hands.'

Sarah's mouth dropped open. Did the woman not realise how intimidating she sounded? And Laura *was* intimidated, it was clear. She looked like a woman who wanted to disappear inside herself.

'Talk of the devil and she shall appear,' she joked wanly, then visibly braced herself and headed off to obey her mother's command.

What an absolute cow the woman was. Aware of what she had gone through – Sarah couldn't imagine how anyone would survive losing a child – she felt bad for thinking it, but the fact was, she was unbelievable. It seemed as if she were deliberately trying to stir up trouble between Laura and Steve.

CHAPTER THIRTY-FIVE

There actually weren't that many guests: just a few neighbours, along with herself and Sherry, who seemed to be dominating the conversation with tales of her fashion assignments abroad. 'Well, I said to Stella, that's going to make headlines, but for all the wrong reasons,' she was telling one of the mothers, who was doing her best to look fascinated while attempting to placate her little boy, Lucas, who was desperate for another go on the slide.

'McCartney, and I doubt she's ever met her, let alone talked to her,' Laura whispered cynically as she headed past Sarah to take Lucas by the hand and lead him away. The mother smiled gratefully, but Sarah was sure she'd much rather Laura led Sherry away.

Laura really was good with children. Sarah watched as she chatted to the boy, bending down to his level and making him giggle before helping him onto the slide.

'All right, Sarah?' Steve asked, his expression cautious as he led Ollie across from the food table, which was laden with party snacks that would rival anything Mary Berry could produce. There were sausage rolls, slices of chicken terrine topped with leeks and apricot, star sandwiches – Sarah had had to hide a smile at those – and a variety of puddings, including an impressive Spider-Man birthday cake in the shape of a four. Laura really had worked hard. She was clearly desperate for Ollie's party to go well.

'Fine.' She smiled, despite the strong words they'd had. The sun was shining. Ollie was happy. She was on her own, but things could be worse. 'How are you two doing?'

'Good, aren't we, Ollie?' Steve looked down at him, and then pseudo-despairingly back to Sarah. 'He's into the volcano cake.'

'So I see.' Sarah couldn't help but laugh at her chocolate-coated child, who blinked innocently up at her as he attempted to lap the evidence from his cheeks. Laura had also made a towering chocolate sponge with molten toffee lava. It was a chocolate-dribbling disaster waiting to happen, but it was definitely a hit.

'No Joe?' Steve asked curiously.

Dropping her gaze, Sarah shook her head. 'No, no Joe.'

'He's on duty,' Ollie provided, pausing in his efforts to free his face of chocolate. 'Catching all the baddies.'

'Ah.' Steve nodded. He was eyeing her narrowly when she looked back at him, though, as if he didn't quite buy it. Her flushed cheeks were probably a bit of a giveaway that things in her garden weren't all rosy.

'We have a swimming pool too, of course.' Sherry's loud tones drifted across the lawn. 'One does wonder how one would manage without one's own pool in these hostile temperatures.'

Eyeing the sky, Steve smirked. 'She thinks she's in the tropics.'

'Pity she isn't,' Laura growled, coming towards them after delivering Lucas back to his father. 'Preferably the jungle, with another poisonous viper for company, or a big fat boa constrictor.'

Steve's gaze flicked awkwardly from her to Sarah and back.

'What's a boa constrictor, Daddy?' Ollie piped up.

'Er …' Steve knitted his brow. 'It's a kind of—'

'In fact,' Sherry interrupted, striding across to him, 'why don't you, little Ollie and Laura come over to us tomorrow? The pool's just been cleaned and I'm sure Grant would love to—'

'No,' Laura said flatly.

Sherry's eyes travelled in her direction. 'But it seems silly not to make use of it, darling,' she said. 'You have a private swimming pool at your disposal, you might as well—'

'Can we, Daddy?' His face lit with excitement, Ollie tugged on Steve's hand. 'Can we?'

'We could have Sunday lunch together.' Oblivious to her daughter's eyes drilling into her, Sherry continued talking to Steve. 'Grant's the cook in our house, of course, with my always being so busy, but—'

'I said *no*!' Laura shouted, causing a hush to fall over the garden. 'We're busy. Tell her we're busy, Steve.' Her eyes were desperate. Sarah would swear the blood had drained from her face.

'It's only an invitation to lunch, Laura.' Steve looked at her, perplexed. 'We could just—'

'We're not going!' Laura was adamant.

'You're drawing attention, darling,' Sherry hissed, her smile tight as she moved bodily in front of her daughter, as if shielding her from their guests. Or their guests from her daughter? Sarah wasn't sure which.

'Laura …' His expression fearful, Steve moved towards her, but Laura backed away. 'Calm down,' he said, clearly concerned. 'It's okay. We don't have to—'

'It's *not* okay,' Laura cried. She appeared to be gasping for breath.

What on earth? Her stomach knotting, Sarah took a step in her direction.

'It's not okay,' Laura repeated. 'Ask *her* why it's not. Ask her *why*!' she sobbed, and then, her frantic gaze pivoting around the garden, she turned on her heel and ran.

'What the …?' Dragging a hand through his hair, Steve glanced at their stunned guests and then started after her.

'Steve, wait.' Sarah took hold of Ollie's hand. He was plainly as bewildered as his father was, but … 'I'll go,' she said, bending to pick him up. If anything could calm Laura down, she was sure it was his presence.

Steve turned back. 'But what about …?' He nodded towards Ollie.

'He'll be fine,' Sarah assured him, giving him a look as she walked past him, hopefully communicating that maybe he should convince Sherry to think about taking her leave. 'I'll call you if I need you.'

She found Laura in Ollie's bedroom, looking small and lonely sitting on the edge of his bed. She was knotting and unknotting her fingers, Sarah noticed, obviously extremely distressed.

'I thought you might like to help me clean this little man up,' she suggested, trying very hard not to notice the new wallpaper, which was identical to Ollie's wallpaper at home. 'I think he liked your chocolate volcano.' She offered Laura a smile as she glanced up, looking disorientated, as if she didn't quite know where she was. 'He might possibly have liked it a little too much though, hey, Ollie?'

Ollie looked worriedly from her to Laura, then, 'It's yummy,' he said, and patted his tummy.

A faraway look in her eyes, Laura took a second, and then, finally, focused on Ollie. 'Oh my God,' she gasped. 'He's in an awful mess.'

Ollie glanced uncertainly up at Sarah again, and then completely surprised her. 'Don't worry, Laura,' he said, placing his small hand gently on her arm. 'I can have a bath.'

Her eyes a kaleidoscope of emotion, confusion, deep sorrow, pain that was palpable, Laura gazed at him for a moment. Then she laughed, a strangled laugh that turned into a sob, and reached out to hug him. 'You're a good boy,' she murmured, breathing him in. 'A good, beautiful little boy.'

She pressed him closer, her gaze drifting up to Sarah. 'Ollie can't go there. It's too dangerous,' she whispered. 'Tell Steve he mustn't go.'

CHAPTER THIRTY-SIX

'Can you swim, Laura?' Ollie asked, around the wet wipe Sarah was scrubbing his face with.

'A little bit.' Laura glanced at him in the bathroom mirror as she dabbed at her eyes. 'I'm not very good, though. We'll have to learn together one day, won't we? But maybe in a small pool.'

'Uh-huh.' Ollie nodded, and yawned. He was obviously ready for his afternoon nap, even with all the excitement. 'With special superhero water wings,' he said.

She smiled. 'That's right. To keep us safe.'

'That's better.' Sarah looked him over, satisfied that he was as clean as he could be. 'I knew you had a face under there some-where. Shall we go back and see how Daddy's doing?' She glanced questioningly at Laura.

Laura nodded. Her face was still drained of colour, but she looked more in control than she had a short while ago. 'Sorry I lost it.' She smiled self-consciously as Sarah took hold of Ollie's hand to lead him to the landing. 'I just couldn't bear the thought of spending a whole day with her.'

Sarah wasn't surprised. She was concerned, though, very. Laura hadn't been just reluctant to accept Sherry's invitation; she'd seemed terrified. And why had her mother exacerbated the situation instead of simply taking no for an answer? The whole episode had been bizarre. Laura was a grown woman, for goodness' sake. Yes, she had some stress-related issues, quite clearly, but nothing she wasn't managing. Yet Sherry insisted on bossing her around, treating her like a child. It was almost as if the woman had some kind of hold over her that Laura was trying to break free of.

'Can I still have some birthday cake, Mummy?' Ollie asked hopefully as, allowing Laura to go ahead of them, they made their way down the stairs.

'Of course you can.' Laura smiled back at him. 'But maybe later, since your tummy is full of chocolate volcano.'

Ollie thought about it. 'Okay.' He shrugged. 'Can Lucas have some too?'

'I think Lucas has some, munchkin,' Sarah said, nodding towards the hall, where Lucas stood with his parents, a birthday gift bag in his hand.

The little boy gave a wave as his parents ushered him towards the front door. 'Bye, Ollie.'

Ollie waved back. 'Bye, Lucas,' he said, looking a little dejected now. 'Can he come and play again, Laura?' he asked, looking up at her.

'Of course he can,' Laura assured him, smiling bravely despite the obvious awkward atmosphere.

'Any time,' Lucas's father said, giving Laura a sympathetic glance.

'Yes, why not?' his wife said sharply, looking daggers at him and then heading off without even acknowledging Laura.

Laura's cheeks flushed furiously. 'I'd better go and clear up outside,' she said, turning quickly towards the kitchen. To hide her embarrassment, Sarah guessed, glancing after her.

'Would you like to snuggle up on Laura's sofa and watch a film rather than go to bed for your nap?' she bent to ask Ollie.

Ollie looked delighted at that. '*Finding Dory!*' he said excitedly, spinning towards the lounge.

As Sarah put the film on and settled Ollie down, she wondered why it was that Laura was so reluctant to go back to her childhood home. It had to have something to do with the disappearance of her brother. The memories around it would be almost unbearable, but was it more than that? Reminders of the precious time Laura had spent with him there perhaps? Something to do with summers playing by the pool? She would bite the bullet and ask her, she decided. Given how today had turned out, maybe it wasn't the best time, but she had to know. There were just too many unanswered questions.

'Comfy?' she asked Ollie, plumping the cushions up around him.

'Uh-huh.' He yawned widely, working to keep his eyes open. He would be asleep in minutes, Sarah guessed.

'I'll be just outside in the garden,' she said, straightening up and pressing a kiss to the top of his head. 'Back soon.'

Noting Sherry's designer bag hanging on the newel post, she gathered she was still here. The woman seemed omnipresent in Laura's life. Maybe Sarah should suggest that Steve have a quiet word with her and ask her to allow Laura to live her *own* life. She would never do that with her mother constantly interfering in it.

She'd taken a step towards the kitchen when the doorbell rang. With no one else around, she supposed she should answer it.

'Afternoon.' A man around middle age smiled charmingly as she pulled the door open. 'Grant Caldwell,' he introduced himself, extending his hand. 'I'm here to collect Sherry.'

'Ah, right.' Sarah shook it and stepped back. So this was Laura's stepfather. Closing the door, she ran her eyes over him. He wasn't what she'd expected. She wasn't quite sure what she *had* expected, but possibly not someone who, stylishly dressed in a blue linen shirt and cream chinos, was undeniably handsome. Slate-grey eyes that looked at her kindly. Dark hair, flecked silver at the sides. He was tall, almost athletic-looking.

'She rang me,' he said, offering an explanation as to why he was here. 'It's a bit inconvenient, I'm supposed to be on the tennis court, but she said it was an emergency, so …' he shrugged easily, 'here I am.'

'Does she not drive then?' Sarah asked.

'She prefers not to if she can avoid it.' He leaned closer, lowering his voice. 'Don't say I said anything, whatever you do, but she has a little problem with her eyes. Can't tolerate contacts and refuses to wear glasses. I told her they would quite suit her, but … Women's vanity is a strange thing.' He sighed good-naturedly and shook his head.

'Oh, I see.' She did, where Sherry was concerned. She'd only met the woman twice, but she struck her as the sort who was definitely vain. 'I think she's out in the back garden. Steve and Laura are out there too.'

'I'd better go and fetch her. Knowing Sherry, she'll be holding court,' he said with an amused wink.

Sarah thought better of pointing out that thanks to Sherry, there wasn't much of a court left to hold. This really was none of her business. Except it was, because Ollie was still here and had already been caught in the middle of it.

'This way?' he asked, gesturing towards the kitchen with another disarming smile.

Sarah nodded, and was about to follow him but paused as her phone rang. She fished it out of her jeans pocket and a flight of butterflies took off in her tummy as she realised it was Joe. Should she answer? Glancing back into the lounge, where Ollie appeared to be fast asleep, she decided she should talk to him. It was immature not to. Whatever he had to say, she had to know where she stood; draw a line under things if necessary, heartbreaking though she knew it would be.

Steeling herself, she accepted the call, then cursed silently as she realised he'd rung off. She headed for the kitchen, out of earshot of Ollie, and called him back.

'Sarah?' Joe answered, breathing a discernible sigh of relief. 'Thanks for calling back. I really need to …'

She stopped listening, her heart lurching as Laura's voice reached her, high-pitched and petrified. 'No!' she screamed. 'I've told you I don't want him here. I don't want either of you here!'

'Laura! Stop!' Sherry's voice, distressed. 'You need to stop this. You're destroying your life. *Everyone's* life. Please …'

'No! Don't *touch* me!' Laura screamed louder. 'Don't … *Steve!*'

What on earth …? Sarah flew to the back door and took in the scene before her: Laura on her knees on the lawn. Sherry looming over her, clutching her daughter's forearms as if trying to grapple her to her feet. Grant … Grant was crouching over Steve, who was lying motionless on the patio. Sarah's heart turned over as she noticed the blood flowering slowly beneath him, staining the flagstones deep crimson.

CHAPTER THIRTY-SEVEN

Joe

'Who were you calling?' Courtney asked.

His phone still in his hand, Joe glanced towards where she stood in the kitchen doorway, dressed in the shorts and vest top he'd pulled from her dressing table. She'd lost weight, and with her arms wrapped about herself and her complexion chalk white, she looked small and vulnerable. Not the effervescent, confident Courtney he knew. She was trembling. His gut clenched.

What the fuck should he do? He'd cleared her bathroom cabinet, searched all the drawers and cupboards while she'd slept. Looked in every conceivable place, including her handbag. There were no more tablets in the apartment, but ... *Christ* ... How could he leave her after physically having to prise the capsules from her mouth? Antidepressants, sleeping tablets; a lethal cocktail. If she'd swallowed them ...

A stark image of his little sister lying still and cold on her bed assaulting him, he sucked in a sharp breath. She'd been beautiful, fragile, like a perfect porcelain doll. At first, he'd thought she was sleeping. She wasn't. Recalling the telltale trickle of fluid on her cheek, her body limp and lifeless as he'd pulled her to him, begging her with his whole heart and soul to please, *please* wake up, he caught another ragged breath in his chest. She'd been broken inside, so devastated by her first love gone wrong, she couldn't find a way to go on. Their parents had split years since, their father pissed off God knew where. With their mother struggling to bring them up, Ellie hadn't felt able to talk to her, while Joe had been too busy with his own life to make time for her. She'd thought she'd had no one.

And now this. History repeating itself. Ghosts coming back to haunt him. Did Courtney realise what it would have done to him to find her …

'Was it Sarah?' She cut through his thoughts, her tone resigned, devoid of any of the raw emotion Joe had heard when she'd begged him not to go, asking him to give her another chance, as if he was the be-all and end-all of her world.

'I can't do this on my own,' she'd sobbed as he'd hesitated by the front door, every sinew in his body tense, a voice in his head screaming at him to walk away. 'Please don't go, Joe,' she'd begged. 'I can't be alone, not now.'

He had gone. Closing the door behind him, his own emotions raw, he'd walked towards the lift and then stopped, his heart hammering a warning in his chest. There'd been something in her voice, that fatalistic edge he'd heard when he'd brought her back from the hospital. *She wouldn't. Would she?*

He'd turned around, his blood pumping as he'd banged back through the front door. She'd been outside on the balcony, sitting on the balustrade. It had taken him a moment to assimilate, to realise she meant it. If she hadn't found the courage to jump, the tablets she was feeding into her mouth would have ensured she fell to her death.

'It's okay, Joe.' She snatched him back to the present, the dilemma he had now. 'You can stop tearing yourself apart. It's not your fault.'

Confused, he glanced again in her direction.

'It's my fault, all of it. I've been selfish. Stupid beyond belief letting you go. I know it's too late. That you've moved on. It's just

… I've been feeling so empty, so lonely. I hoped that maybe … Anyway, I'm sorry.' Stopping, she dropped her gaze.

Joe moved towards her, but Courtney held up a hand. 'I'm okay,' she assured him, a sad smile still curving her mouth. 'I promise you I'll be fine. I'd rather we didn't … you know, hug or anything, though. I can't promise not to get emotional again if we do that. It's probably better if you just leave.'

'Courtney …' He scanned her face. Her eyes were glassy with tears. Would she be okay? He was far from sure she would be.

'Sarah's waiting,' she reminded him. 'Go to her. Don't worry about me.'

Don't worry about her? Joe had to work at suppressing his disbelief.

'I rang the doctor's surgery,' she said. 'I've made an appointment. I obviously need to talk things through with someone. Meanwhile, I've called my friend. She's coming over for a while. I'll be fine, honestly.'

CHAPTER THIRTY-EIGHT

Sarah

Hearing Joe at the front door, Sarah felt a rush of relief. Their call had still been connected. He'd obviously heard the commotion. She wasn't sure what they were to each other any more, but she felt sorely in need of a friend.

'What happened?' he asked, coming straight into the lounge, Sherry close behind him.

'Daddy fell off the ladder,' Ollie answered, climbing off the sofa, where he'd been practically glued to Steve's side, and going over to Joe. 'He broke his head.'

Steve laughed, then winced. 'It's not broken, Ollie,' he assured him. 'Just a bit dented.'

'It was bleeding.' His voice a worried whisper, Ollie slid his hand into Joe's.

Joe gave it a squeeze. 'I'm sure he'll be fine,' he said, smiling down at the little boy. 'Your mother's looking after him.' Glancing at Sarah, who was trying to persuade Steve to keep the cold compress pressed to his head, he smiled tentatively.

Sarah smiled back and pulled herself up from where she was crouching in front of her stubborn ex. He'd flatly refused to allow them to take him to hospital. She hadn't been surprised. He'd always tended to brush things off as 'just a scratch' or 'a little bump' whenever he'd injured himself at work. This was one almighty bump, though. Sarah's heart had stopped beating when she'd seen him lying so still on the patio.

'Did you lose consciousness?' Joe asked, his forehead furrowed in concern as he walked across to him.

Steve glanced up, his expression wary, Sarah noted, as if he wasn't quite sure what to think about Joe. He wasn't the only one. Sarah had been confident she knew him, that he wasn't the kind of man who would mess her around. Now, she wasn't sure she knew him at all. 'I don't know.' Steve shrugged. 'If I did, it was only—'

'Yes, he did,' she confirmed forcefully. 'I've told him he should go to hospital, but he's being pig-headed, as usual.'

Steve laughed wryly at that. 'Don't change much, do you, Sarah?' He glanced at her amusedly and then back to Joe. 'She always was a worrier.'

Joe's mouth twitched up at the corners, indicating that he concurred with Steve's view of her, which Sarah might have been peeved about but for the seriousness of the situation. 'Actually, I think she's probably right on this occasion,' he said. 'You could have concussion. Might be worth getting it checked out.'

'Not much they can do, though, is there?' Steve replied, with another casual shrug. 'I've got plenty of paracetamol. I'll keep an eye on it and get myself there if I need to.'

'Fair enough.' Joe nodded, eyeing him thoughtfully. 'You might do well to get your ladder checked out, though.'

Steve didn't look too impressed at that. 'I'm a builder, mate,' he pointed out. 'I check my equipment regularly, including anything I use at home.'

Sarah knew that to be true. Running his own building company, Steve was always meticulous about health and safety. He'd climbed ladders half his life. She really couldn't understand how it was he'd come to fall, or why he was up a ladder in the first place. Something to do with bunting coming loose and hanging dangerously, Sherry had told her.

'The slabs must be uneven or something,' Steve said, as if reading her mind.

'Grant tried to steady him,' Sherry interjected. 'He saw him wobbling and flew across to him. He was too late to save him, unfortunately.'

'Grant?' Joe enquired.

'My husband. Laura's stepfather,' Sherry provided.

Joe nodded. 'And Laura? Is she okay?'

'As much as she ever is,' Sherry said with a despairing sigh. 'She's hiding away upstairs, for reasons I'll never understand.'

'She's actually not feeling well, Mrs Caldwell,' Sarah reminded her. Laura had been trembling like a leaf. Even when she knew Steve wasn't badly injured, she couldn't stop shaking. It was Sarah who'd suggested she go up and have a lie-down. Privately, she'd thought she would be far better off away from Sherry; it clearly hadn't occurred to the woman to leave and allow Steve and Laura some privacy.

'I can't say I'm surprised after all the melodramatics,' Sherry commented unsympathetically. 'Right, well, I'd better go and see how Grant's getting on. He's hosing the patio down. He tries to be helpful wherever he can. He's a good man,' she obviously felt compelled to point out. 'I do wish Laura would leave the past where it belongs and stop all this childishness.'

Sighing again, most definitely melodramatically, she turned to stride off in the direction of the kitchen.

'And I wish she'd just bloody well go,' Steve muttered once she was out of earshot. 'I'd never have had the woman here if I'd known what a cow she is.'

It wasn't just Sarah who thought that way, then. 'I'll go and make some tea and have a recce through the kitchen window,' she offered. 'See if Grant's close to finishing whatever it is he's doing. Do you want to sit with Daddy, Ollie?' she asked him. 'I think we might need to keep an eye on him and make sure he has a little rest.'

She glanced at Steve, who gave her a small nod, clearly getting her drift. With his afternoon nap so spectacularly interrupted, Ollie looked as if he might be about to fall asleep on his feet. 'Sounds like a plan,' he said. 'Fancy coming over here and giving your old man a cuddle, mate?'

Ollie answered with a decisive nod, and Joe hoisted him back up onto the sofa.

Sarah wasn't sure who looked more exhausted, father or son, as she watched Ollie snuggle contentedly under Steve's arm. Giving Ollie a reassuring smile, she left them to it, beckoning Joe to follow her to the kitchen.

'You knew I was here then?' she asked him, picking up the kettle.

'I gathered, yes, from the commotion I heard on the phone,' he said. 'That's Grant, presumably?' He nodded through the window.

'That's him,' Sarah confirmed. Laura's stepfather was now collecting up the bunting that had come down when Steve had fallen. He'd been nothing but charming, and clearly he was helpful, which made Sarah wonder why Laura had been so insistent that she didn't want him here. This was more than her blaming her parents for the tragedy they'd all had to endure, she felt sure. Laura had seemed actually terrified. Why? And why had Sherry been trying to subdue her when Steve fell?

'Laura said Grant pushed him.' She glanced tentatively at Joe. She felt as if she were betraying Laura, but she needed another perspective on this apart from her own, which Joe hadn't thought was functioning too well, she reminded herself.

'Pushed him?' His expression a mixture of confusion and shock, Joe pulled his attention away from Sherry and Grant, who now appeared to be deep in hushed conversation.

Turning from the window, Sarah walked past him to close the kitchen door. 'I spoke to Laura once I'd managed to prise her mother away from her,' she said, keeping her voice low. 'She didn't say much. To be honest, she wasn't making much sense, but I definitely heard her say, "He pushed him."'

Joe looked at her askance.

'I have no idea what's going on here, Joe, but something definitely is. I spoke to Steve briefly before you arrived. He thinks she blames her parents for her brother's disappearance. I have no idea why. She definitely doesn't get on with her mother. Remember I told you how her stammer kicked in when she called unannounced that day?'

Joe glanced again at Sherry. 'She is a bit daunting, isn't she?'

That was one way of describing her, Sarah thought. 'She's horrible to her.' She followed his gaze to where Sherry was now gesticulating, wagging a finger at Grant, who eyed the skies as if despairing of her. Sarah couldn't help but wonder why someone who was as good-looking as he was, and clearly good-natured, would stay with someone as obnoxious as Sherry. If she had hidden qualities, they were obviously *well* hidden. Was it all down to money? Might he be financially embarrassed, she wondered, and therefore dependent on Sherry's income? It seemed the only possible explanation.

'This thing with her brother,' she looked hesitantly back to Joe, 'I know it's natural to search for someone to blame when something as tragic as that happens, but it's more than that. Laura seems terrified. She was almost hysterical when Grant turned up today.'

She paused, waiting for that weary look she'd seen previously in Joe's eyes, the one that told her he was about to suggest she was reading too much into things.

His expression, though, was troubled. 'Do you think we could go outside and talk?' he asked. 'I owe you an explanation, but aside from that, I have some information that might be important.'

Intrigued, Sarah went with him, poking her head around the lounge door as she did. Ollie was asleep, she noted, his head resting on a pillow on Steve's lap. Her gaze went to Steve. He was massaging his forehead, still awake, thank goodness. He was probably wondering what to do, worried to death about the situation. Sarah felt awful for him.

Once outside, Joe waited for her to ease the front door to. 'About Courtney,' he started.

Sarah stared at him, a hard lump expanding in her chest. She couldn't quite believe it. Did he really think she would want to hear about his ex-wife amidst all of this?

'Please hear me out.' He'd clearly noticed her astonished expression. 'I need you to know what's been happening because …' He paused, glancing awkwardly down. 'I love you, Sarah,' he announced, stunning her. 'I know you won't believe it unless I tell you what's been going on. Will you let me explain?'

She scanned his face. His eyes were full of quiet pleading. Also, something else. Fear? 'Go on,' she said, apprehension running through her.

Joe nodded, relief flooding his features. 'I told you about the pregnancy.'

Sarah braced herself. 'Yes,' she said, studying his eyes intently. Eyes where dark shadows danced, she noticed, her stomach tightening.

'She has something called polycystic ovary syndrome.' He ran a hand over his neck. 'It can cause complications during pregnancy. It can also be one of the leading causes of infertility. Courtney thinks she won't be able to get pregnant again, and … she blames herself, thinks she's being punished in some way.'

Oh no. Sarah didn't know the woman – she didn't sound like the kind of person she wanted to know – but still her heart went out to her.

Joe hesitated before going on. 'She asked me if we could get back together,' he said, trepidation in his eyes as he searched hers.

What? After all she'd done to him? Sarah almost laughed in disbelief.

'I said no,' he added quickly. 'There's no way I would ever consider … The thing is … She tried to take her life,' he continued, his voice thick with emotion. 'I found her on the balcony. She'd taken tablets. I …' He stopped and looked heavenwards.

'Oh God, Joe, no.' Her heart skidded against her ribcage. He'd been through this once with his poor sister. It had almost destroyed him.

He looked back at her, his eyes those of a haunted man. 'Whatever she is, whatever she's done, I can't leave her too long on her own right now. I just can't take that risk. I needed you to know. I hoped you'd understand. I should have been there for you. I wasn't. I need to be here for you now, but I …'

Sarah swallowed. 'It's okay,' she assured him. She hesitated, then stepped towards him to offer him the hug he clearly badly needed. She wasn't sure it *would* be okay. Though she hated herself for it, there was a small part of her that wondered about the woman's motives. Joe would never walk away from her while she was threatening to take her own life. Anyone who knew anything about him would know that.

Dropping his head to hers, Joe pulled her close for a second, and then breathed out a heavy sigh and eased away. 'There's something else you need to know. About Laura,' he said, his gaze now holding a warning.

'Which is?' she asked, a fresh chill of trepidation running through her.

'I checked under the name Jameson,' he went on guardedly. 'It seems she was a teaching assistant before she worked at the hospice.'

'A teaching assistant?' Sarah looked at him curiously. 'And?' There was more, obviously. She steeled herself.

'She was dismissed from her job when a child wandered off on a nature trail on her watch.'

'Christopher Jameson,' she whispered, nausea churning her stomach. 'He said she was dangerous. He said I should ask her about her previous job and why she left it. I was going to, but when Steve told me how abusive he'd been towards her, the lies he'd told about her …' She hadn't mentioned to Steve what Jameson had said about her previous job, and now she wished to God that she had. Which one of them was lying? Laura? Her ex-husband? If it was Laura, why would she?

'It might be nothing,' Joe said, but she could see from the tight set of his jaw that he didn't think it was. 'I'm going to check it out further. Meanwhile, I realise you might want to stay to make sure Steve's okay, but it might be an idea to make an excuse to take Ollie home this evening.'

Sarah glanced back to the house. She could hear Sherry saying her goodbyes. She had an overwhelming urge to go back in, gather Ollie up and leave immediately, but she had no idea what to say to Steve. How much he would believe.

'I'll try to call around later,' Joe offered, 'once I've checked on Courtney. If you want me to, that is?'

She nodded. She wasn't sure whether that was a good idea or a bad one, but the thought of being on her own suddenly scared her. 'I …' she started, about to say that she did want him to, and then stopped, realising that Sherry was in the hall.

'Bye, Laura,' the woman called. 'Do try and eat something, darling.' There was no answer from upstairs.

'I told you this would happen.' Sherry's tones grew louder as she approached the front door. 'We should have nipped this in the bud.'

'Perhaps it's time to stop trying to stifle her,' Grant suggested, his tone weary.

'And what would that achieve? You really do amaze me some-times, Grant. Do you think it's just myself I'm worried about?'

Joe and Sarah exchanged wary glances.

'No,' Grant said eventually, with a discernible sigh. 'But you can't keep doing this, Sherry. Maybe we should think about telling her—'

'Don't be ridiculous,' Sherry hissed, and swung the front door open.

Not wanting her to think they'd been listening, Sarah improvised, wrapping her arms around Joe's neck and yanking him to her.

Sherry huffed past as they kissed. 'Your child has just woken up,' she imparted. 'You might do well to keep an eye on him.'

CHAPTER THIRTY-NINE

Laura

Bile rising in her throat, Laura watched from the bedroom window as her mother strode down the garden path, Grant trailing in her wake. He would always be there, always in Sherry's shadow, always in her debt. She'd guilted him into marrying her. When he'd wanted to leave, she'd guilted him into staying. Laura had no doubt that that was why she'd done the inconceivably wicked thing she had. That had been her aim, to keep a man who was desperate to walk away from her chained to her forever. She would always claim she was protecting him, protecting her daughter. She was a liar. Everything that spilled from her Dior-coated blood-red slash of a mouth was lies. Laura was sure she hadn't been sleepwalking that long-ago dark night. She'd taken the sedative her mother had offered her before going to bed. She recalled doing that. Sherry always made sure she took her sedatives. Sometimes she didn't swallow them, aware that her mother often didn't go to Jacob if he woke in the night. Always leaving him to … Jacob's sobs had woken her. He'd been crying. She could *hear* him. She heard him now, whimpering like an abandoned puppy.

The crying had stopped. Suddenly there was nothing but the rain drumming like fingernails against the windows, the wind whispering through the trees: *You have to save him.* The memory floated back, as others had, hazy and incomplete but slowly forming a picture. Ironically, it was her mother's latest attempts to sabotage any life she might have that had triggered them. How horrified would Sherry be if she knew that?

She wanted to destroy Laura's relationship, to keep her from forming relationships, from trusting herself enough to believe in herself. She'd achieved her aim. She'd poisoned Sarah's mind against her. Her policeman boyfriend would investigate her. Steve would leave her.

Hearing the bedroom door open, she wrapped her arms more tightly around herself, trying to stop the incessant shaking. She continued to watch as Grant drove off, her mother's mouth moving animatedly as she berated him – for failing to successfully do his part in keeping their secret safe, Laura assumed. She should have found the courage to challenge her. Right there in the garden in front of witnesses. She didn't doubt that Sherry's wrath would have exploded. She would have done more than allude to the fact that her daughter wasn't responsible for her actions on the night Jacob had disappeared. She would have tried to convince everyone that she'd been responsible for what happened to the beautiful little boy Laura now knew she searched for in her dreams. But now her memories were returning, Sherry might just have been caught out in her lies.

'How are you?' Steve asked tentatively. Sensing him right behind her, Laura tensed. It wasn't his fault. He'd done nothing to deserve any of this, but she couldn't turn to him, seek the comfort in his embrace she desperately needed. She couldn't offer him reassurances or explanations. There was no way to do that without revealing everything. If she stayed here, Steve and Ollie would both be in danger. If she left, though, her mother might still hold the threat of harming them over her. If Sherry suspected that Laura had remembered details that had evaded her until now, she would stop at nothing to keep her from telling.

'Did he push you?' she asked, her gaze still on the window. 'Grant, did he push you?'

'What?' Steve laughed, incredulous. 'No, he didn't *push* me. For God's sake, Laura. He was trying to grab the ladder. He didn't push the bloody thing.'

She glanced back at him. 'Are you sure?'

His forehead creased into an uncertain frown. He couldn't be sure. Nor could Laura, not one hundred per cent; it had all happened so fast. But wouldn't that have been Sherry's way of sending out a clear warning?

'They're going to take him away from me,' she said quietly.

'Who is?' Steve asked, clearly bewildered. 'Who are they going to take away, Laura?'

'Sarah and her boyfriend. They're going to take Ollie away. They don't trust me after all that happened today.'

'They do,' Steve tried to reassure her, though he sounded far from convinced. Poor Steve. If anyone was a good man, he was. 'Sarah understands you've had some problems,' he went on, attempting to play down her unstable behaviour. Behaviour that to him must appear to border on insane. 'She wants what's best for Ollie, of course she does, but she doesn't not trust you.'

'She's taking him home.' Laura pointed out the obvious flaw in his argument. Ollie had been due to stay, but she could hear Sarah downstairs talking to him, enticing him with the promise of Joe coming to see him later. She'd heard her telling Steve that he was overtired after all the excitement. Steve hadn't argued, agreeing immediately that it might be best if Ollie went home with her, which confirmed that he'd lost trust in Laura too.

She'd heard Joe talking to Sarah before her mother had barged out, all that Joe had said about his ex-wife. He was obviously a caring man. It was clear that he cared about Sarah and Ollie. She felt better for knowing that he would be around to protect the little boy.

She glanced down to where Joe had climbed into his car. He was watching the house, waiting, Laura gathered, to make sure

Sarah and Ollie emerged safely. Did he know, she wondered, that someone was watching him too? Her gaze travelled back to the car parked on the opposite side of the road, two vehicles behind him.

CHAPTER FORTY

Sarah

She'd debated whether to just ask Steve outright. It didn't seem fair to heap yet another problem on his plate. But then she'd realised she had to, if only so she could stop obsessing about it, which she knew she was. On top of everything else, though, she would defy anyone to blame her, including Steve.

'Hi. How are you?' he asked when he picked up.

'Okay,' she said. 'I'm just on my way to nursery to pick Ollie up.'

'How's he doing?' Steve asked, a worried edge to his voice. Clearly he was concerned that the events over the weekend might have upset him.

'He's fine,' Sarah assured him. 'I told him Laura had been feeling poorly. He seemed to accept that. He's making her a card to cheer her up.' She wasn't sure when Laura might see the card, given the circumstances, but she thought Steve would feel better for knowing Ollie hadn't been badly affected. 'So, how are *you*? How's the head?'

'Not too bad. You never know, the bang might have knocked some sense into it,' he joked wryly. 'About the stuff we argued about,' he went on hesitantly. 'I, er, get it. Why you were so determined to find out more about Laura before allowing her to become involved in Ollie's life. I mean, she obviously does have some issues, and, well … I'm sorry for acting like a bit of a dickhead.'

Sarah smiled at his gruff attempt at an apology. 'No problem. I get it too. You love her.'

She waited, wondering whether Steve would admit as much to her.

'I do,' he confirmed after an awkward pause. 'Probably more now, but … It's a bit of a mess, isn't it? This thing with her family?'

'Definitely,' she had to agree. 'Word of advice, if I may?'

'Shoot.'

'I know it won't be easy, but if I were you, I'd keep Sherry at arm's length.'

'I intend to,' Steve said with a despairing sigh.

Sarah hesitated, then, 'Can I ask you something?'

'As long as it's nothing too difficult,' he joked, half-heartedly this time.

'The wallpaper in Ollie's room, did you choose it?'

'No,' he answered, after a pause. 'Laura did. She knows Ollie's into dinosaurs, so …'

He was thinking it was a coincidence. Sarah hoped it was too, because Laura hadn't been to her house. *No, you were the one sneaking about in* her *house*, she reminded herself. Remembering Bunny's ear, she didn't feel any easier. 'Great minds then, obviously,' she said, deciding to leave it there for now. Steve didn't need any more to contend with.

'About Ollie's visits …' he said, and paused.

She steeled herself, guessing what he might be about to say.

'After all that happened, I'm thinking you might be reticent about him coming over.'

She hesitated. 'To be honest, I am a bit. Do you think maybe you could just take him out for the day?' she suggested. 'Just until things are a bit more settled.'

Steve took a breath. 'I suppose that's probably a good compromise,' he agreed.

Sarah heard the reluctance in his voice and felt for him. He loved Laura, that was obvious, but he loved Ollie too, fiercely. He would never knowingly do anything to put him in danger. 'Thanks, Steve,' she said gratefully. He could have been awkward about it, which would have just exacerbated the problem. 'We should make sure to keep talking.'

'We will,' he promised.

She smiled. This was progress at least. However things had turned out between them, he wasn't a bad man. She really hoped things worked out for him and Laura. He'd been wrong to talk to Sherry about Laura having therapy, but it was clear that she did need some help. She obviously hadn't been able to move on at all. Sarah would suggest to him that he approach the subject again, directly with Laura this time, and subtly. 'I'd better go.' She glanced towards the nursery. 'I think the parents are going in. Speak soon.'

Ollie bolted towards her as soon as she walked through the nursery door. 'We have some pretend grass,' he announced as Sarah bent to give him a hug.

'Do you? Well, that's exciting, isn't it?' Easing back, she gave him a bright smile. She presumed he meant AstroTurf. Melanie had mentioned they were getting some fitted in the garden so the children could play safely.

'Uh-huh,' Ollie said, grabbing hold of the hand she offered him. 'They're making a space so we can ride our bikes. Can I ride my bike, Mummy?' he asked with a little jig as they walked back to the car. 'Can I?'

'We have to get you a bike first, don't we?' Sarah laughed. She'd promised him a new one as a belated birthday present. It looked as if he was keen to seal the deal.

Chattering away to himself all the way home about which bike he wanted, he was still trying to decide between the inevitable

Spider-Man model and the fire chief one they'd seen online as they walked through the front door.

Her attention on her son, Sarah didn't realise anything was amiss until they went into the lounge. When she did, her heart turned over. 'Ollie! Leave it!' she screamed, the desecration that greeted her scorching itself on her eyes as she dragged him physically away from the carnage and back to the hall.

CHAPTER FORTY-ONE

Joe

Having knocked on Courtney's door several times, Joe was debating what to do. Her car was in the car park, so she was presumably here. Why the hell wasn't she answering? *Dammit.* His gut tightening, he found the key he still had and let himself in. 'Courtney?' he called. Getting no answer, he checked the kitchen and lounge area, and then, his heart slowing to a dull thud in his chest, he walked towards the bedroom, queasiness gripping him as he considered the balcony beyond it.

His hand shook visibly as he pressed down the door handle, sweat wetting his forehead as his mind painted a graphic image of what he might find inside. His eyes darting from the bed to the large patio windows, relief crashed through him. *Nothing.* She wasn't here. No sign of her on the balcony, though he headed that way anyway to double-check. Wiping a hand over his face, his eyes flicked again to the bed. He couldn't help thinking of the nights he'd spent in it, the long sleepless nights, wondering whether she'd been with the hotshot the night before, that evening, that day. It served to remind him why he couldn't allow his undoubted sympathy for her to cloud his judgement. The same went for the lingerie discarded arbitrarily over the bed, placed almost artistically, he couldn't help noticing. Immediately he reprimanded himself for reading something into it. She would have been trying it on;

she might well be self-conscious about her body after all she'd been through.

As he walked back out, his gaze fell on a note on the dressing table. *Out with a friend,* it read. *Speak soon.* It didn't have his name on, but he guessed it was meant for him. Why would she leave it in the bedroom? Why not the kitchen, the most obvious place, or the hall?

Christ, he was becoming paranoid. Reminding himself that he didn't need to feel that way any more, that it didn't matter where she was or who she was with, he headed back to the hall and opened the front door, sucking in a breath as he stepped into the corridor. Her perfume was cloying. Everything about her had been cloying, he remembered. Their whole relationship had been about her and her needs. Granted, the sex had been difficult to walk away from. It had been spectacular, but it had been just that: sex. No affection. No love. He wasn't sure she actually knew what love was. For her it was more about possession. Everything had to be done her way or no way. He had no doubt it had been her pulling the strings in her relationship with the hotshot, had the man but known it. He'd obviously woken up to that fact, just as Joe had. She was beautiful, undeniably, potent – and lethal.

Taking the stairs in favour of the lift, which took forever to arrive, he tugged his ringing mobile from his pocket. It was Courtney. He rejected the call. He would get back to her at some point. Meanwhile, if it was urgent, he guessed she'd ring again. He needed not to be at her beck and call, he'd decided, for her sake and definitely for his own. He was about to pocket the phone when it beeped with a text. He checked it and stopped dead. *Someone's broken into the house,* he read.

Fuck! Racing to his car, he yanked the door open, threw himself inside and immediately called Sarah back. 'When?' he asked as soon as she picked up.

'While I was out at work,' she answered shakily. 'I've just picked Ollie up from nursery and …' She stopped, a sob catching in her throat.

Christ. Joe breathed in hard. 'Have you called the police?'

'I'm calling you, Joe,' she answered, her voice strained. She was trying hard to hold back the tears. 'I didn't know what I should do. I wasn't sure they would come straight away and … I'm scared, Joe.'

'I'll call it in now,' he said. 'Don't touch anything. Stay wherever you are and … No, don't.' Had she checked all the rooms? There was a possibility someone might still be there, though he tried to reassure himself it was unlikely. 'Go round to one of your neighbours,' he instructed, working to keep the panic from his voice. 'Stay there until I get there. I won't be long.'

'Okay. Thanks, Joe,' she said, her voice small.

Gunning the engine, Joe cursed liberally, wishing to God he could get hold of the bastard who'd done this to her. He'd rip their fucking head off. What the *hell* was he doing here? Yes, Courtney had needed support. He didn't doubt that. But his priority should be Sarah. *Was* Sarah. And he was never bloody there when she needed him.

CHAPTER FORTY-TWO

Laura

'Where were you?' Steve asked the second Laura walked through the front door.

Her heart sank in despair. He was constantly on tenterhooks around her, watching her all the time, treating her as if she were made of glass. Truthfully, she felt as if she was. When she looked at her reflection in the mirror sometimes, it seemed distorted. As if the glass had been shattered and she'd been put back together with part of her missing.

'Just out walking. I needed some space,' she answered vaguely. Then, noting his worried frown, she grew irritated. 'I can't be answerable for my every move, Steve,' she snapped. 'I am capable of looking after myself, you know. I don't need a bloody chaperone.'

He looked shocked for a second, then he sighed wearily. 'I never thought you weren't capable of looking after yourself. I was concerned about you, that's all.'

'But *why* would you be concerned?' she asked him. Why wasn't he angry? His life was turning into a catastrophe, and still he tried to be the soul of understanding. What was the matter with him? Did he honestly think he could fix things for her? That in monitoring her moods and her every move, he could make things right? Did he imagine that he could somehow mediate between her and her mother? He *couldn't* fix this. Didn't he see?

'Why are you so caring, Steve? I mean, don't you sometimes feel frustrated with all of this?' She eyed him uncomprehendingly. If he would only vent his frustration occasionally, it might allow her to vent hers. Didn't he realise that?

'Yes, I'm frustrated,' he answered, his tone calm. She saw a flash of humiliation in his eyes, though, and that just made her feel worse. He was doing his best, she knew he was, but she couldn't deal with being constantly watched, frightened to put a step out of place lest he start believing the lies her mother had been feeding him. She couldn't breathe. 'I'm not sure it would help the situation if I gave in to it, though, are you?'

'Nor does interrogating me help the situation,' she pointed out tersely.

He massaged his forehead. 'I wasn't interrogating you, Laura. You've been gone a while and ...' He stopped, emitting another heavy sigh. 'Your mother came here. About an hour ago.' He looked warily back at her.

'Right.' She felt her jaw clench. 'And I suppose you invited her in for a cup of tea and another cosy chat about *me*.' She eyeballed him accusingly.

Steve held her gaze. 'In actual fact, I didn't let her in,' he said, clearly working now to hold onto his patience. 'I told her she wasn't welcome.'

He'd stood up for her? Laura looked at him in surprise.

'About what you heard us discussing, your mother and me ...'

'My going for therapy.' She felt herself tense.

'Don't you think it might be worth considering?' he asked. 'Family therapy, maybe?'

'What?' She baulked. He couldn't be serious, surely?

'You and me, I mean,' he clarified quickly. 'I know you've been before, but it might help.' He shrugged hopefully. 'It might be useful for me too. At least then I'd know how I could help you, assuming you want me to.'

Laura had no idea what to say. She was being unfair. She knew she was. He wasn't interrogating her. He didn't want anything from her other than for her to be healthy and happy, less troubled. He wanted her to be able to confide in him. He wanted to be able to confide in her. To sleep soundly in his bed without having to worry about finding her wandering about in the garden in the dead of night. A normal relationship was what he wanted. How could he ever have that with her?

'I don't want to lose you, Laura,' he said gruffly, 'but …' He shrugged and trailed off pointedly.

Laura's throat tightened as she realised he was issuing her an ultimatum: sort your mess of a life out or else. 'You don't want to lose Ollie either,' she finished, swallowing emotionally. 'Nor do I.'

CHAPTER FORTY-THREE

Sarah

Keeping a lookout through the lounge window of her neighbour's house, Sarah almost cried with relief when she saw Joe arrive.

'Is he here, Mummy?' Ollie asked as she turned from the window, his voice tremulous and uncertain.

'He's here, sweetheart.' Sarah helped him from the sofa and took hold of his hand. 'Thank you,' she said to Walter, who had kindly taken her in. He was a widower, getting on and a little bit lonely, Sarah guessed. He was always helpful and considerate, keeping a friendly eye on the comings and goings in the neighbourhood. He hadn't noticed anyone coming and going from her house today, though. Whoever it was had somehow managed to get in unseen.

'My door's always open, my lovely,' he assured her. 'You can call on me any time if you need to.' Walking with her to the door, he gave her shoulders a squeeze, which almost caused the tears to spring forth there and then.

Turning to give him a hug, which both surprised and delighted him, she held Ollie's hand tighter and went to meet Joe, who looked as relieved to see her as she was him.

'Are you all right?' he asked, his gaze full of concern as it travelled over her.

She answered with a firm nod. She hadn't been in control of her emotions on the phone. She'd probably panicked him. 'Just a bit shocked, that's all,' she lied. She was shaking inside. She felt violated, imagining some stranger's hands touching her personal things, Ollie's things – that was what had upset her most of all. What kind of animal would do that to a child, invade his world, his safe space, and possibly scar his little mind forever?

'I'm not surprised.' Scanning her eyes, his own growing dark with anger, Joe pulled her to him, holding her close for a second, and then eased away to crouch down to Ollie. 'How are you doing, mate?' he asked him gently.

'Okay,' Ollie murmured, his voice tiny.

'You sure?' Joe searched his face.

Ollie nodded, doing his best to be brave, but then his face crumpled. 'They took Mr Whale,' he cried, tears escaping his eyes to plop down his cheeks.

Looking pig-sick, Joe pulled him close. 'We'll get you a new one,' he said throatily, pressing a soft kiss to his cheek, which almost caused Sarah to crumple.

Whatever Joe had done, however gullible he seemed to have been where his ex-wife was concerned, he cared about her son, cared about her. He *was* the man she'd thought he was. And he was here for her. Buoyed by that knowledge, her heavy heart lightened a little.

Hoisting Ollie into his arms, Joe leaned to brush Sarah's lips with his and then gave her an encouraging smile. 'There's a car on the way. I'm going inside to take a look. Do you think you could look after your mummy while I do that, Ollie? She's looking a bit sad.'

Blinking hard, Ollie replied with another small nod, and then reached to hook his arms around Sarah's neck.

'I won't be long,' Joe assured her, making sure she had a firm hold of Ollie. 'Do you want to go back to your neighbour's?'

'No, I'll wait here,' Sarah said determinedly. This was her home. She wanted to go back inside it. She wanted to clean it – though she doubted it would ever really feel clean again.

Joe's face said it all when he emerged a few minutes later to meet the police car drawing up outside. His expression was thunderous. 'All right, Joe?' a woman police officer asked, looking him worriedly over as she climbed out of the driver's side.

'Hi, Kayla. I've been better.' He nodded to the male officer who climbed out of the passenger side.

'How's it looking?' The man indicated the house.

'Pretty grim,' Joe said, his jaw tight. 'They've trashed the place.' His gaze flicked anxiously in Sarah's direction. 'This is Sarah and Ollie. It's her house, you gathered that?'

'We did.' The woman smiled sympathetically at her. 'Pleased to meet you, Sarah. Joe's told us a lot about you. All good, by the way,' she added reassuringly. 'I'm sorry you had to come home and find this. You must be gutted.'

'I am,' Sarah said, hitching Ollie higher in her arms. Joe had been right. Whoever had done this had trashed the place, just for the fun of it, it seemed. Furniture had been upturned, drawers opened, the contents left spewing out. Cushions had been slashed and strewn about, ornaments and photographs swiped from the shelves. One of her and Ollie laughing together, which she'd loved, had even been trodden on, the glass smashed and ground underfoot. Nothing seemed to have been taken, apart from Ollie's whale. Sarah simply couldn't understand the mentality of someone who would do that. *Why* they would.

'Any signs of a forced entry, Joe?' the male officer asked.

'I can't see any,' Joe answered with a despondent shake of his head.

Sarah glanced guiltily between them. 'The downstairs loo window was open,' she admitted. 'I suppose someone could have squeezed in through that.'

'It would have to have been a small someone,' Joe said, a curious frown crossing his face.

'Kids, most likely,' Kayla commented with a weary sigh. 'The scenes-of-crime officer's on his way.' She looked back to Sarah.

'He'll assess any forensic opportunities. Hopefully we'll come up with something – fingerprints, footwear marks.'

What they actually came up with was nothing. A shiver ran down Sarah's spine as she surveyed the chaos after the forensics people had left. It was as if a ghost had swept through her home. A poltergeist, she thought with bitter amusement as she dusted a splinter of glass from her beloved photograph.

'Will they find Mr Whale, Mummy?' Ollie asked, his little face grave.

'They might,' Joe said, walking across to where the little boy sat on the sofa playing listlessly with his Lego, which Joe had painstakingly gathered together. 'We'll go shopping at the weekend anyway, shall we?' Sitting down next to him, he threaded an arm around his small shoulders. 'See if we can find another toy who needs a warm bed to sleep in at night. What do you think?'

Ollie nodded. 'One like Bunny?' he asked, his eyes hopeful as he looked up at Joe.

Sarah's heart missed a beat. He'd hardly mentioned Bunny since Mr Whale had arrived on the scene.

'Just like Bunny, sweetheart,' she said, feeling choked up all over again as she went across to him. 'We haven't seen him in a long while, have we?' He'd actually been tucked away at the back of the top shelf in her wardrobe. He'd been moved – by the intruder, she assumed – but he was still there.

Ollie looked up at her, his huge eyes filled with guilt. 'He got hurt,' he whispered.

Sarah held her breath. 'How did he get hurt, Ollie?' she asked him carefully.

'I don't know.' His eyes held hers. Sarah could see he was telling the truth. 'Laura was going to fix him, but then she couldn't find him.'

Sarah swallowed back a huge lump of guilt of her own. If she hadn't taken him, Laura most likely *would* have fixed him, and Ollie need never have been without him. She'd acted impulsively, followed her instinct, but it seemed that yet again, her instinct had been wrong.

An hour later, with Ollie tucked up with his T-Rex dinosaur toy and assurances that Joe was staying over, Sarah joined Joe in the kitchen, where he was making a much-needed coffee after their efforts clearing up. She was grateful for one small mercy: that he was on a day off on his shift rota. Her mum's house was a fair drive away, but she could have gone there for a couple of nights – although she was reluctant to worry her – or descended on Becky. She would much rather be here with Joe though.

'Sorry,' she said, going across to him and sliding her arms around his midriff.

'For?' Joe asked.

'Not sure.' She rested her head on his shoulder. 'Everything.'

'You haven't done anything,' he said, turning to face her. 'But I'm liking the tactile apology nevertheless.' Smiling, he kissed her softly, which Sarah definitely liked. 'Okay?' he checked, easing away to scan her eyes.

'Better,' she said, giving him a reassuring smile back.

'Shall we top these up with a medicinal Cointreau and take them through to the lounge?' he suggested.

'Good idea.' She went to fetch the Cointreau from the cupboard while he collected up the mugs. 'Why do you think they didn't find any forensic evidence?' she asked, looking back at him. 'I get that whoever did it must have worn gloves, but I thought they might find some footprints or something.'

'Me too.' Joe sighed. 'Some impressions, too, since the possible point of entry overlooks the garden. Could be that they were wearing protective footwear, I suppose.'

Sarah looked at him curiously.

'The sort the forensics team wear,' he explained, 'or hospital staff.'

Her heart lurched. 'Laura,' she whispered, hardly daring to look at him. When she did, she saw none of the wary disbelief she'd seen before in his eyes. Instead, his expression was one of guarded apprehension. Did he think it was at least a possibility? 'She works in a hospice,' she reminded him. 'Wouldn't protective clothing be available there?'

'Possibly,' Joe said. He wouldn't say he thought it *was* Laura, not outright, not without evidence, but he did think it could be her. She could see it in his eyes.

'She wouldn't have needed to climb through a window, Joe. Don't you see? Steve still has his keys.'

Joe ran a hand over his neck. He didn't comment, frustratingly.

'She has the same wallpaper in Ollie's bedroom as he has here, *exactly* the same, yet she's never seen his bedroom.' Sarah forced the point. 'She must have been in the house before, mustn't she? How else could she have known? And who else would have taken his whale, for God's sake? I've no idea why she would, why she would cut the ear off his bloody bunny, but you have to concede it could be her?'

He nodded slowly. 'I'll make sure it's looked into,' he said. 'I'll need to talk to my DS, but I'll see that she's spoken to.'

Sarah felt a marginal amount of relief, but … *spoken to*? What did that mean? 'Interviewed?' she asked him.

'Probably,' Joe answered vaguely – again – which was infuriating. 'I can't go out on a limb, Sarah. It won't stand,' he added, clearly reading her exasperated expression. 'There are official channels I have to go through.'

Sarah drew in a sharp breath and bit hard on her tongue. She knew he would need to talk to his superior. She knew there were channels. But how long would all that take? She couldn't just leave it, carry on as normal and allow Ollie to go over there. *She* had to talk to Laura if no one else would. Confront her. She would kill her, and her bloody mother, before she would let any harm come to her child.

CHAPTER FORTY-FOUR

Joe

After speaking to his detective sergeant, who told him what he'd thought she might – that anything he thought he had on Laura Collins was circumstantial – Joe waited for the guy he'd called in to fit locks to Sarah's windows to finish, and then made sure the house was secured before leaving. He wasn't sure the extra security, apart from the new lock on the front door, was needed now. What Sarah had said seemed far-fetched, but it was feasible. Laura was a damaged individual, that much was clear. The question was, how damaged? He couldn't verify it without access to her medical records, but as sleepwalking affected only a small percentage of adults, he was assuming it was late-onset, possibly the stammer too, both brought on by emotional trauma when her brother disappeared. He felt sorry for her. He truly had thought Sarah was obsessing about her initially, that she might have been jealous, even unconsciously – she and Steve had had a child together; he'd guessed that the ties wouldn't be easily cut. He didn't think that now. Sarah was frightened, with good reason. He couldn't be sure the break-in had been anything to do with Laura, but if it was, seeing Sarah's house viciously trashed, the ear sliced off the toy she'd shown him, then Laura's problems had to run deeper than post-traumatic syndrome.

Christ, why hadn't he taken her more seriously? Furious with himself, he headed for his car. He damn well should have. Instead, he'd dismissed her concerns, as good as ridiculed her. He would never forgive himself if any harm came to her or Ollie.

He was taking a risk professionally, but he needed to talk to Christopher Jameson, establish why he'd told Sarah that Laura was dangerous. He'd clearly been trying to warn her, but of what? He'd given her vague details, that was all. Joe needed more.

Arriving at the guy's place of work – he hadn't had to do much digging around there; the man's profile had been on LinkedIn – he approached the reception desk and showed his ID. Two minutes later, Christopher Jameson emerged from one of the offices.

'Is there a problem?' he asked warily. He was clean-cut, wearing a business suit; he didn't appear outwardly aggressive, but that was no indication that he wasn't. Abusers, male or female, often seemed reasonable on the surface. He had a slightly guilty look about him, but Joe couldn't blame him for that. Most people did when approached by the law.

'Is there somewhere we can talk privately?' Joe indicated the office Jameson had just come from.

The man scrutinised him cautiously, and then nodded him through.

Joe waited until he'd closed the door, then, 'I'm not here officially,' he said.

Jameson narrowed his eyes. 'So you're at my place of work for what reason exactly?'

Joe guessed he was pissed off at him for turning up here. He had every right to be. 'Laura Collins,' he said, and waited, studying him carefully.

The man emitted a short, scornful laugh. 'Sorry.' Shaking his head, he pulled the door open again. 'I have no wish to discuss Laura Collins or anything to do with her.'

'Right.' Joe stayed put. 'When I said I wasn't here officially, I should clarify that I meant I wasn't here officially *yet*.'

'For fuck's …' Cursing agitatedly, Jameson shoved the door closed. 'Do you realise what she put me through?' He eyeballed Joe angrily. 'She accused me of being *abusive.*'

Joe held his gaze. 'Were you?'

'Only when I threw her out,' the man growled irritably.

Joe pushed his hands into his pockets, trying to keep the whole thing low-key. 'So why did you throw her out?'

Jameson eyed the ceiling, his jaw clenching. 'She's sick,' he said, jabbing himself in the temple. 'She needs help. Not that she'll admit she does.'

'And you think she's sick because?'

Sighing, Jameson drew in a long breath. 'Is this something to do with the woman who accosted my son in the school playground?' he asked.

Accosted his …? That didn't sound like Sarah. But then she had been desperate. 'Could be,' Joe said non-committally.

The man arched a curious eyebrow. 'She has a kid, doesn't she?'

Joe didn't answer. He wasn't about to disclose anything about Sarah he didn't need to.

'She told me she did,' Jameson went on, confirming that he knew anyway. 'I'll tell you what I told her. She needs to keep him away from Laura. She's dangerous.'

'You have reason to think so, presumably?' Joe asked, making sure to keep any inflection from his voice, despite his growing unease.

'And some,' Jameson said shortly. He looked him over cautiously again, and then appeared to back down. 'She was obsessed with my son. I don't mean she tried to compensate for the fact that she wasn't his real mother. It was more than that. She took over care of him completely. She seemed to love him immediately …' Pausing, he laughed wryly. 'More than she did me, that soon became clear.'

'So why was that a problem?' Joe urged him.

'It wasn't,' the guy said, 'at first. But then she started banging on about Liam being in danger, about her having to keep him safe. Christ only knew what from. She started to smother him. Wouldn't let him out of her sight. She called him Jacob a few times. I guessed that was something to do with the kid brother she lost. To me, it seemed as if she was substituting Liam for Jacob, as if she thought he was him. I don't know. It sounds a bit nuts, but I began to think that maybe she was trying to re-create history out of some sense of guilt.'

'I see.' Joe felt the hairs rise over his skin.

'She wrapped him in cotton wool,' Jameson continued, a despairing edge to his voice. 'Liam couldn't go anywhere in the end without her shadowing him. It wasn't healthy. He wasn't happy.'

'And the crunch point?' Joe asked. 'I'm assuming there was one?'

Jameson tugged in a breath. 'She took him swimming. Liam couldn't swim, but she took him anyway. Afterwards, she said she was trying to teach him.'

Joe looked at him, puzzled. 'Isn't that a fairly normal activity for a parent to undertake with their child?'

'In an outdoor pool at midnight?' Jameson eyed him wearily. 'We were on holiday. Liam couldn't swim because he was scared of the water. He gets that from me, I'm aware of that.' Running a hand over his neck, he looked away. 'His mother drowned.' After a second, he locked haunted eyes back on Joe's. 'At a Norfolk seaside resort, can you believe?'

'Jesus.' Joe was taken completely aback. 'I'm sorry,' he said, silently cursing himself for not familiarising himself with the man's history.

'Yeah, me too.' Jameson smiled regretfully. 'She went in to try to save a boy who was in trouble. She hadn't realised there were rip tides. I'd taken Liam for ice cream. He was too young to remember it – at least I hope he was – but he saw it all. The thing is, Laura didn't seem to be aware of what she'd done. As in, completely unaware. She was sleepwalking, I think. She did that, wandering about in the dead of night. I found her outside several times. Anyway, that was the final straw. She refused to get help, and I'd had enough. That's when I realised just how dangerous she was. I made myself a promise that she would never see him again.'

CHAPTER FORTY-FIVE

Sarah

Sarah double-checked with Becky that she was okay to pick Ollie up from nursery and then drove to the hospice. She wanted to talk to Laura face to face, without Steve around and certainly without Ollie. She had no patience left for half-truths and lies. She wanted the whole truth – and she wanted to look Laura in the eye and know she was telling it.

Parked outside the hospice, she'd almost given up waiting, thinking Laura must have left early and she'd missed her, when she saw her come out. She was chatting to a colleague, so didn't see her until Sarah had climbed out of her car and was walking towards her. 'Laura, hi,' she said. 'Do you think we could have a quick word?'

There was a flicker of uncertainty in Laura's eyes, and then she quickly arranged her face into a smile. 'Sure, no problem,' she said. 'See you tomorrow, Marie.'

Giving her friend a wave, she veered off towards Sarah. 'Do you fancy grabbing a coffee? If we walk up to the main road, there's a Costa. Or we could go to a pub if you—'

'No.' Sarah stopped her. 'I have to go and pick Ollie up from my friend's, so I'd prefer to talk in the car, if that's okay with you.'

'Fine,' Laura agreed, her forehead knitting into a frown. 'Which friend?' she asked.

None of your bloody business. 'Someone I've known since college,' Sarah provided vaguely, and led the way to her car.

Once in the passenger seat, Laura turned to her. 'Is everything all right?' Her worried eyes skittered over Sarah's face. 'Ollie's okay isn't he?'

'Yes, considering …' Sarah said, and left it hanging.

'Has something happened? You look a bit stressed.'

'I am. My house was trashed last night,' she announced, studying the other woman carefully.

Laura's eyes sprang wide. 'Oh my God, Sarah. I had no idea. Was anything taken? Is Ollie—'

'Ollie's fine,' Sarah assured her again, growing irritated. Laura's every other sentence seemed to be about Ollie. 'There was nothing much taken, apart from the whale toy you gave him. It appears to have been done out of maliciousness, nothing more.'

'Mr Whale …' Laura's gaze grew troubled. 'But that's terrible,' she said, her eyes flickering down. 'Why would someone do that? I'm so sorry, Sarah. That must have been awful for you. Are *you* all right? Does Joe know?'

'Joe knows,' Sarah confirmed. She was wondering whether all this was an act, but then, seeing the tears welling in the other woman's eyes, she thought she would have to be a bloody good actor. 'He stayed over. Ollie felt more secure with him there.'

Laura nodded. 'Yes, of course he would,' she said. 'If there's anything I can do to help, anything at all, just let me know. I could have Ollie while you—'

'No,' Sarah said, more forcefully than she'd intended. She didn't want to put her on the defensive before she'd started. 'I prefer him to be with me,' she added. 'Can I ask you something, though?' she went on before Laura could steer the conversation back to her son yet again.

'Anything,' Laura said, her face a mixture of sympathy and innocence. Was she innocent? Guilty of nothing but suffering the legacy of a horrific time in her own life?

'Have you used Steve's keys to access my house?' Sarah said it bluntly.

'What?' Laura laughed, her expression now one of astonishment.

'The wallpaper in Ollie's room,' Sarah went on determinedly, 'it's the same as the wallpaper in his bedroom at home. Steve doesn't have any photos, so how could you have seen it unless you'd been in his bedroom?'

Laura stared at her, stunned. '*You* have photos,' she pointed out incredulously. 'You showed me photos – when we first met at the pub. I chose that paper precisely because you had. I wanted Ollie to feel at home when he came to stay. I wanted him to be surrounded by familiar things. Wouldn't you?'

Shit. Sarah cursed silently. She did have photos of Ollie in his bedroom on her phone and she had shown Laura them. But had Laura really studied them enough to take in so much detail? 'His bunny …' She gathered herself. She had to ask, even if the woman ended up hating her. She would never stop worrying about it otherwise. 'How did his ear come to be cut off?'

Laura's gaze flickered down again. 'You really have a problem with me, don't you?' she said, smiling sadly.

'I have a problem with why you told me it was sitting on his toy box and all the while it was stuffed inside it with its bloody ear chopped off,' Sarah replied angrily. It wasn't *her* who should be answering questions here.

'So it was you who took it,' Laura said quietly, somehow managing to turn the tables. 'I thought my mother had. She's such a *sss*spite … vicious cow.'

Sarah noted the stammer and wasn't sure whether to feel sorry for her, ashamed that she'd obviously made her so stressed, or suspicious. 'I did say I wanted it,' she offered, by way of lame defence for doing what she'd just accused Laura of: snooping around her home.

'Lucas cut the ear off,' Laura said after a loaded pause.

'Lucas?' Sarah was disbelieving. How was she to verify that? March around to Laura's neighbour's house and demand to interrogate her child?

'I was keeping an eye on him while his mother took her dog to the vet,' Laura went on. 'I took Ollie with me, naturally. He had Bunny with him. Lucas's mum had left scissors on the coffee table. I didn't see Lucas pick them up. I thought I'd averted a crisis managing to grab them before he hurt himself. Apparently I didn't.'

Oh no. Sarah closed her eyes. She'd done it again.

'I should have told you,' Laura added dejectedly. 'I was going to sew it back on, but …'

'He wasn't there,' Sarah finished, guilt weighing heavily in her chest. 'I'm sorry,' she added, not sure what else to say.

'It's okay. You were suspicious. I understand,' Laura offered magnanimously, 'especially with my mother turning up to spoil everything the way she does. God, wouldn't she just love this.'

Sarah glanced at her, her guilt multiplying tenfold as she saw a slow tear roll down her cheek. 'Why is she so horrible to you?' she asked.

Laura turned to gaze out of the window. 'Because she's frightened,' she said.

'Of?' Sarah urged her.

'Me,' she said simply.

CHAPTER FORTY-SIX

Sherry

'Do you not realise she might tell him everything?' Sherry asked irritably as she followed Grant around the stables. He'd been questioning her again, wondering why she insisted on interfering in Laura's relationships, as if he didn't know.

'Tell him what?' Grant asked patiently. 'She doesn't remember what happened that night. She can't tell what she doesn't know, can she? There's nothing she can say that won't sound highly implausible given her condition. The case is closed. As far as the police are concerned, Jacob went missing. You need to move on, Sherry. It's dead and buried,' he said, causing her heart to constrict painfully.

'We can't guarantee she won't recall something,' she retaliated, as he continued around the stables, lifting his saddle and bridle from the hooks in the tack room, refusing to acknowledge her concerns. 'There's always the possibility that something might trigger her memories,' she went on. 'That she might confide in this latest man she's involved with. Doesn't it worry you that she chooses to have relationships with men who have children uncannily like him? *She* can't move on. She's trying to hold onto him, don't you see; to keep him alive? She's reliving her life with him. She's desperate to know what happened to him.'

Sighing, Grant turned away, carrying his riding gear across to his beloved horse, a thoroughbred Arabian – a flighty, temperamental mare. Sherry was sure he thought more of it than he did her. 'Why can't you just drop it?' he asked, preparing to saddle up. 'Leave the girl alone?'

Standing a safe distance off from the snorting beast, in case lethal hooves should fly, Sherry eyed him with frustration. 'Do you think I don't *want* to?' she retorted. 'Do you imagine for one second that I want to keep going over and over this? That *I* don't want to bury the past and all the despicable things that went on?'

Grant didn't react. He never did. 'How can you be so indifferent?' she asked him. 'So uncaring?'

He looked at her at last, his expression one of astonished amusement. '*Me* uncaring?'

By which he meant she was. As if this cold person she'd become was who she wanted to be. As if she didn't lie in bed night after night, riddled with guilt, haunted by what had happened. 'I hope your fucking horse throws you,' she hissed tearfully.

Grant sighed heavily as she walked away. 'Sherry,' he called after her, 'come back.'

She kept walking.

'Sherry … look, I'm sorry,' he went on, his tone contrite. 'I know you're worried. I am too. I just think you need to stop trying to live Laura's life for her and get on with your own.'

Sherry swiped at the tears on her cheeks. She couldn't get on with her own life. She didn't have one. It was all a front, a sham. A shallow existence. Better this, though, or so she'd thought, than to live a lonely existence in poverty. She'd been there once, living hand to mouth. She couldn't go there again.

She only hoped he was right, that Laura didn't remember and never would. She'd seen that look in her eyes again after that idiot man's unfortunate accident, one of confused disbelief. Sherry hadn't flinched in the face of it, though her heart had been breaking for her daughter. She couldn't. There was simply too much for them to lose, for Laura to lose, if only she knew it. She'd hoped that in the fullness of time, her daughter would see that she'd only ever tried to do the right thing for her, that she did love and care for her, to the detriment of herself. She wasn't getting any younger, though. No amount of Botox or beauty treatment could erase the passage of time on the inside.

She had to stop this once and for all, she realised, her heart heavy with regret. Her only way of doing that was to prove that her daughter was unstable. She would be continuing to protect Laura, too, in a way. She reassured herself with that thought. Her daughter couldn't go on as she was, living a delusional life. That was no kind of existence either.

CHAPTER FORTY-SEVEN

Sarah

Laura hadn't expanded on what she'd told her. Saying she needed to go, stuttering the words out, she'd scrambled out of the car and run to her own vehicle. Sarah had felt terrible. She'd tried to call her on her way to pick Ollie up. Laura hadn't answered. Sarah couldn't blame her. She'd been tempted to try and contact Sherry, but guessed that might only make matters worse, for which Laura wouldn't thank her. She'd decided to ring Steve, then wondered what she would say to him. Then there was the little matter of why she'd been talking to Laura in the first place – to more or less accuse her of desecrating her home. Steve would probably tell her in no uncertain terms to stay out of their lives. She wouldn't blame him, either.

Sighing at her complete mishandling of the situation, she pushed her worries to one side. Ollie would need all her attention after what had happened. He wouldn't get that if her mind was on Laura and the problems surrounding her.

Ringing Becky's doorbell, she was surprised to hear Ollie laughing inside. Becky's husband, Adam, pulled the door open, sweeping a still giggling Ollie up as he did. 'I bet him a cookie I could reach the door before he did. Ollie won,' he said with a wink and a theatrical sigh. 'Becky's in the kitchen.' He nodded her that way. 'Ollie and I are doing something very important in the lounge, aren't we, Ollie?'

'Playing Twist,' Ollie provided delightedly.

'Twister,' Adam corrected him. 'I think he's winning at that too. He's tying me in knots. Say hello to your mummy, Ollie.' He leaned him towards her, enabling Ollie to fling his arms around her neck and slap a wet kiss on her cheek.

'Hello, Mummy,' he said, his cheeks flushed, his eyes excited, clearly keen to get back to his game.

'Hello, little man,' Sarah said, laughing. And then, more seriously, 'Just ten minutes more, Ollie. Becky and Adam will be wanting to have their dinner.'

'She wants a quick word with you first,' Adam said, glancing warily at her as he carried Ollie back to the lounge.

Puzzled at his expression, Sarah headed straight to the kitchen.

'Hi.' Becky smiled from where she was putting a tray in the oven. 'Good day?'

'Reasonable,' Sarah said. 'You?'

'Not bad.' Becky straightened up and went to the kettle to flick it on. 'If you don't count the bit where one of my pupils was sick in the sandpit.'

'Ugh.' Sarah screwed up her nose, imagining the mess that would have made.

'Luckily one of the other teachers offered to clear it up while I took him to the office,' Becky went on. 'Thank goodness, or it might have been two of us who were sick in the sandpit. Coffee?'

Sarah smiled. That was one of the things she loved about Becky. The fact that she was down to earth and always managed to see the bright side of things. 'I'd love a quick one, thanks.' She sighed gratefully and headed over to the kitchen island to take the weight off her feet for five minutes. It had been a long day at the rescue centre – and that was without the emotionally exhausting conversation with Laura. 'Has Ollie been all right?'

'Fine,' Becky assured her, fishing two mugs out of the cupboard. 'Adam's keeping him entertained,' she said with a tolerant smile. 'I think he's gone back to his childhood.'

Seeing a flash of longing in her friend's eyes as she walked across with the coffee, Sarah felt for her. She and Adam had been trying for a baby for over a year, but she hadn't managed to get pregnant yet. 'Adam said you wanted to have a word with me about something,' she said, eyeing Becky curiously.

'I did.' Becky pushed the biscuit barrel in her direction. 'It's to do with Laura.'

'Oh.' About to help herself to a biscuit, Sarah stopped.

'You said she was dismissed from her job as a teaching assistant, so I did a bit more digging around,' Becky went on hesitantly. 'I thought you would want to know why.'

Sarah did, but from the guarded look on Becky's face, she wasn't sure any more.

'Joe said a child wandered off in her care on a school trip …'

Sarah nodded, her imagination already running riot.

'They'd been on a nature trail and then they were going to be spending the afternoon in the children's pool at the water park,' Becky went on, her expression causing goosebumps to rise over Sarah's skin. 'The boy was rescued from the adult pool. The deep end.'

'Oh God, no.' Sarah's heart turned over. 'How old was he?' she asked, her throat tightening.

'Just five,' Becky supplied. 'Blonde hair, blue eyes.'

Sarah waited until she'd tucked Ollie safely up in bed before she called Joe. 'The little boy who wandered off on Laura's watch,' she said as soon as he answered. 'He was rescued from the deep end of a swimming pool.'

Joe didn't reply straight away, then, 'Jesus,' he said, sucking in a sharp breath.

'That man she was married to, Christopher Jameson, he was right,' Sarah went on, cold fear and nausea constricting her stomach. Despair, too, at her own stupidity. Every time she imagined she could trust this woman Steve had brought into Ollie's life – a woman who *she'd* given access to her child, had been persuaded to keep giving her access, despite her reservations – she'd been proved wrong. What else would it take to make people see that Laura wasn't the person she pretended to be? Would they condemn Sarah *now* if she denied her access, which she fully intended to?

'About that,' Joe said, sounding cautious. Everyone was cautious; tiptoeing around Laura's feelings because of her brother's disappearance, frightened of stressing her out. What about Sarah? *She* was frightened. What about Ollie? Shouldn't he, a vulnerable child, be people's first consideration? 'I spoke to him,' Joe continued. 'Christopher Jameson, I went to see him.'

'And?' Sarah asked, cold foreboding in the pit of her stomach.

'She took his son swimming.' Joe delivered another bombshell. 'The boy couldn't swim,' he went on gravely. 'He was terrified of water in fact.'

Sarah's heart slammed into her chest. The dreadful argument at Ollie's birthday party; she recalled it vividly. It had started the second Sherry had mentioned the swimming pool, and ended with Steve inexplicably falling from a ladder. She had no idea what was going on, what had gone on, but it was now very clear that something was terrifyingly wrong. 'Why didn't you take me seriously, Joe?' she asked him, anger rising hot inside her. 'Why aren't you doing something? My son might be in *danger*.'

'I'm trying,' Joe answered, his tone frustrated. 'I've spoken to my DS, but—'

'Not hard enough,' Sarah said furiously, and ended the call.

CHAPTER FORTY-EIGHT

Becky came straight over when she rang her. Sarah thanked God that she had at least one person on her side. 'Are you sure you want to do this now?' her friend asked worriedly as she stepped through the front door.

'I'm sure.' Sarah nodded, determined, her car keys already in her hand. 'Steve needs to know what he's got himself into, the danger he's been putting his child in.' She intended to make it as clear as daylight to Steve that he wouldn't be seeing his son again as long as he was in Laura's company. 'Ollie's sound asleep,' she said. 'He might wake up and fret with all that's being going on, but hopefully he'll sleep through.'

'Don't worry, I'll keep a careful eye on him,' Becky assured her, not looking overly thrilled that Sarah was insisting on going to Laura's house tonight, but accepting that she needed to. She'd had enough of phone calls and being talked down. She didn't want to give Steve or Laura notice of her arrival, give Laura a chance to hone her bloody acting skills.

'Thanks, Becky,' she said gratefully.

'It's not a problem. I know you'd do the same for me. Just take a breath and drive carefully.' Becky looked her over seriously. 'Promise me.'

'I promise,' Sarah said, swallowing emotionally as her friend gave her a firm hug.

'I'll have my phone right by me,' Becky called after her as she climbed into her car.

Sarah nodded appreciatively and made sure to reverse slowly off the drive.

She hadn't gone far when her phone rang. *Joe.* She hesitated, and then rejected the call. He would only try to dissuade her from going, as he'd tried to dissuade her about every suspicion she'd had about Laura. She felt a pang of guilt as she reminded herself that he had been trying, that he had appeared to be supporting her more. He couldn't do anything, though, could he? He did have to follow protocol and would be obliged to try to persuade her out of doing anything rash.

Sarah didn't *intend* to do anything rash, although she just might if Steve refused to see what was abundantly clear to her. She felt a combination of nausea and nerves churn inside her. Laura had a fixation about water. Hadn't she said that Ollie and she would learn to swim together? That she would buy him some water wings? Super-bloody-hero water wings? She'd filled his mind with tales of a superhero called Jacob who swam with the *fucking fish*, for God's sake. Had she been tempting him to go into the water? Sarah couldn't know what had gone on around her brother's disappearance, nor would she ever, probably, but one thing she did know was that Laura Collins, Caldwell … whoever she was … *did* need therapy. Serious therapy.

Leaving the car on the pavement outside Laura's house, she marched up the garden path, rang the doorbell and banged the knocker. She was angry. She needed to stay angry. She wouldn't back down, not this time.

CHAPTER FORTY-NINE

Laura

Hearing someone hammering on the front door, Laura almost shot off the sofa. 'Who's that?' she whispered nervously to Steve. It wouldn't be a sales person calling at this hour, and they weren't expecting anybody. Her mother wouldn't come here, not now. Steve would never allow her in and Sherry would know it.

'No idea.' Glancing at the wall clock, Steve heaved himself up from his armchair and headed curiously for the hall.

Her heart thumping, Laura went to the lounge door, listening as he pulled the front door open. 'I need to talk to you.' Sarah's voice floated in, her tone brooking no argument.

'What, at this time?' Steve asked, clearly confounded. As he would be. Sarah hadn't rung. She'd come unannounced, and plainly wasn't going to go until she had spoken to Steve. About what? Laura worried.

'Yes, at this time,' Sarah insisted.

'You'd better come through to the lounge,' Steve suggested reluctantly.

'No. We'll talk outside,' Sarah replied. 'It's you I want to talk to. Just you.'

It went quiet for a moment, and then Laura heard the click of the latch on the front door. He was going along with it. What would Sarah say to him? What did she have to tell him that had brought her charging around here at this time of night?

Stepping out of the lounge, she checked the hall was empty and then made her way carefully to the stairs and flew up them. Her mind ticking feverishly, trying to think back to the conversation they'd had in the car, anything Sarah could possibly want to discuss with Steve out of earshot of her, she went to the front-facing window of the main bedroom and eased it open.

Sarah was talking fast, her words coming out in a garbled rush. Laura strained to hear. She couldn't make sense of what she was saying at first. And then her heart skipped a beat. She was talking about Christopher, the incident with Liam in the swimming pool, and the little boy at the school. *Oh God, no.* How much did she know? How had she found out? *Joe.* Of course. She would have spoken about her worries to him. He would have got hold of the information. Laura swallowed back a hard knot of fear in her throat.

'Sarah …' Steve stopped her with an exasperated sigh. 'We've already talked about this. Laura has some issues to do with her past, you know she does. She's trying to deal with them. Can you not just—'

'But what about the garden party?' She cut across him, talking animatedly. 'Are you seriously telling me you don't think Laura's meltdown as soon as her mother mentioned the swimming pool is something to worry about? You ended up falling off the *ladder*. It was frightening, Steve. It's bloody terrifying knowing what I do now.'

'It was an accident,' Steve retaliated. 'I fell, Sarah. These things happen. As for the rest, it's probably all just—'

'What? Coincidence?' Sarah laughed incredulously. 'Poor Laura being blamed when she's obviously so innocent and vulnerable? Being picked on by her mother? She's filled Ollie's head with stories about superheroes who rescue fish. Are you telling me you don't think that's odd? She was going to take *him* to the swimming pool. This is not all just—'

'You're getting things out of proportion, Sarah,' Steve interrupted impatiently.

'For God's sake!' Her voice rose. 'Open your eyes! I don't know what or how, but this obviously all has something to do with Jacob.'

He hesitated before answering. Then, 'He disappeared, Sarah,' he said flatly, 'without trace. If he'd been in the swimming pool, don't you think the police would have noticed? If Laura had had anything to do with it, don't you think they would have charged her? And don't you think your boyfriend wouldn't have dug that information up if they had?'

'I … don't know,' Sarah replied, some of the bluster seeming to leave her sails. 'All I do know is—'

'And that's the point, you *don't* know,' Steve pointed out angrily. 'You're making ridiculous assumptions, vicious bloody allegations, and you have no proof whatsoever.'

'Of course I don't have proof,' she snapped. 'How would I have? But if you put all this together with the decoration in the bedroom, his maimed bunny, the fact that Ollie and her ex-husband's little boy—'

'Oh for … You're losing the plot, Sarah,' he growled irritably.

But she wasn't. Laura knew she wasn't. She was putting the pieces together. Steve would realise it at some point and he would wash his hands of her, take Ollie away from her. But still he wouldn't be safe. No child she cared about would ever be safe as long as she had secrets to tell. And if she did tell, then her life would be over. Her mother would make sure of it. She had to stop this. She *had* to keep Ollie safe. Wetting her parched lips with her tongue, she risked a glance out of the window.

Steve's chest was heaving. He was angry, upset clearly. Sarah was eyeballing him furiously. 'Ollie's in danger! I can feel it!' she cried, banging a hand against her chest. 'If you won't do something about it, then *I* will.'

Seeing her gaze shoot to the house, thinking she might be about to barge her way into it, Laura moved swiftly away from the window.

CHAPTER FIFTY

Sarah

'Sarah, come back!' Steve called after her as she strode to her car.

'And listen to you defending a woman who would harm your own *son*?' Sarah shouted over her shoulder. 'No way.' Blinking back tears of sheer frustration, she dragged an arm furiously across her face – and dropped her car keys.

'God!' Her anger mounting, she bent to scramble them from the gutter. The neighbours' curtains were twitching, she noticed as she straightened up. Were it not for the fact that she felt completely out of control, she would bang on their doors too. Ask Lucas's mother if she really was careless enough to leave sharp scissors on the coffee table. That should ensure that *she* challenged poor innocent Laura's lies.

'Sarah, look … just come back, will you?' Steve followed her, his tone more conciliatory. 'Come inside and talk to Laura. I'm sure she can explain—'

'No!' Sarah shrugged him off as, catching up with her, he placed a hand on her arm. 'Do you honestly think she's going to tell you the truth?' She searched his face. Even under the light of the street lamps, she could see his despair. He evidently did think she was the one with the problem. It was almost as if Laura had engineered the whole thing. Well, she might have Steve fooled. But Sarah wasn't. Did he really think she was going to go in there and discuss all this with a woman who was obviously deranged over a nice cup of tea? 'You can't see it, can you?' She narrowed her eyes, studying him hard. 'You're as obsessed with her as she is with Ollie.'

'*Me* obsessed?' He gawked at her in disbelief. 'It's you who's obsessed. I'm beginning to think you need more help than she does.'

Sarah's fury kicked in ferociously. 'You're right. I do need help, Steve,' she seethed, inhaling hard to stop her tears from exploding. 'I'm not getting any, though, am I?'

She looked him over with a mixture of disdain and bitter disappointment, then, willing herself not to lose it, she pressed her key fob and pulled her car door open, climbing in with as much dignity as she could.

'Sarah … look, I'm sorry,' Steve said, as she reached to close the door. 'I'm overwrought. We both are. Please don't go off like this. Come back and—'

'No, Steve. I've said all I have to. If you want to fight me, that's your prerogative, but I don't intend to let my son near that woman ever again.'

'You can't stop me seeing him.' A worried frown crossed his face.

'Watch me,' she retorted, yanking her door closed.

'Sarah!' He yelled after her as she pulled away. 'For God's *sake* …'

The revving of her engine drowning him out, Sarah glanced in her mirror to where he stood in the middle of the road, dragging a hand through his hair, frustrated obviously, but not half as frustrated as she was. Seeing him throwing his hands up in despair, she turned her gaze back to the windscreen and her heart lurched violently.

What was this idiot *doing*? She blinked hard against the searing white light that sliced through her vision. There was a car coming towards her, its headlights on full beam. Coming right at her. 'Dear

God!' Reacting instinctively, she wrenched the steering wheel hard left away from it, her foot slamming down hard on the brake.

Her breath stalling, her eyes going back to her rear-view, it took a second for her to assimilate. When she did, her heart stopped beating. 'Steve!' she screamed, her world slowing, her blood turning to ice in her veins.

She banged her door open and raced back towards him. Tears obscuring her vision, a strangled cry escaping her mouth, she dropped to her knees next to him. 'Steve?'

'Fuck,' he murmured. 'That hurts.'

'Stay still.' Taking hold of the hand he was reaching towards her, Sarah gulped hard against the constriction in her throat.

'Do you think I might be accident-prone?' He laughed, then winced painfully. 'Sorry,' he whispered.

'Yes,' she said, squeezing his hand, praying hard. 'You're a disaster.'

'I know.' He managed another small laugh – and spat blood.

Don't die. Please God, don't let him die. 'Keep talking to me, Steve,' she urged him. 'Steve, *please* … stay awake.' She stifled a sob as his eyes fluttered closed.

Where was Laura? She glanced back to the house, then in both directions along the road. The car that had ploughed callously into him had long gone. She hadn't got her phone. She hadn't got her *phone*. She choked back another sob, and then, seeing a neighbour emerge from his door, she screamed, 'Call an ambulance!'

CHAPTER FIFTY-ONE

Joe

Joe had heard the dispatch come through. Having established that there were no fatalities or critical injuries, he tried to get hold of Sarah. 'I heard what happened,' he said when he finally contacted her. 'Is he all right?' He felt gutted for Sarah and Steve both. Either lightning did strike twice, or her ex was the unluckiest bloke on earth – assuming it was a hit-and-run and not someone deliberately mowing him down.

'Better than he was. He has two broken ribs, though.' Sarah filled him in. 'His arm's fractured too. He bit hard on his tongue and …' She stopped, her voice catching. 'The car just ran straight into him. It bowled him over like a skittle. We'd been arguing and … He was barely conscious when I reached him. I didn't have my phone and … I thought he was dying, Joe. I thought he … Oh God.'

Hearing her tears, deep, heart-wrenching sobs, Joe cursed himself. He should be with her. He should always have been there for her. 'Okay?' he asked softly, after a pause.

'Not really,' she admitted, her voice small and tremulous as her sobs shuddered to a hiccupping halt.

He gave her another minute. Then, 'Did you see the car?' he asked her carefully. He knew she'd already given a statement, and he didn't want to upset her all over again, but for his own curiosity's sake, he needed to know.

'Not clearly,' she said, drawing in a breath. 'It all happened so fast. It was a dark car, a four-wheel drive. It had its headlights on full beam. It was coming towards me, almost straight at me. I swerved to avoid it, and the next thing I saw was …' Faltering, she breathed shakily out. 'It ploughed right into him, Joe. It didn't even stop. How could someone do that? Just drive off?'

'Panic, more than likely. It's possible the driver might come forward,' Joe offered.

'I hope the absolute bastard rots in hell,' Sarah seethed, her anger obviously surfacing after the initial shock, which was a good sign. Better than blaming herself, which he had thought she might, given what she'd said about her and Steve arguing. He should be with her, offering her the support she needed. She shouldn't be dealing with this on her own.

'They're discharging him,' she said, making a monumental effort to compose herself. 'He's insisting on going home anyway. He's worried about Laura being on her own, can you believe? The woman who was mysteriously missing when he almost got killed.'

Joe felt a prickle of apprehension run through him. 'Where was she?'

'She *said* she heard us arguing,' Sarah provided bitterly. 'She *said* she lay down on the bed and put her earphones in.'

He heard the incredulity in her voice. 'You don't believe her?'

'No, Joe, I don't believe her,' she answered forcefully. 'Would you just stuff your earphones in and have a lie-down if you heard Steve arguing with me outside?'

'I wouldn't, no,' he had to concede. 'But then didn't she do that after all hell broke loose at Ollie's birthday party? Could be that she has a tendency to retreat inside herself.'

Sarah hesitated. 'I suppose,' she said, sounding far from convinced. 'She didn't come out for ages, though, despite her neighbour almost knocking her door down. I didn't think Steve had even closed the door. It's just … There's something not right about her, Joe. About her whole family. I'm scared.'

He knew she was. The hard knot of guilt wedged in his chest twisted itself tighter. He was a policeman, and he could do nothing to help her. 'Do you want me to come over?' he asked. 'I could be there in ten minutes.'

'No.' Sarah declined his offer after a second. 'Thanks, but I'm okay. I really need to get home and check on Ollie. Becky's been there with him all evening.'

Joe's heart sank. He understood. She needed to be with her little boy.

'You could come over tomorrow,' she suggested. 'If you want to, that is. I wouldn't blame you if you didn't. I've been pretty awful to you, haven't I? I know none of this is your fault.'

He felt relief wash through him. 'I want to very much,' he assured her.

'Good,' Sarah said, and paused. 'I'd like to see you,' she went on uncertainly, 'to apologise.'

'Now there's an offer a man can't refuse.' Her tactile apology in the kitchen in mind, he smiled. He suspected what she needed was someone to just hold her. He was up for that, if nothing else. 'See you then. Try to get some rest meanwhile. Okay?'

Once he'd rung off, he went across to Kayla who was at one of the desks. 'Do you think you could do me a favour?' he asked her.

'Anything for you, Joe,' she said chirpily, 'as long as you get the drinks in at the pub.'

'Done,' he promised. 'I need to find out what kind of vehicle is registered to a particular person.'

'No problem,' Kayla assured him. 'So, name?'

'Caldwell. Sherry Caldwell,' he supplied.

He waited while she logged on and checked the Police National Computer. He was acting on no more than the proverbial hunch … No, it was more than that. Something was rattling him. Sarah was right. Granted, the family had gone through some horrendous stuff. They were dysfunctional, fractured as a result of it. But Laura's problems, this hostility her mother seemed to have towards her? There was more to it, he was sure of it.

'Nothing coming up,' Kayla said after a second. 'Sure you've got the name right?'

He wasn't, and he had no way of finding out without asking Laura. 'Could you try Grant Caldwell?'

CHAPTER FIFTY-TWO

Steve

Waking with a jerk, Steve attempted to raise his head from his pillow, and then groaned as a sharp pain ripped through him.

'*Shit.*' Remembering he was at home in his own bed, he lay still for a second and tried to gather himself. He'd been dreaming, trapped in a nightmare, a terrifyingly real nightmare: his boy floundering in the deep end of a pool, floating further away from him as he made futile attempts to reach him. The pool grew larger, the water darker, crimson blood seeping from the wounds of a dead rabbit like ink puffed from a squid.

The bang had woken him. The car slamming into him, he'd thought. He'd relived it over and over since it happened. But it wasn't that. He'd heard this sound before, a distinct noise that had dragged him from his sleep on previous bleak nights. He knew what it was: the lounge door slamming to, which meant the patio doors were open, that Laura was on the other side of them.

Perspiration tickling his forehead and running in rivulets down his back, he tried to lever himself up, hindered by the persistent ache across his torso, the plaster cast on his left forearm. Just do it, he willed himself, making another supreme effort.

Finally, his limbs shaking, a sharp cough rattling his chest, he manoeuvred himself to sitting and eased his legs over the edge of the bed. Cursing his feebleness, he waited again – for the pain to subside, for the strength to pull himself to standing. He wasn't sure he could make the stairs. What if he couldn't? What should he do? Call someone? Who? Who the bloody hell was he supposed to call to help him bring his girlfriend in from the garden? He laughed sardonically at the idea that her mother would care. She was the root of Laura's troubles. He was sure it was more than the loss of her brother that haunted her. There were things she wasn't telling him, things she was hiding – Sarah had been right about that. He didn't know how to help her, but he did know he couldn't just abandon her, leave her at the mercy of a woman who appeared to want to keep her trapped in her own nightmare.

Taking slow, shallow breaths, he groped for the bedside table, managed to get to his feet. Then, grimacing with each step, he made it out of the bedroom and along the landing. The stairs took all his concentration, all his willpower, each jarring step sending another searing pain through him.

Eventually reaching the lounge, he pushed the door open. He was right. The cool air hit him immediately when he stepped in. Whipped up by the wind, the white voiles at the patio window were billowing like the sails of a ghost ship. Beyond them, the silhouette of a woman searching aimlessly for the ghost of the child who'd been lost on just such a forbidding night.

Desperate to help her, to know how to, he made his way through the lounge, wincing as he stepped out. 'Laura,' he called quietly. He didn't want to raise his voice and scare her.

She didn't flinch, but continued to stare out into the half-light; at the empty garden before her, which he knew was another place in her mind, the dark, lonely place where the lost little boy roamed.

'Laura …' Moving towards her, he called her name again.

'I have to sssave him.' She responded the way she always did, but Steve knew she wasn't talking to him.

'It's okay, Laura. He's safe,' he replied, hoping to persuade her back to the house. He couldn't lift her if she dropped to her knees. Had no idea how he would encourage her to climb the stairs. Leaving her out here in her skimpy nightclothes and with nothing on her feet wasn't an option, though. He needed to get her inside. Get her warm. 'Let's go back inside, shall we? And then—'

'He's not safe,' Laura said, her voice flat, her gaze faraway. 'He's crying. I can hear him. You have to tell Sarah.'

Sarah? Steve squinted at her, uncomprehending. 'What do I need to tell Sarah?' he asked her, his heart slowing to a dull thud as his mind ricocheted back to his dream.

'Ollie.' She looked at him, her eyes unfocused, filled with palpable fear. 'Sarah can't take him away from me. He's in danger. I have to *sss*ave him.'

CHAPTER FIFTY-THREE

Sarah

Attempting to get her life back in some sort of order the next morning, Sarah was stuffing clothes into the washing machine when Ollie padded past her, heading towards the back door, which she'd left open after hanging the last load out. 'Don't go outside, sweetheart.' She stopped him short of stepping out into the garden. 'You don't have any shoes on.'

'But I want to play in the sand with my friend,' he whined, kneading his eyes with one hand and pointing to his sandpit with his other. His invisible friend, she presumed, burying her irritation as she was reminded of the nonsense Laura had fed him.

'I think your friend might have to go in for his breakfast.' Not wanting her own bleak mood to affect her little boy, she played along anyway. 'He's probably hungry.'

'No she's not,' Ollie said. 'She just waved to me. She's waiting for me.'

She? Frowning, Sarah walked over to the door to peer out. The garden was empty. He'd obviously invented another little friend. She wasn't sure whether that was a good thing or not, but she was glad he didn't appear to be as fixated as he had been on the little boy who swam with the fish. 'The sand's still damp, darling. You can play later when it's dried out and you're dressed,' she told him, closing the door.

'But I want to play now,' Ollie insisted, his bottom lip protruding petulantly. He was clearly fractious from too little sleep after waking several times in the night. Tossing and turning herself, worried about Steve, she'd eventually brought him into her bed. He'd had a nightmare, been crying out for his daddy. He knew something was wrong. He'd picked up on her mood. She needed to reassure him. She would have to take him to see Steve as soon as she'd spoken to him and established that he felt up to it.

'You can't play outside in bare feet, Ollie. Remember when you cut your foot? It was sore, wasn't it?'

'Yes,' he conceded, blinking back the tears that were brimming.

'Well then, you don't want to do that again, do you?' she said more firmly. Leaving the washing, she took hold of his hand to lead him back to the table. He was definitely overtired, having finally fallen asleep as dawn broke. Knowing the chances of her sleeping herself were nil, she'd got up and come downstairs. She'd already cleaned the house once, with Joe's help, but her skin still crawled every time she imagined someone desecrating her space, and she'd ended up cleaning everything again like a woman possessed. The place still felt tainted, as if a bad omen hung over it. She'd been tempted to put it up for sale. But then she'd decided she wouldn't let this hateful person ruin her life any more than she would let Laura endanger her son's. She would fight. She had no other option. Laura should know that was what mothers did to protect their children, to the death if they had to.

'How about you show me how to make scrambly as good as Becky does and then we snuggle up and watch a film together?' she said, injecting some excitement into her voice. She'd made up her mind to spend time with him rather than take him into the nursery today. Her supervisor at the rescue centre had been understanding about her situation when she'd explained, thank goodness. She'd had too much time off lately.

'Can we watch *Land Before Time*?' Ollie asked hopefully.

'Of course we can. We'll have a special day together doing whatever we want to do. I think we deserve it, don't you?' Sarah smiled, immensely relieved that he'd chosen dinosaurs over fish. However cute they were, she wasn't sure she would have been able to watch Nemo and Dory.

'Can I crack the eggs, Mummy?' he asked, looking a little more enthusiastic.

'I think you'd better.' She gave his hand a squeeze and helped him up onto his stool. 'We're bound to end up with bits of shell in it if I do it.'

'Becky gets it out with her stensions,' Ollie informed her with a knowledgeable little nod. 'But she told me not to tell you.'

Collecting the eggs and milk from the fridge, Sarah smiled, imagining her friend doing just that. There were secrets and there were secrets, though. And that one was pretty harmless as secrets went.

They'd cracked the second egg into the bowl, Sarah praising Ollie's expert egg-cracking skills, when there was a knock at the front door. The postman, she assumed, with something that didn't fit through the letter box. 'One second,' she said to Ollie, grabbing the tea towel to wipe her hands as she went to answer it.

Pulling the door open, she was surprised to see a parcel sitting on the doorstep. Strange that the postman hadn't waited, she thought, bending to retrieve it; a nondescript cardboard box that was relatively lightweight. She had no idea what it was – she hadn't ordered anything – but it was definitely addressed to her, the name and address scrawled in capital letters on a plain white label. Furrowing her brow, she scanned the top and sides of the box, peered at the bottom of it. There didn't appear to be any postmark. So who on earth had delivered it? There was a woman walking a dog a way off, but no one visible in the close vicinity, no courier vans disappearing into the distance. Had a neighbour received it by mistake and dropped it off? It seemed odd that someone would do that without stopping to speak to her. Assuming that was the explanation and that whoever it was must have been in a hurry, she carried it inside.

'Won't be long, Ollie,' she called, placing the box on the hall table and grabbing her keys to score the brown parcel tape it was sealed with. She was momentarily startled when, pushing aside the tissue inside the box, she was confronted with a fluffy blue bunny. What on earth …? Laura had dropped it off, presumably, trying to make amends and probably apprehensive about hanging around – with good reason. Sarah hadn't hidden the fact that she wasn't very happy with her when they'd been at the hospital. Not sure what to make of the gesture, she lifted the bunny somewhat tentatively from its nest of shredded paper and her heart lurched violently.

It had an ear missing.

The opposite ear to the bunny sitting upstairs in her wardrobe.

Her mind faltering as she tried to make sense of it, she pulled out the folded sheet of paper that had been tucked underneath it, opening it with trembling hands. *SORRY FOR YOUR LOSS*, she read – and her heart stopped dead in her chest.

Cold terror and nausea churning inside her, she dropped the rabbit as if it might bite her and spun around towards the kitchen.

'Ollie, we need to get you dressed, sweetheart. We—' She stopped inside the door, her world careering off kilter as she realised he wasn't there.

The back door was open. Her blood ran cold. He was obviously in the garden, she tried to reassure herself. Her throat dry, she hurried outside. He still hadn't got any shoes on. She really would have firm words with him when—

He wasn't there either, but the side gate was open. Fear gripping her chest like a vice, she flew through the gate, down the path and onto the road, scouring it left and right. There was no sign of him. No sign of anyone. No cars. *Nothing.*

'Ollie!' she screamed, willing herself not to buckle right there and sink to her knees. '*Ollie!*

CHAPTER FIFTY-FOUR

Joe

Seeing Grant Caldwell heading away from the property astride a formidable-looking horse, Joe debated what to do. Approaching him would probably spook the animal. In any case, he wanted to get a look at his car before speaking to the man, or his not-so-delightful wife. Grant Caldwell, he'd discovered, drove a Range Rover Sport, black in colour. Sarah's description had been vague – it could be any number of vehicles – but it fitted, and this car would certainly be pretty nifty if the need arose, off or on the road.

Negotiating the long drive, he pulled up a way from the house, a detached Georgian farmhouse set in a good two acres of paddock. Impressive, he thought, letting himself through the five-bar gate into a large gravelled parking area that boasted a pond, complete with fountain. The bloke must be making a bob or two just to pay for the upkeep. It was the sort of property most people could only dream of.

Glancing around, he bypassed the four-car garage, heading for the front door. The Range Rover was parked outside. Guessing it wouldn't be there if the man had anything to hide, he decided to take a look at it before knocking anyway. If he was spotted, he could always say he was admiring it. He hadn't quite worked out his story as to why he would be calling unannounced, but he would get to that when he needed to. If they didn't know about Steve's accident – or claimed not to – then that would be a reasonable excuse.

Bingo, he thought two minutes later, surveying a sizeable dent in the bumper. No scratches, he noted, meaning the impact was unlikely to have been metal against metal or the car hitting any other hard object. Impact with an animal might result in that kind of damage, but Joe reckoned it was more likely to have been caused by hitting something on two legs rather than four. No doubt Grant – or Sherry, whichever of them might have been driving it – would have an explanation. He was betting, though, that if he could get the vehicle towed in and examined forensically, it would yield the evidence he suspected was there.

Crouching down, he peered more closely at it. There were no visible signs of blood or fibres, but that didn't mean there weren't any. He wasn't sure he was likely to get a request for a forensic road collision investigation sanctioned, though, considering there were no fatalities or life-changing injuries. The only witness had been Sarah, who understandably hadn't been able to provide much detail. They had no registration number, and the initial responders hadn't come up with much; tyre marks wouldn't help without specific identification marks, and the chances of pursuing that line of investigation was also minimal.

Sighing, he straightened up. Except for the fact that Sarah had said the car appeared to be coming right at her, which had shaken him, he wasn't entirely sure what he was doing here. It could be that the Caldwells were involved, one or both of them. Sherry, maybe, going to see her daughter after imbibing too much wine over dinner? It might be no more than that, an accident, the driver running scared because they'd been drink-driving. Joe couldn't escape the niggling worry gnawing away at him, though, that it wasn't that simple. That what had happened to Steve was malicious intent. Taking into account the definitely weird things going on, his overriding worry was that Sarah might have been the prime target.

So, what could he do about it? Pose a few questions, he supposed. Ideally to Sherry and Grant Caldwell separately. Maybe he would get lucky and one of them would slip up and contradict the other's story.

Running a hand over his neck, he was about to turn to the front door when something cracked into the back of his skull with the force of a sledgehammer. Blinking hard against the blinding jagged lights that danced across his eyes, he dropped heavily to his knees. He didn't have a chance to wonder what the fuck was going on before the second blow floored him.

CHAPTER FIFTY-FIVE

Sarah

'Where is he?' Cutting the call to Joe, whose number she'd rung repeatedly on her way here, Sarah pushed through Steve's front door almost before he'd opened it.

'Who?' His arm pressed to his ribs, Steve took a step back as she stormed past him. 'Sarah, what the bloody hell is going on?'

Continuing along the hall, she banged the lounge door open, glancing in, and then flew to the kitchen. It was empty. No smell of breakfast or coffee, no sign that anyone had even been in it this morning. 'Where *is* he?' She whirled around, back to the hall. 'Where's my *baby*?' she screamed.

'Ollie?' Steve asked, the colour draining visibly from his face.

Oh God, no. Seeing his genuine bewilderment, the alarm in his eyes, Sarah's heart froze. He seemed to have no idea what she was talking about. Snatching her gaze away, she turned to race up the stairs, pushing Ollie's door open, as if by some miracle she would find him playing there, then flew to the main bedroom. The bed was unmade. Steve had clearly just climbed out of it. No Laura. Panic twisting inside her, she stepped inside, glancing around the room, for what she wasn't sure. She wasn't likely to find her hiding under the bloody bed.

Trying desperately to stay calm, she swung back to the door – and stopped, her gaze falling on an oval locket lying on the dressing table. Picturing Ollie making a tiny 'o' shape with his thumb and forefinger when she'd asked him about the photo Laura had shown him, her heart leapt. This had to be what he meant.

Tentatively she picked it up, took a breath to brace herself – she wasn't sure why – and prised the clasp open. For a second, she thought the blue-eyed, blonde-haired little boy looking back at her *was* Ollie. That the tiny wisp of hair in the other side of the locket was his. She'd trimmed his fringe, after all.

It wasn't Ollie, but seeing afresh the striking resemblance to him tore another hole in her heart. Did Laura truly imagine that Ollie was Jacob, that somehow she could replace him?

Gulping back the nausea rising inside her, she returned the locket and ran back to the stairs, coming face to face with Steve, who was making a painful attempt to climb them.

'Where's Laura?' she demanded. She'd been sure she would find Ollie here. Been desperate to. She'd slipped away from the police, who'd tried to console her, assuring her they would find him. She knew they wouldn't. They were moving too slowly, knocking on neighbours' doors, for God's sake, while her innocent child was with a woman who was plainly deeply disturbed. They needed to find Laura. That was where he would be. They hadn't been listening. They'd offered her platitudes. He'd probably wandered off through the open gate, they'd said. He wouldn't have got far. They would find him. Like Jacob? she'd wondered. The little boy who'd disappeared from the face of the earth?

Even after she'd shown them the bunny, still they'd tried to reassure her, offering her tea while they waited for a family liaison officer who would be able to keep her informed. *Tea!* As if that would help, as if she could drink it without choking. Dear *God*, she couldn't do this.

'I need to talk to Laura.' Biting back her fury in the face of a man whose pallor was now the colour of death, she squeezed the words out and tried hard to remain rational. Laura wouldn't hurt him; she loved him – that was the hope she was clinging to.

'She's … not here.' Steve told her what she'd already established, his voice ragged, his breath rasping. 'I took some painkillers, early this morning. I was out for the count. I didn't wake up until I heard you hammering on the door. When I looked for Laura, I realised she wasn't here.'

'And you don't know where she is? What time she went out?' She stared hard at him, saw the rise and fall of his throat as he swallowed.

'No,' he admitted, his gaze drifting down and back. 'What's going on, Sarah? Where's my son?' He took a step towards her, the look in his eyes a mixture of terror and confusion.

'Did she sleepwalk?'

He evaded the question, looking apprehensively away again.

'Steve!' she yelled, causing him to jolt. 'Did she sleepwalk?' She *had* to find her. Ollie had *not* disappeared from the face of the earth. He had *not*! *She'd* taken him. She was the only one who would take him, her fevered mind compelling her to. *Where* had she taken him?

'Yes.' He sucked in a breath. It appeared to stop short of his chest. 'I found her in the garden.' He moved away from her, his face etched with pain as he turned to sink heavily to the stairs.

Sarah wanted to go to him. Wanted to tell him everything would be all right. Wanted someone to tell *her* it would. *Please God* … where was her baby? 'Did she say anything?' she asked past the excruciating lump in her throat.

Steve ran his hands over his face, then nodded slowly and closed his eyes. 'She usually searches for Jacob when she goes out there. She wasn't this time,' he said, his voice hollow. 'She was looking for Ollie.' He stopped, his eyes haunted. 'She thought you were going to take him away from her. She said he was in danger.'

She knew it. She just *knew* it!

'Sarah, wait!' Steve called after her, struggling to his feet as she raced back to the front door. 'Where are you going? Have you called the police?'

'Yes,' she shouted back. 'They'll most likely call here.' Halfway to her car, she didn't stop. She was acting on instinct, drawn to what she knew Laura was drawn to. She'd been reliving her life with Jacob through Ollie, that much was clear. Sarah's heart beat like a terrified bird in her chest as she wondered: would she relive his last moments? Moments she was sure had something to do with water. Why else her morbid fear of swimming pools?

CHAPTER FIFTY-SIX

Joe

Hearing someone quietly talking, Joe kept still, trying to make out what was being said above the pounding in his head. 'Wake up, M-M-Mother. It's time to face the music.' He heard that clearly. Laura, unmistakably.

Pain searing through his neck, he tried to shift his position, to see what the hell was going on, and then groaned inwardly. She had to be joking. He was secured to the leg of a table with his own bloody handcuffs. A weighty farmhouse table that stood in the middle of a large kitchen.

Guessing she would know he'd come round soon enough anyway, he shuffled across the flagstones, manoeuvred the cuffs up the leg and managed to pull himself to a half-sitting, half-lying position. Her back towards him, Laura was kneeling on the floor three or four yards away from him, Sherry Caldwell's body half obscured behind her. His heart rate ratcheting up, he scanned the room. No sign of Grant Caldwell. How long had he been out of it?

'Laura,' he said carefully, 'what's happened? Is your mother all right?'

Jerking, as if she might have forgotten he was there, Laura didn't answer immediately. Then, 'She's just sleeping,' she said with an apathetic shrug. 'She accidentally swallowed some of my tablets. It was a bit of a struggle to get her to take them, but she's so much easier to t-t-talk to when she's quiet.' She leaned further over her. 'Aren't you, Sherry?'

Shit. Joe tugged uselessly on the cuffs. He knew he had no chance of getting out of them. His only hope would be to lift the table. It was possible, but only if he could get his weight under it. His gaze went back to Laura. 'Is she breathing?' he asked her, cold foreboding twisting his stomach as he considered what she might do next.

'Unfortunately, yes,' she answered with an elongated sigh.

He felt his heart clunk back into its mooring as he saw Sherry stir, attempting to raise her head.

'Shush, shush, Sherry.' Laura pushed her back down. 'You're in my care now. We really should get you out of this dressing gown, though. White doesn't flatter your p-p-pale skin tone, darling. You could be mistaken for a corpse.'

Craning his neck, Joe watched in morbid fascination as she reached into a make-up bag on the floor beside her and withdrew a lipstick. She removed the cap to test it against the back of her hand, and then applied it to her mother's lips. Her movements were calm, methodical and unhurried. Trepidation prickled the length of his spine. If she hadn't been out of her mind before, she seemed to be now. Driven there, probably, by the events in her life; thereafter by the woman who was supposed to care for her and who actually appeared not to care at all.

He took a breath. She wouldn't do it, but it was worth a try. 'Do you think you could undo the handcuffs, Laura?' he asked her. 'I can't feel my—'

'She ran Steve over.' Laura glanced at him over her shoulder. 'She hurt you too. She could have killed both of you. You shouldn't waste any sympathy on her, Joe.'

'I'm not,' he said quickly. 'It's you I'm concerned about. You could end up in prison. If you let me go now, I can help you.' Sweat trickling down his spine, he tried to keep her talking, attempting to get at least one shoulder under the tabletop as he did.

'But you're a policeman. You'll feel obliged to help *her*.' She turned her attention back to her mother. 'There,' she said, tipping her head to one side as she surveyed her handiwork. 'You look younger now. You never know, Grant might even stay with you because he wants to; your p-p-perfect man, the man you ruined my *life* for, loved more than me.'

Sherry moved, attempting again to lift her head. 'That's not true, Laura,' she rasped. 'I've never—'

'Whose love you valued above my *life*.' Clutching her mother's shoulders, Laura pushed her down. 'Your *grandchild's* life! You callous bitch!'

Her grandchild? Joe squinted at her, confused. There were no other siblings as far as he was aware. Sherry and Grant had had two children: Laura and Jacob. Unless … Was she talking about *Jacob*?

'She stole him from me,' Laura went on unsteadily. 'Convinced me that he would have a better future with her and Grant as his parents, that Grant would marry her if he thought she was pregnant. It would secure his future, she said. He would be financially secure for life. We all would – meaning *she* fucking well would.'

'Laura, stop this!' Sherry struggled yet again to raise herself.

'Lie *still*, Mother!' Laura growled, shoving her down hard. 'Stay very, *very* still. You're not going anywhere until you tell Joe here what you did. Because, you see, if you don't, I won't hesitate to bury *you* alive, do you understand?'

'Laura, please stop this,' Sherry begged, her voice tremulous and terrified. 'You're upset, darling, confused. You know how muddled you sometimes get when you're stress—'

'That's what she did, you know? She took him away. Buried him in some dark, lonely place all on his own.' Laura glanced at Joe and then back to her mother. 'You told Grant he was dead when you fished him out of the pool, didn't you?'

'Laura, you're being ridiculous, darling. Please don't say any—'

'*My* baby!' Laura glared down at her. 'My p-p-precious Jacob. You told Grant he was *dead*, but you didn't make sure, did you? You didn't fucking well make sure!'

'Laura, stop!' her mother cried. 'You don't know what you're—'

'He *wasn't*!' Laura screeched. 'He wasn't dead! I know he wasn't. He was floundering, trying to swim, but he couldn't! And *you* didn't even try to save him!'

Jesus Christ. Joe's throat was suddenly dry.

'She buried him anyway.' Her tone was flat, cold, unforgiving. 'Do you know why? To have something to hold against that *bastard* she got to marry her. As if his fucking well *abusing me* wasn't enough.'

'She's lying,' Sherry cried. 'She's doing it out of spite. Some sort of vengeance for how she imagines I've blighted her life.'

'You never believed me!' Laura screamed. 'I tried to tell you what he did. You never—'

'Because it was a lie!' Sherry screamed back.

'No, Mother,' Laura seethed. '*You're* the liar. Everything you *are* is a lie. You'll stop at nothing to maintain your pathetic fake image; to keep a man who hates you. He despises you almost as much as I do! You killed my *baby*! You killed me!'

Christ almighty. Joe hadn't noticed the kitchen knife lying on the floor until she picked it up. 'Laura …' He yanked hard against the cuffs. 'I hear you. I heard everything. You don't need to do this. Please …' Seeing a movement beyond her, his gaze shot to the door. *God, no.* His insides turned over as he realised who it was. 'Put the knife down, Laura. Let me help you.' Praying hard, he heaved his shoulder up against the tabletop.

'She destroys things! She breaks things! She ruined my marriage!' Laura wasn't listening. 'It was *her* who led that little boy to the swimming pool. She wanted *me* to get blamed. She wants me to be scared. To keep quiet. She wants to get rid of me. She always fucking well has! *Bitch.*'

Seeing her press the sharp tip of the knife to Sherry's throat, Joe felt his gut clench with terror. 'Laura, don't,' he pleaded. 'This won't bring Jacob back.'

'You shouldn't have tried to make me believe it was me who killed my baby, Mother. I remember, you see. I was the one trying to s-s-save him, and you … I *know* what you did!' Laura's chest heaved.

Fuck! Joe couldn't see any way she wouldn't push that knife home. In her mind, she had nothing left to lose that her mother hadn't already taken away.

'Do you know what the irony of all this is, darling Mother?' she went on with caustic amusement. '*Do* you? He really *was* Grant's child. And he *killed* him.' She paused, watching her mother carefully. 'Oh dear, are you shocked, Sherry? Finally, are you *hearing* me? Jacob wasn't fathered by some boy in the village. I never went out with any boys from the village. Never had sex with anyone else. Jacob was *Grant's* child. He slapped him to stop him crying, and then left him to drown in the pool while he sat pouring brandy down his neck and not giving a shit. And *you* cleaned up his mess, just to hold onto him. You had no respect for me. No respect for yourself either. Where *is* he? Where did you *bury* him?'

'Laura, don't!' Joe's heart slammed against his chest as she raised the knife, and then almost gave out as Sarah stepped into the room.

'Laura,' she said shakily, tears rolling down her face, 'I've lost my little boy. Can you help me find him?'

CHAPTER FIFTY-SEVEN

Sarah

'Ollie?' Laura blinked up at her, stupefied.

Sarah nodded, her gaze swivelling to Joe. She caught his warning glance as he attempted to wrestle the handcuffs that were securing his wrists from under the leg of the table. Understanding that he didn't want her drawing attention to him, she fixed her eyes back on Laura. 'He went missing,' she whispered, her throat thick with tears.

'When?' As she rose unsteadily to her feet, Laura's expression was a mixture of disbelief and confusion. 'Where?'

'This morning. From my house. My garden,' Sarah told her, her heart wrenching with unbearable guilt. Her sweet, innocent boy … *please, dear God, let me find him.* She prayed that Laura might empathise with her in some small way and give him back to her.

'But …' Laura glanced down, her forehead creasing into a frown. 'She couldn't have. She was here.'

'Who couldn't have? Couldn't have *what?*' Sarah asked desperately. 'Laura, *please*, tell me where he is.'

Laura's gaze was fixed dazedly on her mother, who was now on her knees, a hand pressed to her chest and apparently gasping for breath. 'She's been here all morning,' she said. 'I've been here with her. She *couldn't* have.'

Couldn't have taken him? Was that what she meant? Nausea roiling inside her, Sarah searched Laura's face, icy realisation spreading through her as she noted the other woman's shocked bewilderment. Laura truly didn't know where he was. Ollie wasn't *here*. She'd searched the house and the stables. The swimming pool, that had been the first place she'd looked, time seeming to stand still as she'd approached it, stared down into its deep, unyielding depths. He really wasn't here. Dread clutched at her chest as harsh reality hit her. Her little boy was truly missing.

'Joe?' she murmured, feeling the blood drain from her body. Somehow he was there as her legs turned to butter beneath her, supporting her, shouting something to the police officers racing past her.

'She's armed!' he yelled, flailing his arm in Laura's direction as Sarah felt her world crumble. Circling both arms around her, he drew her to him as two officers descended on Sherry, prising her from her knees and leading the gasping woman away.

'We'll find him.' He eased back a fraction. Scanning her eyes, his own dark with foreboding, he tried to reassure her. 'We'll find him, Sarah,' he repeated, his voice raw with emotion. 'I swear to God if it's the last thing I do, I will bring him home.'

How? Sarah wanted to ask, but she couldn't force the word past the acrid grief lodged in her throat.

'Where's your phone?' he asked softly.

Dry-eyed with shock and ice-cold fear, Sarah simply stared at him, her mind racing in terror. Who had taken him? *Why?* An agonised moan escaping her, she leaned back towards him, buried her head in his shoulder, as if the solidity of him could make her nightmare go away. Had they hurt him? *Don't hurt him. Please don't hurt him.* A shudder ripped through her. She could feel her baby's pain. Hear him. See him, no matter how hard she squeezed her eyes closed. Her little boy's face, pale and petrified, his summer-blue eyes recoiling in fear. His small voice filled with terror as he cried out for his mummy. She couldn't bear it. She *couldn't*.

'Sarah?' Gently Joe lifted her chin, urged her to look at him. 'Your phone, it's ringing. You need to answer it.'

For a second, she didn't understand. What did it matter? And then, reading the caution in his eyes, it hit her. Quickly she stepped away from him, scrambled it from her jacket pocket. It had rung off. *Shit! Shit!* She fumbled with it, pulled up the last caller number. She didn't recognise it.

Joe eased the phone from her hands. A deep furrow formed in his brow as he studied it, and then his face paled. 'Jesus Christ,' he whispered. 'Courtney.'

CHAPTER FIFTY-EIGHT

It took a second for comprehension to dawn. When it did, Sarah felt as if the air had been sucked from her lungs. He'd recognised the number: his ex-wife, the woman who'd sought him out to tell him that she'd been pregnant with his child, that she'd lost the child, playing on his emotions, taking advantage of the fact that he would care, something she'd known without doubt. She'd refused to let go of him, pursued him, drawn him back time and again with tales of her woes. Joe hadn't been able to walk away. She'd known he would struggle with his conscience. He'd been trapped like a fly in her web. An intricate web of deceit. Sarah had known what Joe couldn't see. Realising that the man she'd cheated on him with was probably the biggest mistake of her life, Courtney had decided she wanted Joe back. Sarah had been the obstacle in her path, the thorn in her side she'd had to extract.

But she hadn't been able to. And now … she had taken Sarah's baby.

Her heart freezing, she looked towards Joe, who had her phone pressed to his ear, his face deathly pale as he tried again to call the number. Was it possible that the woman imagined that this was a way of luring him back? What then? she wondered; what did she hope to gain? And more importantly, what did she intend to do now?

Pulling the phone from his ear, Joe handed it back to her and then moved suddenly, shouting instructions to one of his colleagues as he raced to the hall, something about family liaison officers and making sure Sarah was taken home. Home to wait alone? Leaving him to … what? There was no way she was going to do that. Sarah followed him. She needed to be with him. She needed to be in the vicinity her son might be. She would know he was there. She would *feel* him.

'Will do,' the man shouted back. 'Joe, you should know we've lost Laura Collins. She did a runner through the back door. Simon gave chase but he lost her. I'll keep you posted.'

'Great,' Joe muttered, and ground to a halt at the front door. Dragging a hand over his face, he turned to face Sarah. 'You need to go home. This might all be nothing. I'll call you if—'

'It's not *nothing*.' She held his gaze determinedly. 'You know it's not. Unless you gave it to her, how would your ex-wife have my mobile number? And why would she call me?'

'I didn't give her your number. I … I don't know.' He kneaded his forehead.

'I'm coming with you. I have to.' Determined that he wouldn't stop her, she moved past him towards his car.

'Sarah, please, just let me deal with this.' He was close behind her. 'If she has anything to do with this, which I'm struggling to believe, it's highly unlikely she'll be at home. Please trust me: you being there won't help. It might even make matters worse.'

Incite her to do something? Was that what he meant? He was frightened, the fear in his eyes tangible.

'She does have something to do with it, I'm sure of that.' Sarah hesitated. 'She lost *her* child, Joe. I'm going on nothing but my gut feeling, but it seems to me she wants me to suffer the same loss. I have to *be* there, don't you see? If she's … If he's still …' She faltered, her heart wrenching unbearably. 'She might realise that he needs me, that he needs his mummy.'

Joe nodded sharply, released the locks and yanked the driver's door open. 'Make sure to fasten your belt,' he said throatily.

CHAPTER FIFTY-NINE

Joe pulled up close to the building where he'd shared an apartment with Courtney. 'That's hers,' he said, nodding through the windscreen.

Sarah looked up to the apartment he indicated, a corner penthouse on a development of waterside properties refurbished sympathetically to preserve the history of the area. It had large Victorian windows overlooking the deep basin and huge locks where canal and river combined. There was a straight drop into the basin under two of the windows, Sarah realised, her breath stalling. On the other outer-facing wall of the apartment, running the length of two windows and a set of patio doors, was a long balcony. The one where Joe had found his ex-wife attempting to take her own life, she thought, cold foreboding washing through her.

'You might do better to stay here.' He turned to her, his eyes filled with trepidation, sending a fresh prickle of fear down her spine.

'Joe, I *can't*. I have to know.' He couldn't stop her, he wouldn't try, but she willed him to understand. 'I might be horribly mistaken. I—' She stopped as her phone rang again, causing her heart to jolt in her chest.

She checked it. 'It's her,' she said, her stomach turning over.

Joe nodded tersely. 'Can you put it on speaker?' he said, his eyes growing a shade darker.

Her hands trembling, Sarah did as he asked, then breathed deeply to stop the tears flowing. 'Courtney?' she said, trying to relate to her while her world was collapsing around her. 'Do you have him? Please tell me. Is Ollie—'

'He really is a beautiful little boy, isn't he?' The woman cut across her.

'What do you want?' Sarah swallowed back the shard of glass in her throat. 'Why have you—'

'You know what they say.' The woman sighed expansively. 'Fair exchange is no robbery. You stole what's mine ...'

Oh God. Nausea burning her throat, Sarah locked petrified eyes with Joe.

Inhaling hard, Joe reached for the phone. 'Courtney,' he grated. 'What in God's name ... *Courtney!* Fuck it!' Ramming his door open, he pulled his own phone out, radioing for help with one hand as he raced towards the apartments, calling someone on his phone with the other.

Her heart pelting in her chest, Sarah spilled out after him, catching up with him as he punched a security code into the intercom at the entrance. 'Kayla? Joe,' he said into his phone, swinging the door open and pushing through to the foyer. 'She's fine. She's here with me. I've called it in, but I need backup fast, no sirens. My old address, Severn House apartments. I think Ollie may be here.'

Jabbing the lift buttons, he cursed liberally. 'Where *is* the fucking thing?' Glancing up at the elevator display, he dragged a hand over his face, then, 'Jesus, Sarah, I'm sorry,' he said, his voice choked. 'Why the *hell* didn't I—'

'The stairs,' Sarah stopped him. The lift wasn't coming. It was stuck, sitting on the third floor while ... She would kill her. She would *kill* her if she harmed one hair on her baby's head.

'*Shit!*' Stumbling as she climbed, her shin screaming with pain, Sarah limped upwards, waving Joe on as he faltered. It was taking too long. Much too long. The woman's mind was twisted with some need to seek vengeance. What was her warped reasoning urging her to do? What was going through Ollie's mind? *Don't let her have hurt him. Please don't let her have hurt him.*

Her heart splintered as Joe rammed the front door open and went straight to the bedroom, each piece piercing her chest like an icicle. 'Ollie …' she said, her voice trembling, her body shaking as she took in the scene before her. He was on the balcony, standing on the balustrade. He hadn't been there a short while ago. She must have brought him out to stop them… Stop them *what?* Her blood froze as she noticed Mr Whale tucked under his arm. Sitting next to him, one arm around him, her legs facing out over the water, was the woman who'd taken him for reasons Sarah could barely comprehend.

'We've come out to look at the pretty boats. We can see them better from here, can't we, Ollie?' Courtney said, her voice light, harmless – unthreatening.

He's just a child! My baby. Sarah almost crumpled.

'Tell Mummy which one is our favourite, Ollie,' the woman urged him.

'The red one.' Ollie pointed out at the water. 'It has Donald Duck on it. See, Mummy?'

'Yes!' Sarah lurched forward as he twisted to look at her. 'I see it, Ollie. Keep still, baby. Please …' She forced back the sob that racked her body. 'Keep still, sweetheart.'

'Courtney,' Joe took a tentative step towards her, 'it's cold up here. How about you let Ollie come inside and we'll talk, just you and me?'

'You came, then? I thought you might, my very own hero,' Courtney said, her voice still deceptively light. Smiling, she glanced over her shoulder and then back at the water. 'Who will you save, Joe, I wonder, if I let go of him?'

CHAPTER SIXTY

Her heart frozen with fear, Sarah sank to her knees. She couldn't stop the tears. Couldn't breathe.

'Mummy, what's wrong?' Ollie asked, his small voice quavering.

'Mummy banged her leg, Ollie, that's all,' Joe tried to reassure him. 'Don't worry, we've called the paramedics. She'll be fine.'

'Will I see them?' Ollie asked, his voice filled with awe as he anticipated blue flashing lights.

'No!' Joe said quickly, taking another step onto the balcony as Ollie leaned forward. 'They're friends. They're coming in their car. They'll be here soon.'

'Oh.' Ollie sounded disappointed. 'Can we go inside now, Courtney?' He looked at her. 'I want to hug Mummy and make her feel better.'

'Soon,' Courtney said. 'We don't want to miss the long boat coming through the lock from the river, do we?'

'No,' Ollie said uncertainly.

Joe took another small step. 'Why are you doing this, Courtney?' he asked, his throat hoarse.

'Do you remember our honeymoon?' she said.

'Venice,' Joe answered, sucking in a tight breath.

'It was beautiful, wasn't it? This view always reminds me of it. We were good together then, weren't we, Joe? The perfect couple, everyone said.'

Joe kneaded his temples. He didn't reply.

'I thought we could go back there. You know, try to fix things,' she went on. She was completely delusional, living a fantasy. Sarah stared hard at her, taking in her long flowing hair. She was a beautiful woman, competent and confident on the outside. Successful. Bereft and broken on the inside. She couldn't have Joe, so she would destroy him. Destroy everything he loved.

'You chose *her*, though.' Courtney shrugged. Ollie teetered. Sarah's heart stopped beating.

'I was carrying your child, and you chose her over me,' the woman continued insanely.

'I had no idea.' Joe edged towards her. 'About the pregnancy.'

'Would it have made any difference?' she asked him.

He took another sharp breath. 'Possibly,' he ventured.

Courtney didn't reply for a second. Then, 'I think not,' she said. 'You love him, don't you?' She glanced towards Ollie. 'You love him more than *our* child. I know it's him you've come for. Not me.'

'Shit! Courtney, *don't*!' Joe moved fast as she relaxed her arm around him.

Laura, though, was faster. Emitting a cry like that of an enraged animal, she hurtled forward, snatching Ollie from the brink of certain death before Sarah could blink. Whirling around, she pressed his face close to her shoulder, stroking his back, whispering to him as she carried him back towards the apartment.

'Jesus Christ, no.' Joe gazed in horror over the balcony he'd reached a split second too late to save the woman whose twisted love had almost destroyed him.

Heaving herself stumblingly to her feet, Sarah saw him bury his head in his hands. She wanted to go to him. He needed her, but … *her baby.*

'Laura!' She flew after her, and stopped.

Laura was in the lounge, Ollie still in her arms. She looked past him to Sarah, her green eyes wide, those of a frightened kitten. 'I had to *sss*ave him,' she said, handing him carefully to his mother.

EPILOGUE

Sarah

Her heart bleeding for the little boy who'd finally been laid to rest, Sarah read the inscription on the simple white heart Laura had chosen.

My Love Will Find You Wherever You Are
Night, Night, Little One

It was right, appropriate, she thought, profound in its simplicity. Jacob wasn't a lost little boy any more. Laura's love for him had found him. She'd never given up searching for him. Sarah would never fully understand all that had happened, what had driven Sherry Caldwell to such callous evil, but she did understand now why Laura had sought out children who looked like Jacob. Through Ollie, and Liam before him, she had been able to feel close to him, reach out and touch him, keep the essence of her child alive until she was able to bring his tiny body home.

Watching Laura reach tremblingly out to trace the delicately chiselled inscription with her fingertips, Sarah wiped away a tear and lowered herself to the grass beside her. 'Okay?' she asked her, even though she knew she never could be with part of her heart missing; her child stolen cruelly away from her. She hoped, though, that she might now be able to move forward in some way, forge a relationship with Steve based on a future together, whilst never forgetting the life that was so fundamentally part of who she was. Steve would help her to do that, she was sure, help her to stop blaming herself for something that had been beyond her power to prevent.

Squeezing the hand Sarah offered her, Laura nodded and brushed her own tears away. 'He didn't like people to be sad,' she said, leaning to arrange the soft toy she'd brought against the stone. A lop-eared fluffy white rabbit, it was remarkably similar to the snuggle toy that had been Ollie's favourite. She'd been tempted to give it to Ollie after Bunny had been damaged, she'd told Sarah as they'd driven here, but couldn't bring herself to. She'd held onto it since Jacob had gone missing apparently, taken it out occasionally. Sarah's heart had constricted as she'd pictured her, a mother who was as lost inside as her child, pressing the toy to her face, breathing in the special smell of him. She knew that was exactly what she herself would have done.

'He never would go to bed without it,' Laura confided with a heart-wrenching smile.

Sarah guessed that her fervent desire had been to reunite Jacob with the toy. She guessed also that despite not being able to recall what had happened to him, she'd known he was dead. Her constant search for him was what had kept her going, her mind driving her to keep looking, even in her sleep.

'Sleep tight, my precious baby,' Laura whispered above the soft rustle of the leaves in the trees overlooking the tranquil place she'd finally laid her baby to rest. 'Mummy's heart will always be with you.'

She'd almost broken when the police had told her they would be exhuming his tiny body from the grave Sherry had buried him in. Laura had always known she had buried him. She'd never known where, until now, hence her endless search for him. Her own heart feeling as if it might fracture inside her, Sarah had held her while the sobs had racked her. Laura had known they would have to exhume him, why they would. It hadn't made it any less painful. She hadn't wanted him to stay there, she'd told Sarah, once her sobs had slowed; buried in the family plot that Sherry had occasionally visited, pretending to care about the mother she'd lost. 'I doubt she ever did care about her. I don't think she was capable of caring for anyone,' she said cynically. 'She was probably only visiting to check the ground hadn't been disturbed.'

Sarah supposed that love had many guises. Sherry Caldwell had loved Grant, a twisted, obsessive, unrequited love, clearly. Her solicitor had claimed it had driven her to madness, resulting in her 'criminal act of despair'.

'It wasn't an act of *despair*,' Laura had fumed in the toilets when the court had taken a break. 'She *was* driven, though.' She'd choked back angry tears of frustration. 'She buried Jacob to save her precious reputation.'

Sarah believed it: that a woman who had also cold-bloodedly sought to keep the truth from her daughter, the child's *mother* – feeding her sedatives, robbing her of the right to grieve for her child, driving her almost to the brink of insanity – had been in full possession of her faculties when she'd carried him from the pool that dark night and dug him into the cold, clay-sodden earth.

She'd told Grant he'd killed him. He'd slapped him to stop his crying, it came out, left the poor frightened child wandering in the garden, where he'd blundered in the dark into the pool. Released from his purgatory to face a yet more terrifying one, Grant hadn't been about to lie to the police for her. He'd said in his statement that Sherry had sworn she would keep his secret, stay by his side until death did them part. Death had parted them before prison could. Grant, Sarah supposed, hadn't relished the idea of spending the rest of his life as a convicted child killer and paedophile, at the mercy of those who would dish out their own punishment. Laura's only regret when she learned that he'd ended his miserable life before he could be brought to justice was that he'd never found out that his wife wasn't the mother of his child; that he'd been duped into marrying her.

Rocking silently to and fro as she sat by her child's grave, Laura placed a hand on her tummy. 'I remember the first time I felt him kick,' she recalled. 'Gentle flicks, like soft butterflies. I was mesmerised … but terrified of her, even then.' Her eyes were filled with long-suppressed anger and raw sadness. 'She was parading proudly around the lounge, a hand pressed to her "pregnancy bump", can you believe? I think she was hoping Grant would be more attentive. He wasn't.'

'How did she get away with it? I mean, how …' Sarah trailed off. Surely he must have suspected something?

'She made me wear baggy clothes.' Laura anticipated the question she'd wanted to ask but hadn't known diplomatically how to. 'Shapeless monstrosities brought back from her trips. She's made a point of bringing me unflattering, supposedly on-trend stuff ever since. She never was comfortable with me showing off my figure.'

Sarah felt disgust for the woman roil inside her. Laura had problems, major problems, which, given the determination Sarah now knew she possessed, she had no doubt she would do her best to overcome. The fact that she'd survived at all, though, to be the caring person she was, was a miracle.

'She dissuaded him from attending the birth, obviously,' she went on, fiddling distractedly with the arrangement of freesias and roses Sarah had brought. 'I don't think Grant was too devastated. They weren't exactly a loving couple, always at each other's throats. He never really had much to do with Jacob once he was born, could never abide him crying when he and Sherry argued, which was often.'

Burning anger rose thick in Sarah's throat as Laura recounted the lengths to which Sherry had gone to get the man who would fund her lifestyle to marry her. 'He was reluctant to commit,' she told her falteringly. 'He did, though, eventually, naïvely believing everything she told him. I don't think I'll ever understand how she could have been with a man who'd abused her own daughter. I think she must have always hated me.'

'Because there's something wrong with *her*, Laura. Not you,' Sarah said forcefully.

Laura smiled, but the look in her eye said she didn't quite believe it. Sarah prayed she would, in time. Laura had Steve, who loved her without question. Sarah was determined to be a friend to her. How could she not be to the woman who'd saved her child?

'She was never going to go back to a life of poverty having tasted the good life.' There was a hint of regret in Laura's voice, as if she'd hoped …

Sarah had no doubt that that was the truth. That Sherry Caldwell had valued her lifestyle above her daughter. The price Laura had had to pay was obviously a small sacrifice.

'I hope he burns in hell,' Laura said. She hadn't gone to Grant's funeral. There hadn't been many in attendance, Joe had said. But she had gone to see her mother – to try to lay her ghosts, Sarah assumed.

'How was she?' she steeled herself to ask.

'She looked old,' Laura said after a second. 'Her real age, I suppose. She doesn't have the amenities available to ward off the ravages of time any more, does she? I told her she should find some solace in the fact that she no longer has to struggle so hard to maintain her image. At least *she* can see the bars of her prison,' she added, a bitter edge to her voice.

'Will you go again?' Sarah ventured. She hoped dearly that she wouldn't. She needed to be free of her.

Laura shook her head. 'I don't need a mother I never had. I have everyone in my life I need.' She paused, reaching out to rearrange the flowers yet again. Then, 'Can you forgive me, Sarah?' she asked, her eyes averted. 'For all I put you and Ollie through?'

'You saved his life.' Sarah reached to still her hands. She didn't think she needed to say more. If it hadn't been for Laura following them to Courtney's apartment, her own little boy wouldn't be alive today, of that Sarah was sure.

Laura turned to her, her smile one of immense relief. 'I know he's your child, but I truly do love him,' she said hesitantly. 'I'll always watch over him. Always keep him safe. I promise.'

A LETTER FROM SHERYL

Thank you so much for choosing to read *My Husband's Girlfriend*. I really hope you enjoyed it. If you did enjoy it, and would like to keep up to date with my new releases, sign up at the link below:

www.bookouture.com/sheryl-browne

If I was asked to sum up *My Husband's Girlfriend*, I think I would say it's about how we perceive people. Not judging a book by its cover, if you like. I think many of us tend to judge people by their appearance. Firstly, their physical appearance, the clothes they might wear; the 'self' they present to the world. We assess them by the way they speak, their mannerisms, their confidence or lack thereof. We make judgements based on information they might share about their life, their relationships, qualifications, career. If a person admits to being in an abusive relationship, would we perceive them as vulnerable? Would we think them strong for ending that relationship? How would we judge a person who might withhold information precisely because they don't want to be judged? With suspicion, perhaps? Would we condemn our judgemental selves if we jumped to wrong conclusions? As parents, our instinct to protect our children is powerful. Naturally, therefore, we assess anyone who might come into contact with them. But do our own preconceptions and life experiences come into play? As human beings, we send out so many complicated signals. Are we always reading body language and the signals a person is sending out correctly? If someone is hiding something, not making eye contact, is it because they are being deceitful, or are they simply shy or uncomfortable?

In short, the book is about appearances being deceptive. Or are they? Should we trust our instincts?

As I pen this last little section of the book, I would like to thank those people around me who are always there to offer support, those people who believed in me even when I didn't quite believe in myself. To all of you, thank you for helping me make my dream come true.

If you have enjoyed the book, I would love it if you could share your thoughts and write a brief review. Reviews mean the world to an author and will help a book find its wings. I would also love to hear from you via Facebook or Twitter or my website.

Stay safe everyone, and happy reading.
Sheryl x

SherylBrowne.Author

@SherylBrowne

sherylbrowne.com

ACKNOWLEDGEMENTS

As always, massive thanks to the fabulous team at Bookouture, whose support of their authors is amazing. Special thanks to Helen Jenner and our wonderful editorial team, who not only make my stories make sense, but make them shine. Huge thanks also to our fantastic publicity team, Kim Nash, Noelle Holten and Sarah Hardy. Thanks, guys, I think it's safe to say I could not do this without you. To all the other authors at Bookouture, I love you. Thank you for being such a super-supportive group of people.

I owe a huge debt of gratitude to all the fantastically hard-working bloggers and reviewers who have taken time to read and review my books and shout them out to the world. It's truly appreciated.

Final thanks to every single reader out there for buying and reading my books. Knowing you have enjoyed my stories and care enough about the characters to want to share them with other readers is the best incentive ever to keep writing.